D0449431

A PERILOUS TRAIL

Gazing at Rodney Meredith, Tony Carew had seen love shining in his eyes. Why, then, had Rodney suddenly refused to see her anymore? Why had he left her alone to fend off Carter Holbrook's persistent advances? Why was the man who had won her heart tortured by the mystery of an unsolved crime?

Plagued by these questions, Tony threw caution to the winds in a desperate attempt to save her crumbling romance. Little did she suspect that her every move was being closely observed. How could she know that while she followed the trail of a five-year-old mystery —ever closer and closer—danger was stalking her!

EMILIE LORING

FOREVER
AND A DAY

A NATIONAL GENERAL COMPANY

NORTHEAST COLORADO REGIONAL LIBRARY
325 WEST 7th STREET
WRAY, COLORADO 80758

The characters in this story are fictitious.
Any resemblance to persons living or dead
is purely coincidental.

*This low-priced Bantam Book
has been completely reset in a type face
designed for easy reading, and was printed
from new plates. It contains the complete
text of the original hard-cover edition.*
NOT ONE WORD HAS BEEN OMITTED.

🐤

FOREVER AND A DAY
*A Bantam Book / published by arrangement with
Little, Brown and Company*

PRINTING HISTORY
Little, Brown edition published February 1965
2nd printing .... May 1965
Grosset and Dunlap edition published March 1966

Bantam edition published March 1968

2nd printing ...... March 1968	5th printing ...... March 1969
3rd printing .... May 1968	6th printing ...... August 1969
4th printing ..... October 1968	7th printing .... May 1970

New Bantam edition published January 1971
2nd printing
3rd printing
4th printing
5th printing

All rights reserved.
*Copyright © 1965 by Robert M. Loring and
Selden M. Loring.*
*This book may not be reproduced in whole or in part, by
mimeograph or any other means, without permission.
For information address: Little, Brown and Company,
34 Beacon Street, Boston, Massachusetts 02106.*

Published simultaneously in the United States and Canada

*Bantam Books are published by Bantam Books, Inc., a National
General company. Its trade-mark, consisting of the words "Bantam
Books" and the portrayal of a bantam, is registered in the United
States Patent Office and in other countries. Marca Registrada.
Bantam Books, Inc., 666 Fifth Avenue, New York, N.Y. 10019.*

PRINTED IN THE UNITED STATES OF AMERICA

i

It all began on a June day with a long line of seniors walking slowly across the beautiful campus with its towering elms, crossing the platform, one by one, to receive the diplomas indicating that they had earned their degree of bachelor of arts. To Tony Carew that stiff parchment with its great red seal represented four years of work and play, of friendship and adventure of the mind. It was, in a way, a passport to the future. It was also the end of something: the end of college, the end of carefree girlhood.

Sitting among her classmates she listened to the President's address. At first, engrossed in her own thoughts, she barely heeded the words. Then they caught her attention.

The graduation from college, he said in his deep voice, was not the end but the beginning of education if the young women who had just received their degrees intended to grow as human beings. It was not the end of a journey. Rather, it was like a station stop on a long journey that had barely begun. Beyond the quiet campus lay the turmoil, the perplexities, the challenges of the world. How each of them would meet that world and its challenges would depend less on circumstances than on the attitude of the individual. If there were obstacles there must be hope; if there was fear there must be courage. But they should remember, now and always, that life was a great adventure and that it was up to them to meet it greatly.

The President had smiled. "Not long ago," he said, "a group of people in England initiated classes to teach young people the spirit of adventure. I cannot

1

bring myself to believe that such classes are needed here. That spirit is a seed in every child, a seed that must be nurtured if it is to be allowed to develop. To let it die, to stifle it, is to commit a crime against life, against the human spirit.

"For each of you that journey through life will be different because each of you is a separate person. Learn to accept and to understand your difference, your separateness; find the task that is yours to perform and then perform it with all your heart. Learn to respect your fellow human beings, with malice toward none, with charity for all."

The graduation ceremonies were over and the girls, so much a part of her life for four years, fluttered away across the beautiful green velvet of the grass to be welcomed by family and friends and then to scatter to the four corners of the country. And Tony Carew was left alone as she had been basically alone ever since her parents' death when she was fifteen.

No, not quite alone. Across the campus she saw bright red hair and answered the wave of her closest friend, Rosamund Perry. The young man who had been talking earnestly to Rosamund turned away abruptly, striding off the campus, and the small red-headed girl ran toward Tony. There were tear stains on her cheeks and she angrily wiped her eyes and blew her nose.

The two girls provided a striking contrast. Antoinette Carew, who had been called Tony as long as she could remember, was tall and slim, with a shiny cap of blue-black hair and long eyelashes. She had the carriage of a high-fashion model and a bone structure that would keep her beautiful as long as she lived. Rosamund Perry, inches shorter, with red hair and green eyes, was as vivid as an emperor tulip in a bed of daisies. The two friends were like still water in contrast with a rippling brook but, in spite of their vast differences in appearance, their contrasts in personality, they were as devoted as sisters.

"Do you want to tell me about it?" Tony asked

gently. "Would you rather I didn't ask any questions?"

"It's Hal," Rosamund said in a choked voice. "Did you see him?"

Tony nodded. "Shall we drive him back to New York with us?"

Rosamund shook her head. "He has already gone. He's furious with me. He said he—he's not going to see me again." She was crying soundlessly, the tears pouring down her cheeks.

"What's wrong?" Tony asked. "I thought he was so terribly in love with you."

"He is. He wants me to marry him. I tried to explain but he wouldn't listen. He thought I was ridiculous. He said I had a right to my own life. He said if I really loved him I would put him first. I tried to make him understand—but—" She was shaken by sobs. "So he said if that was how I felt it would be better not to see me again. Ever. I was first with him, but if he couldn't be first with me he wouldn't take second place. Not for anyone."

"He'll come back," Tony said confidently. "If he really loves you, he'll trust you and be willing to wait. He'll realize that if you were to fail your mother now you'd be the kind of wife who would fail in that job, too."

"Do you really think so?" Rosamund asked, brightening.

Tony smiled. "I really do." She glanced at her watch. "If we're going to get back to New York tonight we had better start. We'll pick up our weekend bags and then go collect Mister Duffy."

"It seems silly to ship back everything but one bag apiece when we could have taken it all in your car," Rosamund said.

Tony laughed. "You've forgotten Mister Duffy. He really needs to have a freight car to himself."

They stopped for the last time at the room they had shared so long, remembering the talks, the confidences, the long hours of study, the dreams, the parties, and then closed the door gently behind them on their college years and went out to face the future and the unknown.

At a kennel three miles from the college Tony drew up. "I won't be long. They're expecting me."

A few minutes later she returned, leading a great Dane on a heavy leash. At first there was a tug of wills. Mister Duffy saw no point in traveling on wheels, penned inside a moving room that allowed no scope for exercise. He tried to convince Tony that what she really wanted was to have him take her for a walk. Laughing and breathless, she finally got him into the back of the long, sleek Lincoln and then slid under the wheel.

"Heavens!" Rosamund exclaimed. "I always forget how enormous he is."

"Are you sure that it will be all right to keep him at your house, Rosamund? It would be such a joy to have him with me for a change, instead of just going to the kennels to walk him."

"We have the garden in back, you know. Room for him to get some exercise without being in traffic." After a moment Rosamund added. "It will be all right for the present, anyhow."

For a while Tony drove in silence, her eyes on the busy turnpike with its lanes of speeding traffic.

It was Rosamund who broke the thoughtful silence. "I've been thinking," she said soberly, "perhaps, even if Hal comes back, I ought to set him completely free of me."

"What on earth are you talking about?" Tony exclaimed in dismay.

"His salary as a newspaper photographer would be plenty for the two of us but it isn't fair to ask him to support Mother, and I love her too much to marry until she is taken care of. She brought up four children single-handed after Dad died, and she denied herself everything she wanted in order to give us a start. Well, as you know, only Catherine and I are left, and she has her child to support, and only a tiny part-time salary, since she lost her husband. So I must provide for Mother before I can think of myself." As Tony was silent she asked anxiously, "You do see that, don't you?"

"Yes, of course I see."

"It isn't as though she'd ask for a thing; she'd just about die if she thought I'd make a sacrifice for her. But there is so much she could have enjoyed, her drawing and painting, all the pretty things she loved. And now even the house will have to go, sooner or later."

"Oh, no!" Tony cried in protest.

The old brownstone on Irving Place in New York City was the only real home she had known since the death of her parents. From the day, four years earlier, when she had entered college and acquired as a roommate a redheaded girl on a scholarship, with shabby clothes, a merry heart, and a hair-trigger temper, she and Rosamund Perry had adopted each other. In the run-down brownstone house in New York, Mrs. Perry had taken the lonely girl to her heart.

"We can't possibly keep it up," Rosamund said flatly. "We'll have to rent the lower half as a store or shop of some kind, I suppose; maybe the second floor could be used as a loft or storage place or something for one of the Fourth Avenue offices. That would still give us two rooms on the third floor. Of course, we'll have to mortgage the house to afford the alterations. If I could only get a decent job! But I'm not really trained for anything. All I know is a lot about books, a little about painting, and less about music. That's not much."

"Isn't it?" Tony asked oddly, an undercurrent of excitement in her voice.

The long twilight of June never really darkened into night for, as they approached New York, the sky was bright with millions of lights. Lights that outlined the sweep of bridges over the dark rivers; lights that carried the line of towering buildings up into the sky; lights that marked out miles of streets and avenues. Gleaming headlights on endless automobiles; the red and green of traffic lights; lights on theater marquees and in Fifth Avenue store windows; in offices where women mopped floors and in apartments where they were getting dinner; lights on Park Avenue where uniformed doormen signaled for taxis; and blinking lights on the trucks that rumbled all night, bringing food to maintain an island population.

"New York," Tony said, expelling a long breath. "It's all here. Beauty and art and music and theater; business and foreign trade and the United Nations. The future to build the way we want it. Right now I feel as though I could tackle it single-handed."

"What on earth is happening to you?" Rosamund said in amazement. "Tony the untroubled, the quiet of heart. Do you know you carry an aura of peace around with you? Anyone would expect that such an incredibly beautiful creature would—well, she'd stir things up, somehow."

Tony laughed. "You just wait," she said darkly. "I'll stir things up yet." She slowed as a taxi ahead of her jammed on brakes without warning. "Make the monster get down, will you? When Mister Duffy stands up I can't see what's behind me. He stands as high as a camel."

When Rosamund had cajoled a bored Mister Duffy into flopping down on the floor Tony said, "New York is happening to me, I guess. That and the words the President spoke this afternoon. This is our battleground, Rosamund, and we are going to make the fight of our lives. Make it together."

For a moment there was an uneasy silence. Together. Each of them was unexpectedly aware, in a flash of insight, of her separateness, her difference, her individuality.

It's different for her, Rosamund thought. She is rich and beautiful. She has everything. There's nothing she has to fight for.

It's different for her, Tony thought. She has Hal Perkins and her mother, two people who love her dearly. She's not alone. There's nothing she has to fight for.

The car went down the ramp below Grand Central Station onto Park Avenue South, turned left, circled

Gramercy Park, sleeping behind its iron fence, went down Irving Place, drew up at the curb before a shabby little three-story brownstone house.

"I wish you'd look at that," Rosamund exclaimed. "We have a beauty parlor right next door. That's new since we came home for the Christmas holidays."

While Rosamund took out the weekend bags and Tony extricated Mister Duffy from the back seat, the door was flung open and a small woman with hair like a silver halo above a young pixie face that resembled Rosamund's called eagerly, "Welcome home, children. Just put the bags anywhere. The rest of the luggage has already been delivered and it is in your rooms. There are chicken sandwiches and fruit salad and some iced coffee waiting for you in the garden."

She kissed her daughter. "Rosamund, how intelligent you look, darling! Is it that brand-new degree showing?"

She turned to put her arms around the tall, slender girl who was struggling with the great Dane, looking into the lovely face. "Tony," she accused her, "you are up to mischief. I can see it. Take that young pony of yours for a walk, if you can manage him, and then come in, darlings. Come in!"

ii

The garden to which Mrs. Perry had referred so proudly was one of those surprises that New York constantly affords. At the back of the house, surrounded by office buildings, there were a neatly tended lawn about the size of a living-room carpet, a stunted and rather dusty tree, and a rose arbor that scented the June night. A Japanese lantern provided the only light except for the glow in the sky from the great unsleeping city. Here the noises of traffic came muted.

The three women sat in canvas lawn chairs and Mister Duffy dropped down at Tony's feet with a heavy sigh. This, his manner declared, was much more sensible than jolting for hours in an automobile.

After a quick discussion of news they had already exchanged by letters and an account of the graduation ceremonies, they fell silent.

It was Tony who spoke first. "All my life this garden will seem to me like an oasis. So hidden from the world. So private."

Rosamund laughed. "Private! We counted once and discovered that there are nearly three hundred office windows that have a good view of it. However, they're practically all deserted at night, thank heaven!"

"We've always loved it," Mrs. Perry said. "I'm going to miss it. I'm that strange animal, a native New Yorker, you know. Sometimes I think no one believes that people are actually born, live out their lives, and die in New York City. Americans are so restless, always moving on, but I was born in this house, married in a church a few blocks away on Fourth Avenue, lived in this neighborhood all my life."

After a pause she added briskly, "I suppose it's bad for people to get set in their ways. It will be rather fun moving somewhere else."

"I have an idea," Tony said. "All the way to New York I've been thinking about it. Partly because of what the college president said. Partly because I think it would be a rewarding thing and fun to do. I'd like to start a bookshop. A real one where books are the important things, not just greeting cards and a gift shop. A place where people can browse if they like and gossip about books. Not one of those big impersonal places like a supermarket where everyone hurries, but a place like a—well, like a home library—with easy chairs and reading lamps and soft music; with open fires in winter and a garden in summer."

She leaned forward in her eagerness though it was too dark to make out the older woman's face clearly. "Mrs. Perry, would you consider letting me take over the ground floor here and make it into the kind of shop I dream of? You'd still have the garden to yourself in the evenings. I could have the second floor equipped with a kitchen, the front bedroom with its fireplace could be the living room, and the middle room a dining room. You'd still have the bedrooms on the third floor.

"We could make this a place where—oh, where people could discover what good companions books are. Between us, Rosamund and I could handle the business and the buying and the customers. And we might even use one room for exhibits to introduce and encourage young artists."

"Tony!" Rosamund squealed. "Do you really mean this?"

"My dear," Mrs. Perry protested, "have you stopped to consider what this would cost you?"

"We'd get estimates, of course," Tony said.

In the darkness, Mrs. Perry smiled to herself. That crisp, clearheaded business sense had never ceased to amuse and surprise her in the girl who looked as though she served only a decorative purpose. But then it was possible that Timothy Carew's granddaughter had inherited some of his business ability. As long as his great fortune had come into her hands it would be all to the good if she developed the qualities necessary to handle it.

"Actually," Tony went on, "the remodeling won't be so extensive except for ripping out the kitchen and installing another one on the second floor. We'd need a carpenter to build a number of bookshelves, of course. Perhaps a bow window off the living room would be attractive for displays. Naturally there would be a certain amount of redecoration necessary, just so it would look bright and fresh, but I'd like the living room, as far as possible, to maintain its present identity; then the dining room could be made to look like a private library rather than a bookshop.

"We'd need professional advice on selecting our stock and we'd have to be a bit tentative in buying until we learned the tastes of our customers. Perhaps we might even have a small section of rare books to attract collectors, and I don't see why we couldn't have open stalls outside for secondhand books. People simply can't resist them and, after all, we're not too many blocks away from the secondhand bookstores on lower Fourth Avenue."

"Tony, child," Mrs. Perry said, half laughing, half distressed, "you'd be running into thousands of dollars."

"Not as much as you may think. Anyhow, I could spend more than we'd need here on a fur coat or a piece of jewelry or a cruise. But this is something to build from scratch, something to invest in that could be—well, a Mecca for booklovers all over the city."

"You're serious about this?" Mrs. Perry asked slowly, and Rosamund, who had been clenching her hands, relaxed with a long sigh of relief.

"I've never been so serious—so sure—about anything. How about you, Rosamund?"

"It would be heaven," her friend said shakily. "Absolute heaven. And then we could keep the house."

"So you could," Tony said, as though that had not occurred to her. "But," she added warningly, "we'd have to work, you know. Work like mad."

For the first time since the man she loved had walked away from her on the college campus, Rosamund's laughter was lighthearted. "Of course it would be work. But that's what you said this afternoon. Remember? That we were going to fight it out together."

"That's settled, then." Tony stood up and yawned. Mister Duffy looked at her reproachfully. Humans could be very unreasonable. Even his pet human, the one who belonged to him was constantly disturbing him for frivolous reasons. "Where can we put the monster?"

"In the kitchen for tonight," Mrs. Perry decided. "Good gracious, it's nearly two o'clock. Off to bed, both of you. Sleep as long as you like in the morning."

Three months later, in the former dining room of the house on Irving Place, whose walls were now lined with shelves, Tony stood on a ladder, putting in place the books Rosamund handed her. Even in dark slacks and a daffodil yellow shirt, low-heeled shoes so that she could climb up and down the ladder without danger, a smudge of dust across her cheek, Tony managed to remain beautiful.

Rosamund kicked aside an empty cardboard carton and straightened up with a groan of relief. "That's the lot! Twenty-six cartons of books we've unpacked and arranged in the past three hours."

"I can hardly believe we've actually done it!"

"Tomorrow at this time," Rosamund said, "The Good Companions Bookshop will be in business. I'll feel terribly let down if we don't have any customers, won't you?"

"Rome wasn't built in a day."

"Just the same," Rosamund said threateningly, "if people don't come of their own accord I'll feel like going out and dragging them in." She looked at her grimy hands in dismay. "Heavens, I'm filthy. I've got to scrub before I start leaving fingerprints all over our beautiful fresh paint."

While she ran upstairs to wash, Tony climbed down from the ladder, picked up the last of the cartons, and stacked it neatly with the others to go into the basement. Slowly she walked through the ground floor of the little brownstone house. It was incredible to see how much had been accomplished in those three months. But they had worked. How they had worked!

Recalling excitement and interest that had been packed into those busy weeks, Tony wondered, as she had wondered so often before, why people complain about work as man's curse instead of his blessing, his reward, his meaning in life. What leisure-time occupation could possibly have been as rewarding as the creation of this charming little shop?

The work had served another purpose, too. Rosamund had been kept so busy with the decoration of the shop and the replanning of living quarters on the upper two floors, with ordering paint and checking invoices, with talking to publishers' salesmen and carpenters, that she had been too occupied to give way to grief over the fact that Hal had not reappeared, that he had not even telephoned. In spite of Tony's prophecy that he was bound to come back, he had stuck to his word. Whether he was still angry with Rosamund or whether he had found another girl, one with no family commitments, was a question that neither of the girls ever dared to mention.

Occasionally Tony was tempted to write or telephone and explain the real situation to Hal, but she knew that this was a problem that only he and Rosamund could solve. No matter how much she wanted to help, she must not interfere.

As often happens in New York City, September had opened with a heat wave that sent the temperature soaring into the nineties, day after day. Electric fans were whirring in the living room. Garden chairs were scattered around an iron table in the small garden, which was shaded by a huge umbrella gaily striped in blue and yellow. At this moment the leaves of the tree drooped and the metal table would be scorching hot to the touch.

Tony walked through the first floor, checking for any last-minute oversights. The butler's pantry was now a small, businesslike office with a plain desk and steel filing cabinets. The kitchen, its walls painted a fresh cream, held an exhibit of etchings and lithographs of young artists. The dining room, where a record player was ready to produce quiet music by Scarlatti and Mozart and Schubert, held most of the books. The living room contained a locked case of rare books and open shelves of new ones, but on the whole it maintained its private-home atmosphere, with easy chairs and lamps. Only at second glance would anyone observe that the few oil paintings on the wall each held a discreet price tag.

Mrs. Perry watched Tony's progress through the shop. "Satisfied?" she asked, smiling.

Tony nodded. "I think it's perfect! All that bothers me is that we're too late to do well with Christmas cards and they are a big selling item. We have so much to learn! I should have realized that bookstores order them practically six months in advance."

"How are you going to manage?"

"We'll get them somewhere," Tony said confidently.

Mrs. Perry began to laugh. "I can always tell when you're up to something! Your whole face comes alight. Now what plan are you hatching?"

"Well, I was just thinking that it would be nice if we could have cards that were representative not only of Christmas but of our neighborhood. Remember those sketches you made of Gramercy Park last winter? And those water colors you did of people walking past the house, their arms filled with Christmas packages? Why can't you design some special cards for us? And I'll see that they are printed in time if I have to stand over the printer with a shotgun."

Mrs. Perry laughed and then said wistfully, "Oh, Tony, I'd love to do it! There's nothing I'd enjoy more."

"That's settled, then," Tony said briskly, and continued her inspection tour, her heart swelling with pride at the attractive little shop she and Rosamund had created.

A bow window extending out to the street held an etching on an easel and half a dozen new books in bright jackets. Outside, an open bin on rollers contained old books marked, ten, twenty-five, and fifty cents. The shop would not be opened officially until the next day, but there was no place for the bin in the living room.

Tomorrow has to be clear, Tony told herself fiercely. It simply has to be. Sunshine and fair weather would be a bright omen for The Good Companions Bookshop.

For a moment she stood looking at the bow window. Only one thing was lacking, the sign which was to be hung on an ornate metal arm that had already been installed. The sign read:

The Good Companions Bookshop
Carew & Perry, Prop.

Mrs. Perry had been greatly amused by it, but the girls had insisted. It had such a businesslike sound, they declared.

Tony dragged the ladder into the living room and lifted it with some difficulty into the window, for it was tall and heavy. She was about to climb the steps when the front door closed and Mrs. Perry came in, a troubled expression on her charming face. Tony realized then that she had been dimly aware of voices, of some sort of altercation.

"What's wrong?" she asked quickly.

Mrs. Perry's mouth twisted in a rueful grimace. "Oh, dear, it's Mister Duffy!"

"What on earth has he done?"

"Nothing, really. That blond operator from the beauty parlor next door has complained that he nearly knocked her down when she was walking past this house."

"Mister Duffy? Never!" Tony said indignantly.

"I know." Mrs. Perry's face was flushed with anger. "I know as well as you do how gentle he is. But that girl seems determined to make trouble."

"What did you tell her?"

"That's the worst of it. It wasn't the girl herself who came over to make the complaint. It was the owner of the shop, a Mrs. Hazelton. She said the operator had told her that customers were staying away because they were so afraid of Mister Duffy."

"That's more serious," Tony said soberly.

"I know it is. I don't blame the owner. She's a

pleasant, forthright sort of woman. She said she didn't like to make trouble but she couldn't afford to lose her customers." Mrs. Perry's voice trailed off in distress.

"No, of course not," Tony said flatly. "It's my fault. I should have known I couldn't possibly keep a great Dane in the city. I suppose I'll have to find him a home in the country somewhere." Her voice shook in spite of herself.

"Oh, my dear." There were tears in the older woman's eyes. "You've done so much for us and done it so gaily; saved the house and given Rosamund a chance to earn her living at something she loves, and provided me with an opportunity to go back to painting again. Everything. Now the house is so altered that there's not even a room for you, except that living-room couch, as long as you absolutely refuse to take Rosamund's room—and we've made you lose Mister Duffy! I can't bear it."

"Don't worry," Tony told her gently. "We'll work it out somehow."

"Of course," Mrs. Perry said thoughtfully. "There's Catherine. You saw her ad in the *Times* this morning?"

Tony nodded. Mrs. Perry's widowed daughter had advertised two rooms for rent in her home in Westchester: "Plain rooms with few luxuries but good food. Shade trees in the garden for daydreaming and a brook for lazy fishermen." Catherine Cathcart had given her mother's New York address to handle inquiries.

"Would she be willing to take Mister Duffy?"

"She'd love having him, not only because he'd be a perfect companion for a four-year-old boy but because he's a fine watchdog and her house is rather isolated."

As footsteps clattered down the stairs, Mrs. Perry said quickly, "Don't tell Rosamund what has happened. She'll be furious about Mister Duffy and she doesn't like that beauty parlor operator, anyhow, with that phony Southern drawl of hers."

"Phony?" Tony said in surprise.

Rosamund darted into the room. She always moved like quicksilver. "Phony? You-all discussin' that Civil Wah belle next doh? If she's been closer to the Mason-Dixon line than South Brooklyn I'll eat my hat." Green eyes flickered from one distressed face to the other. "What has she been doing now? I'll bet it's Mister Duffy!"

"That red is showing," Tony warned her.

"I know I've got a temper, but—"

Tony explained. There was no use in trying to placate Mrs. Hazelton. If the great Dane was frightening away her customers he would simply have to go.

"I don't believe he ever frightened anyone in his life—except a burglar," Rosamund said hotly.

The gay jingling bell that Tony had arranged for the front door rang merrily and Mrs. Perry went to open it. "Tomorrow," she told the girls, "this will be your job." She opened the door and they heard her cry out joyously, "Jane! How lovely."

"That's Mrs. Haven," Rosamund told Tony in a whisper. "She's Mother's dearest friend and she lives just around the corner on Nineteenth Street in the darlingest little house."

In a moment Mrs. Perry reappeared, her face glowing, accompanied by a slim, alert-looking woman in her middle forties, her brown hair dusted with gray. She wasn't pretty but she had something better than prettiness, for there were lines of humor around her eyes, of compassion around her mouth.

"Rosamund, my dear!" She kissed the red-haired girl.

"How nice to see you, Mrs. Haven. Where have you been all summer? New York isn't the same place without you."

"In Boston, visiting my brother. But it is good to get back to my own little house."

"Jane," Mrs. Perry said, "this is my other daughter, Antoinette Carew. Tony, Mrs. Haven is my oldest friend."

Mrs. Haven greeted the girl smilingly and then

looked around her. "What on earth has been going on?"

"This," Rosamund said grandly, "is the Good Companions Bookshop and you may have the privilege of a preview." She offered her arm with an exaggerated gesture.

Mrs. Haven accepted it with equal exaggeration and let Rosamund lead her on a tour of inspection, the girl's words tumbling over themselves in an amusing burst of jubilant excitement.

When Rosamund had led her friend out of hearing range, Mrs. Perry said in a low tone, "Jane Haven is a wonderful person, Tony. I've known her all my life. She has had a lot of trouble. She married a young poet without any money, but they were wildly in love. He never earned much, of course, and her brother and sister-in-law were bitter about it. Then he had a long and expensive illness of which he died a few years ago."

"She has such a happy look, such an eager, interested look," Tony said in surprise. "You wouldn't think she had had so much trouble and disappointment, would you?"

"She is one of those rare people who think more about others than about themselves. She's truly a gallant woman."

Mrs. Perry broke of as Rosamund returned, triumphantly leading Mrs. Haven.

"This is a wonderful idea!" the latter exclaimed enthusiastically. "I wish you girls every success with it."

"Now, if my daughter will release you," Mrs. Perry said, "it's my turn. I'm going to show you what we have done—or rather what Tony has done—with the upper floors. She has really performed miracles. The only awful thing is that she has designed it so perfectly for Rosamund and me that there's no spare bedroom for her."

"I'll stay on at the hotel temporarily," Tony said. "As soon as I've settled about Mister Duffy I'll start apartment hunting. There must be something in the neighborhood that will do."

"Why can't you come to me, Miss Carew?" Mrs. Haven said impulsively. "I'd delighted to have you becamse I simply rattle around in the house, small as it is."

"Jane," Mrs. Perry exclaimed in delight, "that would be perfect! Tony, you'd love it. The house is a joy. It's a regular museum of fine old furniture."

"Which," Mrs. Haven said lightly, "will probably have to end in a museum. I simply can't keep up the house much longer with taxes the way they are."

"Oh, no, Jane! You couldn't give it up," Mrs. Perry wailed.

"Heaven knows I don't want to. Not just for the sake of the house itself and its associations, but can't you hear Betty's 'I told you so'?"

"Your sister-in-law—" Mrs. Perry began in a tone that showed from whom Rosamund had inherited her temper. She checked herself.

"Do you mean it?" Tony asked. "About letting me rent a room from you?"

It was clear that Mrs. Haven meant it. They settled the arrangements in record time, Tony insisting that it was unnecessary for her to inspect the room first.

"Then I'll expect you for dinner," Mrs. Haven began.

"Not for dinner," Rosamund cried. "Tony has to have her last meal with us!"

Mrs. Haven laughed. "It sounds as though she were preparing for execution. Then shall we say about nine o'clock?"

When Mrs. Haven had gone, Mrs. Perry said, "If we can't keep you here, I'd rather have you with Jane than any place else. She's such a darling. But that impossible sister-in-law of hers—"

"Mother!" Rosamund warned teasingly. "And you're the one who brought me up not to gossip."

"Betty Holbrook would make a saint gossip," her mother retorted. "Jane's brother Tom is a big, impressive-looking man who has developed an important business. His wife, Betty, is one of those small, tight-lipped women who keep their big husbands on a chain as if—as if they were Mister Duffy."

All Betty Holbrook cared about, she said hotly, was money and social position, and she had never forgiven Jane for marrying a man without a large income or the ability and desire to make one.

"At least," Rosamund pointed out, "Carter Holbrook will be all his mother expects of him."

Carter, Mrs. Perry explained, was Jane Haven's nephew, an attractive young man, unspoiled by his good looks, and already, in his early thirties, making an exceptionally fine income.

"He's one of the handsomest men I've ever seen," Rosamund said. There was a kind of weariness in her voice, and Tony was aware that she was thinking again of Hal and his heartbreaking silence.

Mrs. Perry was aware of it, too. She looked from Rosamund to Tony and then said to the latter, with an attempt at brightness, "Why don't you take a cool shower, child, and then go and pack?"

"I'll put up the sign first," Tony decided. "Then we'll be all ready for the Grand Opening."

She climbed the ladder and reached down to take the sign Mrs. Perry handed her. For a moment she looked out into the street. She saw the blond beauty operator whom Rosamund so disliked come out of the shop next door, pause to look into the bow window, and then walk briskly away. Her hair was almost brassy from many tintings; she had large, appealing blue eyes and a sulky mouth. Her pale blue dress was backless, a tasteless dress for a woman in business; her heels were so high that her ankles wobbled awkwardly as she walked.

A young man strolling past the new bookshop halted to look for the number over the door. Then Tony's movement as she reached up precariously to fasten the sign to the bracket caught his attention and he stood looking at her. She moves like a ballet dancer, he thought in delight. His eyes traveled up to the girl's profile. She's beautiful. Good lord, she's beautiful.

He saw the girl lean back, trying to balance the sign, to fasten it to the bracket, saw a pocket of her slacks snag against the easel that stood in the bow window, saw the ladder sway. He flung himself into the shop, dimly aware of a merry jingle of the bell, thrust Mrs. Perry aside, and caught the girl as she pitched forward.

For a moment his arms tightened around her, holding her close, and then he set her on her feet, one arm around her shoulder to steady her.

"Tony!" Mrs. Perry cried. "Are you hurt?"

The girl's face was drained of color. She swayed a little and the young man lifted her out of the window and eased her into a deep chair.

"Just shock, I think. Perhaps a glass of water would help." He had a quiet voice but it carried a note of authority.

While Rosamund hurried away, Mrs. Perry bent over Tony anxiously. The latter opened her eyes and looked up at a tall young man with wide shoulders and slim hips. He had steady blue eyes in a blunt-featured, pleasant face.

"Thank you," she said. "If you hadn't moved so quickly—"

"Glad the old training still operates," he said lightly.

"Football?"

"Princeton. Good lord!" he exclaimed, as Rosamund, accompanied by Mister Duffy, hurried in with a glass of water. The great Dane observed the young man for a moment and then came to rest his head against the stranger's side.

"I never knew him to do that before," Mrs. Perry exclaimed. "What's your secret charm, young man?"

He had a slow, grave smile that warmed his face. "My name is Rodney Meredith and I have no secret charm."

Mrs. Perry looked at Tony's rapt expression, her eyes widening in surprise. Haven't you indeed, she thought in some amusement.

"I am Mrs. Perry," she said, looking the young man over carefully. Tony's life was her own business, of course, but she intended, nonetheless, to form her own opinion of anyone who aroused the girl's interest. This young man, for all his quiet manner and the fact that he was not particularly handsome, had the kind of attraction—an attraction of which he seemed to be unaware—that would catch and hold any girl's imagination.

"Mrs. Perry?" he said in a tone of surprise. "Oh, I was looking for a Mrs. Cathcart."

"She is my daughter."

"There was an advertisement in the *Times* this morning about some rooms with meals in a house in Westchester."

"My daughter is a widow," Mrs. Perry explained, "with one small son. Her husband left her the house, which is too big for her now, so she'd like to have some of the extra rooms occupied. It's a simple place at the end of a country lane, very quiet, with a big garden. Catherine is a marvelous cook. I think you'd be comfortable there."

"It's not for myself," he explained. "I'm looking for some place where my older brother could live, at least for a few months. He has a man to look after him but—"

"He's an invalid?"

"He is blind." He went on quickly, to prevent any expression of sympathy, to ask for details about the accommodations.

At length he said, "It sounds ideal for Jerome. Is there—do you think your daughter would let me drive him up tonight? I know it's short notice, but we moved out of our apartment early this week because the building is being torn down, and he's so restless in a hotel. He needs to be where he can get some exercise without all the hazards of city traffic. Anyhow, he's extremely, almost abnormally, sensitive about appearing in public places."

"I'll call my daughter at once." Mrs. Perry introduced him to the girls. "Miss Carew and my daughter Rosamund."

He took Tony's extended hand and when he had released it, rather reluctantly, he spoke to Rosamund and then patted the great Dane.

"This is Mister Duffy," Tony told him.

He looked down smiling at the enormous dog. "How do you do, Mister Duffy?"

The big dog flopped at his feet with a long sigh.

"Good heavens, he's practically adopted you," Rosamund said with a laugh.

"I wish I could adopt him," Rodney said. "I've been looking around for a dog for Jerome, one that would force him out for exercise."

Tony and Rosamund exchanged glances and Tony explained the problem that had arisen about Mister Duffy. "So I can't keep him here and, anyhow, it's hardly fair to have him cooped up. I was thinking of asking Mrs. Perry's daughter to keep him for a while." Her hand went out to touch the dog's head. "I'm going to miss him a lot."

"He's a lot of dog to miss. Miss Carew, can't we make some sort of arrangement? Mister Duffy would be well taken care of if he were with my brother, and I'd guarantee to bring him back whenever you like. Or you could come to see him, of course."

With a thoughtful look from one face to another, Mrs. Perry signaled Rosamund with raised eyebrows, picked up the glass, and they both went out of the room.

"Well I—I don't know," Tony said.

"I can give you personal references: my bank, my lawyer, my minister. And Mister Duffy would still be yours, of course."

Tony looked at the quiet young man who was so large and yet could move so swiftly, looked at the steady eyes whose expression brought color flaming into the face that had been so white with shock, looked at Mister Duffy who shifted his position and laid his head on Rodney's shoe.

"I guess that settles it," she said with a laugh. "Mister Duffy has decided his own fate."

Mrs. Perry came back to say, "Catherine is delighted, Mr. Meredith. She will expect you and your brother tonight. And she said she'd love to have Mister Duffy."

"Then suppose I pick him up some time this evening. I'll bring my car and take him up with my brother and his man to Mrs. Cathcart's. Will that do?" He spoke to Mrs. Perry but his eyes were on Tony.

The girl's hand went out again wistfully to the great Dane and then dropped. "All right," she said at last. She gave him the number of Mrs. Haven's house on Nineteenth Street.

"About nine-thirty?"

"That will be fine."

Rodney Meredith bent over to dislodge Mister Duffy's head from his shoe. "We could take him for a walk before I drive up to Westchester," he suggested, "so that he could grow more accustomed to me. That's important, don't you think, if he's to be happy up there."

Tony nodded. "Very important," she agreed. "At nine-thirty then, Mr. Meredith."

With a long, steady look at her he was gone, closing the door quietly behind him. Through the bow window Tony saw him walk down the street. He was whistling softly. He stopped, turned and came back.

"I'd forgotten what made you fall." He picked up the sign, attached it to the metal arm, lifted the ladder out of the window, smiled at her, and was gone again.

"And who," Rosamund demanded from the staircase, "is that man? He has enough charm to turn the head of any woman and yet he's not exactly handsome. How does he do it?"

Tony bent over Mister Duffy, her face hidden, and said casually, "He's going to take the monster up to Kathy's for a while. I think it will work out rather nicely. Mister Duffy seems to have fallen for him."

"So I noticed," Rosamund said, a glint in her green eyes. "Quite a man he must be. I hope he's going to keep you in close touch with Mister Duffy."

"Naturally," Tony said.

"Naturally," Rosamund echoed. She laughed. "What goes on around here? According to Mother, you fell right into his arms."

"Just for that—" Tony began, but broke off as the telephone rang.

Rosamund ran to answer it. They heard her say incredulously, "Hal? Hal! I thought you were—mad at me. . . . Of course I do. . . . Of course you can. . . . Of course I will. . . . Seven o'clock? . . . Of course."

She came back, spots of color flaming in her cheeks. "That," she said unnecessarily, "was Hal."

"Of course."

The two girls looked at each other and began to laugh.

The house on Nineteenth Street was three stories in height and just one room wide, with an areaway and steps leading down to a basement. The front door was painted a bright red.

Tony parked the long Lincoln at the curb, lifted down suitcases, and then urged Mister Duffy to get out.

The red door opened and Mrs. Haven stood smiling. "Welcome home, Miss Carew," she said warmly and Tony's eyes stung with tears. In spite of all her good resolutions, she had been feeling like an outcast, desolate and sorry for herself. Partly it was the inevitable letdown from completing her work on the bookshop and the ebbing of the initial excitement. Partly it was the knowledge that she must part with Mister Duffy. Partly it was the feeling that she had no home of her own.

With a few simple words and a smile Mrs. Haven had restored her usual serenity. The older woman looked in some alarm at the great bulk of Mister Duffy and Tony explained that he would be there only half an hour. A young man was coming for him.

Mrs. Haven escorted her through the house. There were an old-fashioned kitchen and storerooms on the ground floor; the first floor had, beyond the small entrance, a formal living room and behind it a dining room. On the second floor there was a library at the front and an informal sitting room at the back, while the third floor contained two bedrooms.

"I've put you in the room at the back," Mrs. Haven explained. "It's quieter away from the street, and it has more sunshine. I do hope you'll be comfortable."

Tony looked at the charming room with its four-poster bed, a highboy that belonged in a museum, petit-point chairs, a chaise lounge, and polished floors with wide boards and rag rugs. There was also a tiny but immaculate bathroom.

"It's perfect," she exclaimed. "I'm going to love it here."

While she unpacked her suitcases and hung her clothes, Mrs. Haven sat chatting with her. It was apparent that she had been accustomed to a great deal of money and an active social life, to servants and comforts that she was now forced to do without, but it was also obvious that she found life interesting and rewarding.

Until Tony was ready to go downstairs they talked of travel and museums and strange customs they had seen on their trips abroad.

In the cozy sitting room on the second floor, Mrs. Haven waved her to a chair and then got up to rummage in a desk drawer and bring her some keys.

"You are to consider this your home, my dear," she said, "for as long as you like. Come and go as you please. Here are keys for the house and for Gramercy Park. Now when would you like breakfast?"

"At eight o'clock, if that's not too early for you."

"That will be fine."

Tony looked at a photograph on a table beside her, the face of a man with a sensitive mouth and smiling eyes.

"That was my husband," Mrs. Haven said. "I lost him five years ago and yet in a way I've never really lost him at all."

"It must have been a good marriage," Tony said huskily.

"It had everything: love and companionship and shared interests. Someone once said a good marriage was a long, uninterrupted conversation. Ours was like that. There was always so much we had to say to each other."

"That's the kind of marriage every woman dreams of," Tony said softly.

There was humor in Mrs. Haven's smile but no

bitterness. "Not every woman, my dear. To my sister-in-law it was a most disastrous affair, because Jack wasn't a money-maker. My kind of marriage wouldn't have made sense to Betty. She wants the things money can buy: social position, status. Sometimes I feel very sorry for her."

She laughed outright. "And she's sorry for me! But Jack and I meant it—you know: for richer for poorer; for better for worse; in sickness and in health; to have and to hold from this day forward."

The doorbell rang. "That will probably be the young man for that monstrous animal of yours." She got up, hesitated for a moment. "This is childish of me," she confessed, a faint flush on her cheekbones, "but would you mind very much—that is, Betty would think it was another proof that Jack failed as a husband—I mean—well, would you mind saying you're my guest here, not a paying guest?"

"But that's what I feel I am!" Tony exclaimed. She fastened the leash on Mister Duffy's collar. "Come on," she told him, "we're going for a walk."

Mister Duffy trotted down the stairs, with Tony running after him, for the great Dane knew quite well that it was his function to lead the way and take charge of proceedings.

Rodney Meredith was waiting at the door, and parked at the curb was a shabby Chevrolet that had seen some years of service.

For a long time he looked at Tony without speaking. Beautiful as she had been in slacks and shirt, with a streak of dust across a cheek, she was breathtakingly lovely now in a slim green sheath, with a twist of gold for a belt around her slender waist. Like most men, he disliked seeing women in slacks, which had so unfortunate an effect on concealing their femininity and charm. She's the loveliest thing on earth, he thought.

However, his voice was quiet as he said, "I talked to Jerome, who is delighted." He reached for the leash, saw the girl's expression, and his hand dropped. For as long as possible Mister Duffy must belong to her.

"I have a key to the park," Tony said. "Shall we walk there?"

Gramercy Park lies in a little backwater of New York City, a tiny park only a block square, enclosed behind ornate iron gates that can be opened only by people who live in the buildings around the square or by a few privileged outsiders. When Tony had unlocked the gate on the south side of the park they went in and she unfastened the leash.

"There's no one here for him to frighten," she said, "so I'll let him run free."

"Frighten?" Rodney sounded rather surprised.

She told him about the hairdresser in the beauty parlor who claimed that Mister Duffy frightened away the customers.

"That's why I have to send him away."

"That's odd. Ever know him to do that before?"

"Never. Of course, if he were ordered to attack he would do it, but as a rule he's the gentlest dog I ever knew."

They walked slowly up and down the gravel paths. In the distance came the long-carrying hoarse sound of boat whistles on the East River. Nearer at hand there was the electrifying and heart-chilling sound of sirens as ambulances, fire engines, and po- lice cars raced to meet some emergency. Lights glit- tered on the Chrysler Tower, a slim spire to the north, on the buildings on Fourteenth Street to the south. For some reason it seemed to Tony that every impression was more vivid tonight than she had ever known it to be.

Sauntering beside her, Rodney drew a long breath. "The end of summer," he said at last, regret- fully.

"I wouldn't like a one-season climate," Tony said. "I love the change of seasons, the return of life in the spring, and the song of birds; the lush splendor of summer; the autumn leaves in the fall; the white canopy of winter."

"So do I," Rodney agreed. "I was really thinking of Jerome."

"That's your brother? The one who's going to look after Mister Duffy?"

"My older brother. He's—rather special as a person. He used to be the gayest human being I ever knew and then, a few years ago, everything changed for him."

There was a long silence while they walked along the paths and Mister Duffy, too dignified to romp any longer, returned to pace sedately in front of them.

"There was a—burglary in his office. Apparently Jerome tried to intervene and he was struck. He lost his eyesight. He lost everything else along with it," Rodney went on bleakly, "his profession and the girl he loved, whom he had planned to marry."

"You mean she broke the engagement after he was blinded?" Tony was aghast.

"She certainly did," Rodney said grimly. "What she actually said to him I'll never know, but from that day I don't think he has cared much whether he lived or died. He shrinks more and more inside himself. I've got a good guy to look after him, take him for exercise, read to him, all that, but—" He broke off and said more cheerfully, "Sorry, I didn't mean to bring you a sob story. I only wanted you to have some idea of what Mister Duffy will mean to Jerome. He's never known that much dog in his life and I have a hunch Mister Duffy is going to take a firm hand with him—if you can say that about a dog—and make sure he gets out into the air, takes walks, begins to have an interest in life again."

"I hope he will," Tony said huskily.

"I'll bring him back, you know, once a week, or as often as you like, but some time, I hope—would you mind coming out to see my brother? He—he's a nice guy."

Abruptly Rodney shifted the conversation away from Jerome and himself to the bookshop. Tony found herself talking eagerly about the plans she and Rosamund had made for creating a shop that would have a personal touch, a place where people could browse at leisure and in comfort.

"Books aren't just commodities like soap flakes and tea. They are companions and friends, a world in which the imagination can soar—and sometimes a guide to the real world, an aid in helping a person to find himself."

"It's a grand idea," he told her. "'I wish you every success with it. But it's quite an undertaking, isn't it, for two girls? Are you and that pretty redhead alone in this?"

That pretty redhead. For a moment Tony was aware of a twinge of jealousy. Then she was ashamed of herself.

"Rosamund Perry. Yes, we're partners."

From the big clock on the tower at Fourteenth Street Tony saw that it was ten-thirty. Where had the time gone? She didn't want this evening to end. She supposed it was because she was going to miss Mister Duffy.

She gave Rodney the key and he unlocked the park gate. Then she put Mister Duffy's leash in his hand. "From now on—"

He looked down at her, a sober, intent look. "I think we'd better go around the block a few times, don't you? So he'll get used to me."

Tony agreed quickly. It was essential that Mister Duffy learn to accept Rodney Meredith. Wasn't it? They walked more and more slowly, Tony's voice chattering eagerly while Rodney's deeper one chimed in now and then. And then, unbelievably, the clock showed eleven-thirty.

"And you've still got to drive to Westchester!" she exclaimed.

"It's not far," he assured her. "I wouldn't have had the evening end sooner."

They returned to Mrs. Haven's charming little house. Together they persuaded Mister Duffy to climb into the right-hand seat of the shabby old Chevrolet. Tony leaned forward, her arms around the dog's neck, her cheek pressed against his head.

"Be a good dog," she said cheerfully, though her tears left glistening marks on the dog's coat.

Rodney took her hand, smiled down at her. "Don't

worry about Mister Duffy. He'll be in good hands.
And all you need to do is to call me and I'll return
him within a few hours."

She nodded.

He hesitated. "Well, I'd better be on my way. I'll
call you in a few days to tell you how he's making
out. All right?"

"Of course."

He slid under the wheel, released the brake, and
the car moved off toward Irving Place and turned
right at the park. The big red warning light at the
park gate illuminated the front seat, the large young
man at the wheel, the large dog beside him. Mister
Duffy settled down, his chin resting on the man's
shoulder. Smiling faintly, Tony went back to unlock
the flaming red door and let herself in to her new
home.

iv

At a modest hotel in midtown, Rodney parked at the curb and spoke gently to Mister Duffy. "Just a few minutes, old boy, and we'll be on our way."

He tapped at the door of a room on the fifth floor which was opened by a rough-looking man in his early forties, wearing dark slacks and a turtle-neck sweater.

"Oh, it's you," he growled, trying to keep his voice low. "Thought you'd forgotten all about us. Know what time it is? Jerome's asleep."

"No, I'm awake," said the man who was lying on the bed. His voice had a curiously lifeless quality.

"Sorry to be late," Rodney said. "The car's downstairs, right in front of the hotel. We can be up there in less than an hour." He turned to the rough-looking man. "Packing done, Sam?"

"Sure it's done," Sam said truculently. "Everything ready but the transportation. You said ten o'clock."

"Stop riding him, Sam," Jerome Meredith said as he got off the bed.

Sam thrust a stick into the groping hand. "You go ahead with Rod. I'll bring the suitcases."

Rodney took his brother's arm as unobtrusively as possible, guiding him to the door, down the corridor, and into the elevator.

"I'm sorry to be so late," he said.

"It doesn't matter," Jerome said. It was easy to tell from that flat, colorless voice that nothing mattered.

"Brace yourself for a shock," Rodney said with an attempt at heartiness. "Wait until you meet Mister Duffy, the dog I told you we're taking up to Mrs. Cathcart."

32

"If we're going to nursemaid a Pekingese—" Jerome began irritably.

Rodney chuckled. "Mister Duffy is more dog than I've ever seen before. A great Dane."

When Jerome and Sam were in the back seat and the suitcases had been stowed in the trunk, Rodney turned around.

"This," he said, "is Mister Duffy."

Jerome leaned forward, his hand touched the massive head of the great Dane. "Good lord! Where did you find this elephant?"

"He belongs to a girl who has a bookshop at Mrs. Perry's house," Rodney said casually. "Mrs. Perry is the mother of your new landlady. And by the way, Jerome, if the daughter, Mrs. Cathcart, is anything like her mother, you'll be in luck. Anyhow, there was some trouble about Mister Duffy. The shop next door claimed he scared away customers—"

"Hey, what are you getting us into?" Sam said belligerently.

"Keep your shirt on, Sam. Mister Duffy won't give you any trouble."

They rode in silence. Sam kept a watchful and dubious eye on Mister Duffy while Jerome sat quietly in a corner, his sightless eyes concealed behind dark glasses. Rodney wondered whether he was asleep and then, as he had to brake sharply, saw his brother's thin hand grip the back of the front seat and relax again. Awake, then. But what thoughts were going on behind the unrevealing face?

Why, Rodney wondered, was he unable to reach the brother whom he so deeply loved and admired. Never, since the accident which had resulted in his brother's blindness, the loss of his law practice, and the breaking of his engagement had there been any real confidence between them. Jerome had stubbornly refused to discuss what had happened, withdrawing more and more deeply into some silent world of his own. Even Sam, who had been a handyman in the old days and was now his faithful companion, was unable to reach him.

The night was hot and muggy and breathless, the

air tainted with gasoline fumes, dust, and the assort-
ed smells of a great city on a summer night. Beyond
the Bronx with its apartment-lined streets, Rodney,
following Mrs. Perry's directions, found a quiet road
and then a narrow lane of arching trees.

"It's real country, Jerome," he said jubilantly.

"Good."

The toneless, apathetic voice made Rodney's
hands close tight on the wheel. How long was it since
he had heard Jerome's joyous great blasts of laughter, since his voice had rung with interest and a boy's
confidence that his world was good, the future in his
own hands?

At the end of a lane there was a big, sprawling,
ugly Victorian house, with unnecessary turrets and
balconies. A period piece. But there were elms and
maples in the well-kept lawn; a child's abandoned
tricycle lay on its side; at the back, where the garden
sloped down to a running brook, there was an old-
fashioned summerhouse. Rodney was delighted. It
might have been made to order. Space and privacy
and freedom from traffic hazards.

For the first time he felt a pang of uneasiness.
Suppose Jerome were to dislike his new landlady?
Remembering the days, not so long ago, when his
brother had been tremendously popular and always
had a string of girls at his command, it was hard to
recognize this new Jerome, with his quiet but implac-
able resentment against women, his dislike of them,
which only his impeccably good manners could conceal.

He hoped that Mrs. Cathcart would understand
the situation, would know by some mother wit how
to deal with it. A lot to expect, he acknowledged to
himself.

O Lord, let it be all right, he prayed silently. Let
Jerome find a refuge here and heal those bitter
wounds that he won't even discuss with me.

As he turned into the driveway a light flashed on
the porch and a girl flung open the door and came
out.

"Mr. Meredith?" she called.

Rodney was aware of Jerome's sudden attention, the strained way in which he listened to her voice.

He eased himself out from under the wheel. "I am Rodney Meredith. Mrs. Cathcart?"

It didn't seem possible that she could be the mother of a four-year-old boy. She looked about twenty. Like her sister Rosamund, Catherine Cathcart was small, with a vivid face and a daring sort of grace. Unlike Rosamund, she had hair of so pale a blond that it was almost flaxen.

"I'm dreadfully sorry that we are so late. It's inexcusable."

"It doesn't matter in the least," she assured him. "The evening has been so beautiful I've been sitting on the back porch, listening to the brook and the rustle of the trees." She broke off for a moment as Sam eased Jerome out of the car and handed him his stick. Then she went on warmly, "You must all be tired. I'll show you your rooms. Where is Mister Duffy?"

The great Dane came toward her with his usual dignity and submitted to having his head patted.

"Good evening, Mister Duffy," she said politely. "Mr. Meredith, I've given you and Mr. Baxter—"

"I'm Sam," the attendant told her gruffly.

"I've given you and Sam adjoining rooms on the first floor. There's a bath attached." She went on hastily so he would not feel that she had considered his handicap in making the arrangement, "You see, I do hope you'll like it here and want to stay, so I've given you the rooms where you can hear the brook." She added in dismay, "Oh dear, perhaps you don't like that sort of thing. In that case, it wouldn't take me ten minutes to fix some rooms upstairs."

"I'd like the brook," Jerome assured her

She turned to Rodney. "For tonight, I can put you—"

"Not necessary, but thanks very much. I'm going back to New York. I have an early appointment in the morning." He started to shake hands with Jerome, broke off with a laugh. Mister Duffy had pushed against the blind man, whose hand was resting on the big head. "Well, I'll be darned!" he exclaimed.

Jerome's sensitive fingers explored Mister Duffy's head. The great Dane nudged him insistently.

"I guess," Jerome said, "he wants to have a walk."

Without a word Rodney put the leash in his hand. Sam was about to protest but stopped as Rodney shook his head violently. Mister Duffy set off sedately across the velvety smooth lawn, leading Jerome, who followed him with cautious, tentative steps, guiding himself with his cane.

Rodney turned to see Catherine Cathcart blink tears out of her eyes.

"He'll be all right," she told him, a little catch in her breath. "Mister Duffy will look after him."

"Keep in touch, Sam," Rodney said and went back to his car.

As he drove to New York he thought with gratitude of the sanctuary he had found for his older brother. Surely it would work out. When he had been out in the open air for a while both Jerome's health and his spirits would improve. In time he would be willing to restore Rodney to his old confidence, tell him about the thing that had happened that had so crippled his life.

It wasn't often, Rodney thought, that brothers had been so close, had built so warm an understanding and companionship. As the older, Jerome had looked after him from the time he was ten, at first with the oversevere and dominating attitude natural in a boy three years the senior. Afterward, they had become the closest of friends. Even when life had inevitably set them on separate paths, with Jerome preparing to follow his father's career in the law and Rodney studying to be an industrial designer, they had never lost their enjoyment of each other's company.

For the first time it occurred to Rodney that, while he had followed the profession of his choice, Jerome had, without apparent reluctance, abandoned his own chosen field to please his father.

"Don't worry, Windy," he had said with a laugh, "there is no real sacrifice involved and it will please the old man. And, after all, he'd never understand why a grown man prefers writing children's books to drawing up briefs."

"But that book was darned good," Rodney said. "Not just because the critics liked it, but look at the way it sold."

"Just a fluke, probably. Anyhow, if I'm any good I'll be able to go on writing at night."

Both of them had known it wouldn't work out.

Windy. It was a long time since Jerome had used his favorite name for Rodney. He had started it because Rodney was so quiet, so monosyllabic in comparison with his own natural exuberance and talkativeness.

"All I'm sure of," Rodney said between his teeth, "is that Jerome never did a dishonorable thing in his life. The very idea is ridiculous. Ludicrous. But then—why won't he discuss it with me? Something to do with Eve, of course. That's the only explanation."

His mind went over and over the mystery of Jerome's behavior. He tried to put the whole subject aside but it persisted in nagging at him. There was, he knew, too much guesswork involved. He had been away at college at the time, and later had done his stint in the armed services. Jerome had fallen madly in love with a girl named Eve Cranshaw and was engaged to marry her. He had been deliriously happy.

Rodney went back over his memories but there was little concrete information to be dug up about the girl whom his brother had so deeply and so disastrously loved. She was a blonde and apparently extremely pretty. Her uncle and Jerome had been involved in some kind of business together. It seemed possible that Cranshaw had been a client of his. But even that Jerome had never been willing to discuss.

He had had a small office in Manhattan with a rather elderly woman secretary who, years before, had worked for his father. Miss G. Burns. In spite of his somber thoughts, Rodney found himself grinning as he remembered Miss G. Burns. In all the years they had known her, neither Jerome nor Rodney had ever discovered her first name. They had made up preposterous names to fit that G: gorgeous, gluttonous, glamorous. But Miss Burns, quiet, dependable, businesslike, aloof, had remained Miss Burns to the last.

Rodney remembered her as a rather heavy woman in her fifties with iron-gray hair drawn into an uncompromising knot, and severe tailored suits. Jerome often said that she knew more law than he did. Now and then he had commented with a laugh that it would be a relief if sometime she made a mistake, even a small one. But Miss Burns never made mistakes.

Then, without warning, she quit her job, leaving only a brief note to say that the job no longer suited her. And the following day Jerome's office was broken into. The burglar had struck Jerome, blinding him, and got away. But what, Rodney asked himself as he had done so often before, was there in the office of a struggling young attorney to tempt a robber? What was there to steal that had caused a bitter quarrel with his client, if he was a client, the man Cranshaw, and that had led to the breaking of his engagement with Eve?

Rodney sighed, signaled for a turn, and drove into the garage where he kept his car. Tomorrow, he thought, he would call Antoinette Carew and tell her that Mister Duffy had been safely delivered and that he was going to take wonderful care of Jerome.

Tony wrapped the book and handed it to her customer. "And if that doesn't cheer up your invalid," she declared, "I don't know what would. It's gay and lighthearted and—oh, a sort of hopeful book."

The worn-looking man smiled at her. "You've been of great help, Miss Carew. Whenever my wife gets discouraged—and it's been such a long convalescence!—I come to The Good Companions Bookshop, knowing you'll find just the right thing to cheer her up."

"Fine! That's what we're here for," Tony told him.

The bell jingled merrily as he went out, and she looked around the shop proudly. Just the way I hoped it would be, she thought. Although it was only October a bright fire crackled in the open grate. Before it two people were arguing hotly about modern poetry. In front of the rental shelves a couple of young housewives were picking out books before going home to get dinner. Rosamund was unlocking the case that held rare books and listening with deferential attention to the scholarly man who was describing the particular edition he was seeking to round out his collection.

In the small room at the back Mrs. Perry was hanging pictures for a local exhibition that was to open the following day. This was to be the work of neighborhood painters, with the prices kept low to encourage sales and so help the unknown painters.

We've built a living, meaningful thing, Tony thought happily.

A few minutes later the last of the customers had gone. Mrs. Perry called Tony, who went back into the exhibition room. For a moment she looked around her.

"This is just perfect," she declared.

"And now," Mrs. Perry began, a soft color in her cheeks. Half embarrassed she opened a drawer and began to spread out some water colors on a table. They were delicate scenes of Gramercy Park under snow; the neighborhood church with its windows glowing in the dark; a woman with her arms piled high with gaily wrapped packages; two small children with their noses pressed against a window, looking at some toys.

"They're charming! They're exquisite! Oh, Mrs. Perry, what a pity you haven't been doing this all these years!"

Mrs. Perry flushed with pleasure but she shook her head. "First things first," she said firmly. "I had other jobs to do, bigger jobs. Looking after my family. And it was all there, waiting for me when I was ready. And thanks to you—" She leaned forward to kiss Tony's cheek. "Thank you from my heart, my dear."

"I'll see the man about having these printed right away," Tony said, turning away to conceal her emotion.

Rosamund came running out to the exhibition room. "I sold it! I sold it! Steak for dinner."

Tony pretended to grumble. "There you go again, eating up all the profits."

Mrs. Perry laughed. "That means Hal is coming to dinner. I thought I'd make a chocolate soufflé, Rosamund."

"Good. Heavens, it's nearly six and I want to change."

"And I have an appointment for a permanent wave," Tony said. "Oh, by the way, Rosamund—" she tried to keep her voice casual—"I'm going up to see Mister Duffy tomorrow. Rodney Meredith says the autumn leaves are wonderful now. Why don't you and Hal come along?"

"Love to," Rosamund agreed enthusiastically. "Kathy has been at me for weeks to go up. She tells me that Mister Duffy is thriving. He not only looks after

Dennis the Menace but he takes care of that poor man. She says Mrs. Meredith seems to be in much better health and he walks with so much more confidence."

"It's working out, then?"

"Well," Rosamund hesitated, "I think Kathy is sort of baffled. She says Mr. Meredith is perfectly charming but remote. She doesn't feel she knows him any better now than she did when he came six weeks ago." She broke off to ask, "Is that blond bombshell doing your hair?"

"No. Mrs. Hazelton will do it. She's staying on just for me. I think she feels rather badly about forcing me to get rid of Mister Duffy."

"Well, she ought to," Rosamund said hotly.

Mrs. Hazelton, the manager of the beauty parlor next door, was a pleasant-looking woman with a Middle Western accent, her comfortably plump body fitting tightly into her crisp white uniform.

"*Bonjour, madame,*" she said, somewhat to Tony's amusement. She settled the girl in front of a mirror and began to brush her hair. "I'm not really French, of course, but even a sentence or two gives a place class. I think. What beautiful hair! It's going to be a pleasure working on you."

Tony settled back in resignation, prepared for an endless flow of words.

"Head comfortable? . . . That's good. I do like my ladies to be comfortable when they come here. I always say if you can't relax while your hair's being done you can't relax anywhere. And I've had this place done real nice, I think, to set off my ladies. You notice? The walls are a pale pink to flatter a customer's skin. Not," she added hastily, "that you need any help like that. But most of my ladies are a mite older. Well, in their forties and fifties, really. Their skin needs all the help it can get."

Tony closed her eyes, letting the words wash over her like a wave. When her hair had been shampooed and the chair was straight again, she became more aware of what Mrs. Hazelton was saying.

"My husband, François—well, really his name is Frank but I think he's silly to mind being called François—gives the place class. He's a chemist and, if I do say it, he's a wonder. He's worked out a new cream that gives the skin a beautiful smooth glow and lasts for hours. Absolutely new. Believe me, it is going to revolutionize make-up. Before long, when we've learned how to exploit it the right way, it's going to put me in the top bracket, one of the great ones, along with Elizabeth Arden and Helena Rubinstein. Because you ask any woman who's begun to age what she needs most and she'll tell you right off it's something to hide the wrinkles and keep the skin young-looking. And this does."

Tony's mind floated off to the following day and the trip, her first trip, to see Mister Duffy. Rodney had brought him to New York several times and they had walked for hours in Gramercy Park, but this visit was going to be different. Tony did not try to explain to herself in what way it would be different.

"Yes, it's a new discovery in cream, *madame*. Of course, until we're ready to market it ourselves, we're keeping the formula a dead secret. It's the kind of thing other people would give a lot to get their hands on. Now and then, of course, I've tried it out on a few favorite customers. I gave some to my operator, Cecily Ann, to try on her aunt. She was crazy about it, said it made all the difference. Ten years younger. Those were her very words. But when she wanted a bigger supply, Frank—François—put his foot down. He says we've got a fortune in it, if we can just keep it a secret. Not that there's much danger of someone getting hold of it except by accident."

"Accident?" Tony said, puzzled.

"Well, there've been a couple of attempts to break into the shop. Someone looking for cash might get this out of the safe, figure out what it is. Anyhow, I'm not going to give out any more of it until we're ready. Though I must say, it seems different with Cceily Ann. My own operator. And the best one I ever had."

Tony roused herself. "Cecily Ann? That's the blond girl, isn't it?"

"Cute little trick," Mrs. Hazelton said. "Pretty as she can be and does excellent work. My ladies all like her. And that Southern drawl of hers—real cute." Mrs. Hazelton sighed. "I don't suppose I'll be able to keep her much longer. I saw her out last Saturday night riding with a good-looking man. Had a car about a mile long. So one of these days she'll probably tell me she's all set to get married."

"Perhaps she'll go on working for you," Tony suggested.

"Not if she marries a man with a car like that. Won't need to turn her hand."

"Mrs. Hazelton," Tony said abruptly, "did you ever have any trouble with Mister Duffy?"

"Who's he?"

"My great Dane."

"Oh. No, I never did. But Cecily Ann said he scared off the customers."

"Did any of the customers ever complain to you about him?"

"Well, no, I can't say they did." After an awkward pause, Mrs. Hazelton said apologetically, "I was really sorry about that. It was Cecily Ann who said she would quit if the dog didn't go. And you don't get operators with her flair every day in the week. I can tell you that. I couldn't afford to lose her. I hope you found a home for him."

She adjusted the dryer and handed Tony a magazine. "Now you can just rest. Best part of having your hair done, I always say. Resting. But some operators are such talkers you can't hear yourself think."

She switched on the dryer and its sound mercifully drowned out her voice.

ii

As usual in the Northeast, Columbus Day was brilliant, with a warm sun, crisp cool air, and a deep-

blue sky. Hal and Rosamund were waiting in front of
the house on Irving Place and climbed into the front
seat of the Lincoln beside Tony.

Hal Perkins was not over medium height and a
little over medium weight, with a round cheerful
face. Regarded as one of the best newspaper
cameramen in the field, with a flair for spotting news
stories, and a capacity for taking dangerous risks to
get his shots, he was one of the nicest persons Tony
knew.

Since he had come back the night before the
Grand Opening of The Good Companions Bookshop,
he and Rosamund had been seeing each other with
increasing frequency. Now that the bookshop was
proving itself to be a going concern, they were beginning to talk about marriage. Rosamund was to
continue her work in the shop and Hal was to move
into the Irving Place house. Rosamund's happiness
was like sunlight around her.

"So," Rosamund said, as the car turned north, "we
are going to be married in February. There should
be a slack season in the shop then, don't you think,
so we could have a two-weeks honeymoon. Oh,
Tony, isn't it wonderful?"

Hal slid an arm around her shoulders. "Hark to the
wench! You'd think she was marrying a millionaire. I
hope you realize, my poor deluded girl, we are going
to be poor but honest. If you think I'll ever provide a
car like this, you need your head examined."

Rosamund laughed. "What's wrong with taxis?"

"Taxis, indeed! I'm afraid you have delusions of
grandeur. It will be subways and buses for you."

The car turned onto a narrow country lane. "Look
at the maples," Rosamund cried. "Aren't they glorious!"

Hal's kindly, shrewd eyes swept over the bright
face of the girl he loved, moved on to Tony's face,
which was usually so quiet, so serene. Now it had a
glow, a radiance, he had never seen on it before.
She's unbelievably beautiful, he thought, but what
has brought such a change in her?

He followed her eyes, saw the towering elms, the

maples flaming with color under the deep blue of the sky, saw the large young man climbing out of a shabby gray Chevrolet ahead of them. His lips puckered in an astonished if silent whistle. So that's it, he thought. Tony the remote has fallen in love.

Rodney turned and saw the long Lincoln, saw Tony at the wheel. For a moment his face lighted up and then he took another look at the expensive car and the bright look faded. At least, Hal thought in satisfaction, the guy isn't a fortune hunter.

He came toward them slowly. The three got out of the car and went to meet him.

"Rosamund," Tony said, "you already know Mr. Meredith. Mr. Perkins, Mr. Meredith."

The two men shook hands, summing each other up quickly, liking what they saw.

The front door opened and Catherine Cathcart came running across the lawn. "Rosamund! How are you, darling? Hello, Hal! Tony, dear, you get more beautiful every day. Come round to the terrace. It's such a perfect day we're able to sit out there. At least, I've been sitting there at intervals. Dennis has fallen into the brook twice so far this morning. I fished him out the first time and Sam rescued him the second time. Sam has more than he bargained for. Dennis has adopted him. In fact, Dennis has adopted them both."

There was the shadow of a frown on her face. "I do hope Dennis isn't making a nuisance of himself, but Mr. Meredith can spin the most entrancing yarns and not only Dennis but all the small children in the neighborhood hang around, simply fascinated, as long as he will talk to them."

Around the corner of the house raced a small boy in blue shorts and shirt, with pale hair like his mother's, his short legs moving like pistons. He flung his arms around Rosamund's knees, nearly upsetting her. "Aunt Rosamund! Aunt Rosamund!"

She knelt to take him in her arms, to kiss the soft flushed cheek. "Hello, urchin."

He tugged at her hand. "Come see the bridge we're building over the brook. Me and Sam."

Rosamund let him take her hand and lead her around the house.

"Hal," Mrs. Cathcart said, "Rosamund tells me you're going to be married. I'm so terribly happy about it." She kissed his cheek.

He beamed at her. "I know what a lucky guy I am, Kathy. You don't have to tell me. Half the time I have to pinch myself to be sure I'm not dreaming."

While the two talked quietly together, Tony and Rodney followed Rosamund and the little boy.

"How is it working out?" she asked him in a low tone.

"Couldn't be better," Rodney assured her. "Mrs. Cathcart is a marvelous cook and she makes Jerome comfortable but she leaves him completely free, too. He's gained weight and he looks better than I've seen him look in years. But Mister Duffy has been the most important factor. He keeps him up to the mark. As I told you, first night we got here Jerome took him for a walk." He shut his eyes for a moment as though trying to blot out the scene. "He was just groping his way along and using that stick of his. You should see him now. He strides off as though he could see as well as anyone, and with so much more confidence."

"I'm terribly glad," Tony told him.

"And I'm terribly grateful," he said. He hesitated, stopped, turned to face her. "I hope—that is, I'd like you to understand about my brother. He's—well, he's rather distrustful of women. There's nothing personal in it. So—"

"I'll understand," she assured him.

For a moment he looked deep into the wonderful clear gray eyes. "Yes, I believe you will."

They rounded the house, saw the flagstone terrace, saw the lawn sloping down to the brook, saw Dennis and Rosamund and Sam examining the tiny bridge, consisting of two planks and a narrow railing, discussing it as solemnly as though it were a cathedral.

They saw, too, the man who sat in a deep chair on the terrace, dark glasses covering his eyes, with Mister Duffy at his feet. The great dog got up, gave one sharp bark, and went to meet Tony. At the sound of the bark the blind man sat erect, his hand tightening on the arms of the chair, straining to hear.

"Down, Mister Ruffy," Tony said laughing. "Down, sir!" She dropped to her knees and wrapped her arms around his neck, her cheek resting on his head. "I've missed you."

"Miss Carew," Rodney said, "this is my brother Jerome."

Jerome stood up, his face turned toward the girl.

"How do you do, Mr. Meredith."

"Miss Carew." His tone was polite. Detached. "How are you, Rod?"

"Fine. Mrs. Cathcart's sister and a friend of hers came up with us. Wonderful day, isn't it?"

"Fine." Jerome's voice was toneless again.

Tony dropped into a lawn chair. "Do sit down, Mr. Meredith."

Rodney took half a step forward and then deliberately waited while his brother put out a hand, guided himself into a chair.

"Nice ride coming up?" the latter asked, still in that remote, indifferent voice.

"Lovely, but not like this, of course." Tony leaned back in her chair, dappled light on her face and her hair, her expression serene. She had a capacity for complete relaxation, Rodney thought. Something of the peace she engendered seemed to reach the taut man in the big chair. His tense hands relaxed, dropped on his lap.

"The country has such lovely sounds," Tony went on softly. "The brook chattering away to itself; the leaves whispering; the woodpecker knocking his brains out against that tree."

The quiet voice, as much a part of the day as the merry, chuckling brook, went on to describe the deep blue of the cloudless sky, the autumn colors in the trees over their head, red and crimson and scarlet, bronze and gold and brown; the small boy who was practically standing on his head to supervise Sam's work; the great Dane who had flopped down at Tony's feet; Rosamund lifting a board with grave concentration.

"Rosamund has red hair, you know," Tony said easily, "and the sun has turned it to flame. She has a vivid pixie sort of face and now it's radiant because she's in love."

There was a bitter twist to the blind man's mouth. "Just a temporary aberration," he said. "She'll get over it sooner than she expects."

Rodney moved. Was silent with an effort.

"Not Rosamund," Tony said quietly. "Not Hal Perkins, the man she is going to marry. They want the only kind of marriage that is worth having—to have and to hold from this day forward."

"You'll like Perkins," Rodney put in.

"Will I?"

"He's merry and brave and he has a lot of the best quality in the world," Tony added.

"And what's that?" Jerome asked, still with that faint mocking smile.

"Just simple human kindness."

The smile faded. "Yes. I see." After a moment Jerome said, "Redheaded. Is Mrs. Cathcart redheaded too?"

"No, she's blond."

"Oh."

"Her hair is so pale a color that it is almost silvery."

"Oh," he said again.

In a moment Catherine Cathcart came around the house with Hal. "This is Mr. Perkins, Mr. Meredith," she said.

Tony, who had been watching their approach, saw Hal's usual kindly smile fade, saw the look of puzzled and half-startled recognition on his face.

Rosamund had come running back to them. "Why must we be so formal?" she demanded. "This is Hal Perkins."

"And you, I think," Hal said in a curious voice, "are Jerome Meredith."

There was a strained silence. Then Jerome said, "That's right."

Sam started toward them, looking at Hal with open

hostility. Mrs. Cathcart averted the impending scene.

"Jerome," she said quickly establishing the first-name basis, "will you lend me Sam for a few min-'utes? I thought we could have a buffet lunch here on the terrace."

Sam was still advancing on Hal, the light of battle in his small eyes.

Rodney began to laugh. "You're taking a risk if you let Sam in the kitchen. He's the original bull in the china shop."

Sam stopped, looked at Rodney, read the urgent message in his eyes. He controlled his anger with a visible effort. "Okay, Mrs. Cathcart, let's show 'em." He opened the kitchen door for her.

Everyone had tried hard but somehow the day was a failure. Perhaps, Tony thought, the trouble was that they were trying too hard. None of them was willing to admit that anything was wrong.

When at last they prepared to leave they were all conscious of a sense of relief.

Tony said good-by to Mister Duffy after taking him for a walk and then came back to slip his leash into Jerome's hand.

Rosamund and Kathy Cathcart walked toward the two cars together, arms around each other, talking in low voices.

Hal, after a somewhat awkward leave-taking of Jerome, strolled away. Only Rodney lingered for a moment.

"Everything all right?"

"Of course." Unexpectedly Jerome asked, "What is she like?"

"Who?"

"This Carew girl you brought up here. There's something different in your voice when you speak to her."

"She's tall and slender, with hair that is almost black and clear gray eyes. Remarkable eyes. An exquisite nose like the one in that youthful painting of the Empress Josephine. She's the most beautiful woman I've ever seen in my life."

Jerome's laugh was without humor. "Quite a build-up."

For the first time since his brother's accident Rodney found himself unreasonably angry with him.

"Well—good night, Jerome." He left rather hastily to join the others.

Hal Perkins was looking at the long, sleek Lincoln. "It would be fun to drive that car."

"Why don't you drive it back?" Tony suggested impulsively. "You know where my garage is on Irving Place. You can leave the keys with Rosamund and I'll get them in the morning. Rodney, may I go with you?"

"Of course. Delighted."

When Hal and Rosamund had driven off, after an exuberant fanfare on the horn, Rodney helped Tony into the shabby Chevrolet. They drove in silence along the country lane, the wider quiet road, and then back through the bustle and the noise and the crowded streets of the Bronx.

"It's queer to think there's so much country right at New York's doorstep, isn't it?" she said when the silence had been prolonged.

"Tony—" Rodney began. Stopped.

"Yes?" She turned toward him.

"Oh, Tony, I do love you so!" he burst out. "Not just because you're the most beautiful thing on earth but because—you're you. A still pond that is sunlit. A—" He lifted a hand and let it drop in a helpless gesture. "There's no describing you. No describing how I feel about you. Just—I love you so terribly."

"Then—" Her voice trembled. In spite of her deep emotion, happiness bubbled up into laughter. "Then—must you be so fierce about it?"

He made no answer. She waited while he passed a car that was double parked, while he paused for a stoplight. Then she turned to look at the blunt profile, at the set mouth, at the lines of stark unhappiness in the face that had grown so inexpressibly dear to her.

"I thought," she began rather shyly, "that love made people happy."

"There's no happiness in this for me," he said heavily. "I love you with all my heart and I can't ask you to marry me."

The happiness that had bubbled up in her like a fountain was abruptly stilled.

"I sound like a fatuous, conceited fool, don't I?" He gave a sharp bark of laughter. "Why should I think you'd dream of marrying me? Not just because of your—incredible beauty. But that—" He nodded toward the big Lincoln ahead of them.

"Money?" Tony said incredulously. "Do you think that matters?"

He laughed again, without amusement. "It matters all right."

"Why, Rodney? Why is it so important to you? I didn't know you were like that."

"It matters all right," he repeated. "If I had enough money I could set to work to help Jerome. And until he is—all right again, I don't belong to myself. I have a job to do."

"You mean his sight?" Tony asked, bewildered.

The Lincoln picked up speed, turned the corner, went out of sight. The Chevrolet moved slowly ahead.

"His sight?" Rodney said slowly. "No. And yet, the ophthalmologist who treated him told me that his blindness was not organic, it was a result of shock. He consulted other specialists about it. They agreed with him that the blindness is—well, a kind of retreat from life. Something happened, something so ugly, so intolerable, he didn't want to see it. Not a deliberate kind of escape, you know. Something buried deep down in his subconscious mind. But it's possible his vision might return someday. When he takes off those dark glasses you'd swear his eyes are perfectly normal."

"Then what is wrong? Is it anything you can tell me?"

"I've got to make things right for him," Rodney said desperately, "and I simply don't know how to do it. I can't reach him. I can't talk to him. He's shut up in a private world of his own and all the barriers are up."

He stopped the car and Tony realized that he had parked before Mrs. Haven's house on Nineteenth

Street. He got out to open the door for her. "It's all my fault. I should have kept away from you, Tony. I might have known what would happen. *Would* happen! It happened the minute I saw you." He said abruptly, "Good night."

Before she could speak he had returned to the car, the door slammed, and he drove off like a man in flight.

ii

In her bedroom in Mrs. Haven's house Tony undressed quickly, slipped her arms into the sleeves of an apricot velvet robe, slid her feet into matching satin slippers, and drew a chair toward the window. She switched off the light and looked out into the darkness.

Rodney loved her. Of all the things that had happened during that disturbing day this was the only one that mattered. He loved her. Once more happiness bubbled up in her exulting heart. Never again would she feel utterly alone. Almost from the first moment she had been more powerfully attracted to the big, quiet-spoken young man than to anyone else she had ever known. And from the beginning she had trusted her own heart. Whatever happened in the future, no one could take this from her, this wonder, this deep-seated joy, this happiness.

Then the sunshine left her face, which clouded over. This love that filled her with happiness had given none to Rodney. Something was deeply, profoundly wrong, and at the core of the trouble was his brother with his strange aloofness, his mockery, his distrust and dislike of women, the cloud that hung over him and which Rodney had set himself to remove.

Why didn't he confide in me? Tony wondered with a pang. Why, at least, didn't he ask me to wait? I'd wait forever. Surely he must guess that. A deep blush burned in her cheeks. How obvious had she been about her love for him? And if he loved her,

why had he not so much as stretched out his hand to
accept the love that awaited him?

She got up to pace the floor, her satin slippers
whispering over the rugs, over the polished wide floor
boards.

She had seen the change in his face when he saw
her big expensive car. He had known then that she
had money, the money he needed so desperately.
Why wouldn't he let her help? Why?

She tossed her robe over the chair and got into
bed, pulling the blankets up over her shoulders. In
vain she tried to hold the happiness that had flooded
her earlier in the evening but it was slipping through
her fingers. Blankly she stared into the dark. There
was only one thing she was sure of. Rodney did not
intend to come back.

iii

At the wheel of the Lincoln, Hal was intent on his
driving. Beside him Rosamund moved restlessly.

"What went wrong, Hal? I thought it was going to
be such a wonderful day and then it was just—
uncomfortable. I think Kathy felt it too, and she was
trying so hard to make it pleasant for us."

He answered slowly, "I'm afraid that it means trouble, darling."

"What kind of trouble?"

"Trouble for Tony."

"Oh, no," she cried in pain and protest. "Not Tony.
Not my lovely Tony."

"I'm terribly afraid so."

"But why? I don't understand. I didn't understand
anything that happened today except that there was
all that uncomfortable strain. What caused it?"

"I guess I did," Hal told her in a worried voice.

"You!"

"Well, you see, I recognized him."

"What are you talking about?"

"Jerome Meredith. I was just starting, five years
ago, and I'd dropped by a police station, a routine

visit, looking for stories, when the call came in. Burglary at Jerome Meredith's office. Didn't seem to be of much interest but I hadn't anything else to do at the time and I trailed along. Meredith was a young lawyer with a tiny office on a court. Place had been pretty well torn up and he had been knocked out and, as it turned out later, blinded."

"Well?" Rosamund said, her voice puzzled.

"Well, there was no clue to the burglar, but the police were interested because of the way the place had practically been torn apart. A lot of trouble to go to in the office of a struggling young attorney. What had the burglar expected to find there? And why in the name of heaven had he broken in at a time when not only Meredith but his office girl were in the place?

"There were a couple of other points that were odd. Meredith had had a secretary who had been with him since he started to practice and who had been with his father before that. The day before the burglary she went on vacation, sent word that she was not coming back, and he got a temporary replacement who was there when I got to the office with the police. Meredith was still unconscious and they were taking him away to the hospital. I got some pictures of him, of the office, and the girl."

Abruptly Hal pulled up to the curb, shut off the motor, and turned to face Rosamund. "A while later, a man named Simon Cranshaw reached New York, breathing fire, saying that he had entrusted two hundred thousand dollars in bearer bonds to Meredith and that the burglary was a put-up job by Meredith himself to cover their theft. I'd hardly have noticed the case if I hadn't known that something was wrong with the setup from the time I entered Meredith's office. Anyhow, the case came up for a hearing and it turned out that the new office girl had disappeared. Not a trace of her. She never showed up. And then— God knows why!—Cranshaw dropped the charges. At least, when the case came up for trial, he had gone somewhere and there was no case against

Meredith. Though the stigma lasted, of course. No smoke without fire. That sort of thing."

"So?" Rosamund said impatiently. "How does all this affect Tony?"

"She is head over heels in love with Rodney Meredith," Hal told her. "You can't miss that look."

They sat silent for a long time. Then Rosamund said, "There's something wrong somewhere."

"There certainly is, my sweet."

"No, wait, Hal," she said eagerly. "Tony is—she has a kind of awareness about people. I don't think she could be taken in or misled by anyone phony. If she's in love with Rodney Meredith, then he is all right."

"I think he is, myself," Hal agreed. "He struck me as a square shooter, a dependable type."

"He also has simply terrific charm," Rosamund said.

"Just the same, there was something all wrong about the burglary in which those bearer bonds were lost. All wrong. Whatever Rodney may be, the chances are that his brother was in it right up to his neck."

"Hal!" Rosamund clutched his hand feverishly.

"Well, darling?"

"Why am I able to earn a living at something I love? Why did we save our house? Why can Mother go back to painting? Why are you and I planning to be married? Because of Tony. She made it all possible. We've got to help her, Hal! We've got to."

"But how?"

"We'll just have to find out the truth about that burglary."

"And how do we do that?" he asked in some amusement. He leaned over and tousled her hair.

"Let's start," she said, "by assuming that Jerome Meredith was innocent, that he was a victim in more than one way."

"More than one way?"

"He lost his sight," she reminded him. "And you can't make me believe he was any party to that just to get his hands on some money."

"Oh." After a long pause Hal said thoughtfully, "I wonder. Now I wonder. But where can we start?"

"Let's call Rodney and put it squarely up to him," Rosamund said.

Hal chuckled. "The direct-action girl. My darling, you are assuming an awful lot."

"Such as?"

"Such as that Rodney won't paste me one for interfering; that he won't tell me to go climb a tree; that he'd welcome an attempt to solve that robbery; that he believes his brother is innocent."

"He does," Rosamund said confidently. "He's completely devoted to him."

"He could be devoted to him, loyal to him, and still believe him to be guilty."

Rosamund shook her head. "No."

"You're as sure as that?"

She nodded emphatically.

He tipped up her chin and bent to kiss her. "That's my girl. I'll call Rodney tomorrow and put it squarely up to him."

Rosamund flung her arms around him. "I'm a lucky girl. A lucky, lucky girl."

He grinned. "Just what I've been telling you."

"If only we could repay Tony in happiness. Help Jerome get back his sight."

"You know, my darling," Hal said slowly, "if Jerome was framed, there may be some people who would not want him to get back his sight. People to whom he could be a danger if he were in a position to point the finger at them."

Rosamund laughed. "Of all the melodramatic nonsense. No one would *want* Jerome to be blind!"

"I hope you are right," Hal said soberly.

iv

In his bed at Kathy Cathcart's house, Jerome Meredith tossed restlessly. The day had gone badly. From the moment when Rodney had brought the girl out on the terrace, he had known from his voice that he was in love with her. Poor Rodney! Well, he'd have to learn the hard way that girls were not to be trusted, to discover bitterness and disillusionment for himself.

He groped for the bedside table and a glass of water. Groping in darkness. That was all his life held. Darkness. And he spread it around him. He had clouded Rodney's young life. Sam had refused a good job to stay and take care of him.

Jerome tensed. He had been aware of the night sounds, the brook that sounded so much louder now, rushing over pebbles, the leaves rustling so that they sounded like rain. Now there was a curious crackling as though someone had got stuck in the big barberry bush under his window.

Mister Duffy, from the first night, had established his right to sleep in Jerome's room. He stirred now, growling deep in his throat. Jerome's fingers groped for the dog's head, felt the rising hackles at the back of his neck.

He got out of bed, found robe and slippers, and groped his way to the door. At once Mister Duffy was on his feet, half following, half guiding him. In the hallway Jerome's hand touched the wall and he walked toward the door at the end of the hall, which opened on the terrace. He moved the bolt, which to his dismay made a loud grating sound, flung open the door.

"Get him, Mister Duffy!"

The huge dog launched himself into the darkness. There was a thrashing sound, someone cursed softly, then feet pounded across the lawn. Mister Duffy's bark seemed to tear holes in the black fabric of the night.

A door was flung open and Sam called, "Jerome! What are you doing?"

"There's a prowler around. I sent Mister Duffy to get him."

"Go back to bed. I'll handle this." Sam lunged back into his room for a flashlight and then past Jerome, who could hear his feet pounding along the terrace.

Then from the staircase behind him Kathy Cathcart said sleepily, "What's wrong?"

"You go back to bed," he told her. "There's a prowler. I sent Mister Duffy after him and now Sam has gone. Everything is under control."

"P—p-prowler?" she said through chattering teeth. "We've never had any trouble here. Dennis!" She ran frantically up the stairs and he heard a door open and close.

In a few minutes she returned. "He's all right," she said. "Sound asleep. I couldn't bear it if anything happened to Dennis." She listened. "There's someone coming." Her small hand clutched his arm and she moved closer to him, seeking protection.

For the first time in several years he was more aware of someone else's needs than of his own. His hand covered the small cold one that held his sleeve.

"It's all right, Kathy," he said quietly. "Sam and Mister Duffy can tackle anything between them."

"Someone's coming." She released her breath in relief. "Here they are."

Sam came in with Mister Duffy. "He got away," he said in disgust.

"He must have taken alarm when I slid back that bolt. It made an awful racket."

"I'd better oil that tomorrow," Sam said. "He sure tangled with that barberry bush. It will break your heart, Mrs. Cathcart, as you seem to set so much store by it." He bent over. "Here, Mister Duffy. What have you got? Give it up."

"Where on earth did he get that?" Kathy asked.

"What is it?" Jerome demanded.

"A dark-blue silk scarf," she told him. "A man's scarf. The prowler must have dropped it."

Sam looked at it. "Mister Duffy tore it off his neck. That guy had a mighty close shave. Or it was pulled off when he struck that bush."

Somewhere a car motor sprang to life, a door slammed, a car moved off. Mister Duffy hurled himself at the door, barking.

"Quiet," Jerome told him.

"So prowlers come in their own cars," Sam said. "It's getting to be a mighty fancy world."

"And what a prowler," Kathy commented.

Something in her voice made Jerome say quickly, "What do you mean by that?"

"That scarf, believe it or not, retails for over forty dollars. I saw one the last time I was in New York and nearly fainted."

"Well!"

"You might as well get back to bed," Sam advised Jerome.

"We're all so wide-awake now," Kathy said, "I don't think we could sleep anyhow. Let's go into the kitchen and have some scrambled eggs."

A half hour later she broke off in the middle of a hilarious story about Dennis with a tremendous yawn.

Jerome, who had been listening, his face alight with amusement, broke into delighted laughter. "You'd better get to bed before you fall asleep."

She yawned again. "I'll just clear up the dishes first."

"I'll do that," Sam said. The look he gave her was filled with gratitude.

It was nearly a month before Hal Perkins was able to carry out his project of calling Rodney Meredith. An epidemic of influenza had drastically cut the staff of photographers on his paper and he was worked off his feet. Each time he called Rosamund or was able to steal a few minutes to be with her, he had to admit that, so far, he had done nothing. Each time Rosamund grew more pressing.

"Tony looks just awful, dear. She gets paler every day and Rodney hasn't called or come near her. He hasn't even brought Mister Duffy down to New York. Kathy says the dog is just fine and so is Jerome. He takes walks for miles every day and he looks like a different man. He and Dennis have become inseparable. Dennis loves Jerome's stories and he's much more obedient than he was. I suppose a little boy needs a man's authority the way he needs brothers and sisters to help him grow up properly."

Early in November Hal and Rosamund sat before the fire in the second-floor living room of the Irving Place house. For some time they had been silent, staring at the blazing logs. Then Hal turned to the girl with a smile.

"All right, honey, I know you're just on the verge of throwing something at me, but all's clear now and I can go ahead with this—what shall we call it?— Project Rescue."

"It's not a bit funny," Rosamund snapped, her green eyes blazing.

He grinned and leaned over to kiss her. "My little firebrand." He sobered. "I know it's not funny. In

61

fact, it might prove to be even less funny than you might think it is."

"What do you mean?" she asked, seeing the gravity of his kindly face.

"We're proceeding on the theory that Jerome Meredith can be proved to have a clean bill of health so far as his professional honesty is concerned. Now all we have to go on in support of that idea is the fact that Tony is in love with his brother. Suppose—just suppose, mind you—the guy is guilty. Instead of rushing in to the rescue we might simply end by stirring up a lot of mud and making matters worse than they were when we found them."

"But—"

"Wait, darling. This is important. Think about the Meredith brothers for a moment. They aren't stupid or helpless. They are highly intelligent and they are fighters. But—they aren't fighting. Why?"

Rosamund curled up in his chair, her mouth drooping. "I don't know."

"Still want to go ahead with this?"

Her hesitation was brief. "Yes," she decided. "Nothing venture nothing have. Let's go ahead."

After a long thoughtful look at her he nodded. "Okay, here we go, then." He crossed the room to the small desk which held the telephone, flipped the pages of the Manhattan directory until he found Rodney Meredith's telephone number and an address in the Village.

After a short wait Rodney's voice said, "Hello."

"This is Hal Perkins."

"Oh." A pause. "How are you, Perkins?"

"Why don't you find out for yourself? Rosamund Perry and I have been having a long talk this evening and we'd like very much to have you sit in."

"Well, that's—you're alone there?" The question *Is Tony with you?* hovered in the air.

Hal turned to give Rosamund a quick look. "We're quite alone. This isn't exactly a social call but—it's friendly."

There was a long pause. Then Rodney said, "Okay. I'm on my way."

When the doorbell rang, twenty minutes later, Rosamund clutched Hal's hand. "I hope we're right about this."

"I hope so, too," he said gravely. He went down to open the door, shook hands with Rodney, and brought him up to the living room. There was a curiously wary expression on Rodney's face as he acknowledged Rosamund's greeting and took the chair she offered him.

After a brief silence she said, "Hal, you begin, will you?"

Hal turned to face the big young man with the steady blue eyes that, at this moment, held a watchful look.

"All right, here it is. Before you take a poke at me or anything like that, let me speak my piece, will you?"

Rodney looked at the photographer's kindly face and some of the hostility went out of his own. "Go ahead."

"The day we went up to Catherine Cathcart's house I recognized your brother."

The muscles along Rodney's jaw rippled but he did not move, his eyes remained steadily fixed on Hal. Rosamund clenched her hands in her lap. It has to be all right, she told herself; it has to.

"Five years ago, I was breaking in on my job. When I had no special assignment I went looking for one. I was an eager beaver in those days." Hal told how he had been in the police station when the call had come from Jerome's office about the burglary and how he had followed the police when they went to the office.

"Even then, when I still hadn't learned the ABC's of my job, I knew that setup was all wrong. Here was the office of a struggling young lawyer and yet it had been literally torn apart by the burglar. Now, on the surface, there was no sense to it. A burglar wouldn't expect to find any valuables in such a place. Unless he was demented, he wouldn't break and enter when there were people working."

Rodney was silent.

"So then the Cranshaw man appeared and claimed

that he had turned over two hundred thousand dollars in bearer bonds to your brother for safekeeping, that they had disappeared, that your brother staged the whole thing to get his hands on the bonds. And then, before the case went to trial, Cranshaw pulled out and left no explanation. The impression that was given to anyone who had followed the story was either (*a*) that your brother had turned over the bonds to him; or (*b*) that the burglary had been a put-up job between them."

Rodney had not moved. He was still watching Hal, but his brain was whirling. Two hundred thousand dollars in bearer bonds belonging to Simon Cranshaw, uncle of the girl Jerome had intended to marry. Two hundred thousand dollars! But why had he never heard of it before? Oh, of course, he'd been in the service then, stationed in Germany. He had never seen the newspapers and Jerome had not told him.

"Now here," Hal said, "is where you can tell us, Rosamund and me, where to get off. The thing is this. Your brother lost just about all he had—his eyesight, his income, his reputation, his profession—because of that burglary. We don't think he was guilty and we've set up a very select committee of two to try to get to the bottom of the thing and clear him."

"Why are you doing this?" Rodney asked.

"Our Boy Scout deed for the day," Hal said lightly. "Shall we let it go at that? For the time being, at any rate."

At last Rodney moved. He got to his feet, held out his hand. "Room on that committee for a third person?" Their hands gripped.

ii

"What we'll have to do," Hal said, "is to pool our information and go on from there."

"Tell me what you found in the office at the time of the burglary," Rodney said. "That seems to be the most logical place to start."

Hal shut his eyes as though trying to summon up a picture.

"Who called the police?" Rodney asked suddenly.

"A man's voice, they said. By the time we reached the place, your brother was unconscious from the head wound that had blinded him. As a matter of fact, he was in a hospital right up to the time when the case was marked closed."

"Go on."

"Well, the prowl car got there first, of course. The police found Jerome lying in a pool of blood in the front office. At first they thought he'd been killed. His office girl was just leaving to get help. Actually, she was waiting for the elevator when the police got out of it. She was hysterical and they couldn't get anything useful out of her at all. She just kept screaming until the doctor they sent from the police department gave her a sedative and they told her to go home. And that," Hal added significantly, "was the last anyone ever saw of her."

"So you think the girl was in on the deal," Rodney said thoughtfully. "Somehow I can't see that. Jerome is a big, powerful man. While he had his sight he was as quick on his feet as a panther. I simply can't see a woman being able to knock him out."

"She may have been in on it. She may not. This is no time to jump at conclusions. You know how people are. They panic. They think it doesn't concern them. They 'don't want to get mixed up in anything.' She may simply have been scared stiff, so she ran away."

"I can't believe any woman would do that," Rosamund exclaimed. "Not just walk out with a man injured, lying unconscious."

Hal laughed without humor. "Remember that shameful case in New York not so long ago? A woman was murdered within hearing of nearly thirty-five people, and not a single one raised a hand to save her. It didn't concern them. Sometimes I get disgusted with the so-called human race. Sorry, I didn't mean to get sidetracked. Anyhow, that office had simply been taken apart. The files, the desk drawers, the safe—everything in the place had been ransacked. They had even torn up the leather cushion on Jerome's desk chair."

"So," Rodney said in his quiet voice, "they were looking for the bearer bonds."

"It has to be that way. But the queer part is that Cranshaw swore not a single human being knew that Jerome had them."

"And then Cranshaw disappeared too," Rodney said thoughtfully.

The three were silent for a long time.

"Anything else?" Rodney asked at last.

"Well, for one thing, it strikes me as a strange coincidence that your brother's secretary resigned without notice one day and the burglary took place the next day. What do you know about the woman?"

Rodney's face was transformed by his smile and Rosamund recognized the quality that had made Tony love him. The smile was irresistible.

"Miss G. Burns. She worked for my father for twenty years. He always said he couldn't have run a law office without her, that she knew more law than he did."

"What kind of person was she?"

"She'd be about fifty-five now, very tailored, very severe, very kind, meticulous, never forgot a detail, loyal—that is," Rodney broke off to say, "I'd have gone to the stake to prove that she was loyal."

"G. Burns?"

Rodney laughed. "Always Miss G. Burns. I've known her all my life and I never knew her first name. Jerome and I used to make up outrageous names to fit that G—glamorous, ghastly, ghoulish, glorious, gorgeous—but to this day all I know is G. Burns."

"And she just—walked out." Hal frowned. "Something wrong there. Well, it's your turn, Rodney. How much have you to contribute?"

"Nothing," Rodney said succinctly.

Hal and Rosamund stared at him.

"That's literally true. Jerome has never said one word about the burglary or his blindness or—"

"We can't help if we don't know the facts," Hal said, "or if you hold out on us."

"I'm not holding out. I know Jerome was engaged to Cranshaw's niece, a girl named Eve. He was head over heels in love with her. She broke the engagement after his accident. He hasn't discussed that either. But he—sometimes I think he almost hates women."

"And there's nothing you can add that would help us, that would give us a lead, however slight?"

"Heavens knows I'd do anything on earth," Rodney said with a violence that surprised them both. As a rule he was a quiet man who spoke little. "I've watched what is happening to my brother and there hasn't been a single thing I could do."

For a long time there was silence in the room. Then Rosamund said, "Kathy has asked us all up for Thanksgiving dinner. Will you come with us, Rodney?"

He hesitated for a moment. "Is Tony Carew going to be there?"

"No, just Mother and Hal and me. And you, if you will come."

"Thank you, I'd like that."

"Why don't you want to see Tony?" Rosamund asked, ignoring the warning in Hal's eyes.

"I don't dare," Rodney answered simply.

Rosamund smiled. "When we get up there," she said, "Jerome is going to talk. In fact, he is going to tell all."

Rodney grinned at her. "And how are you going to accomplish that?"

"I have a secret weapon," she told him and she refused to say anything more.

Hal moved restlessly. "Ten days to Thanksgiving," he grumbled, "and we'll be able to see Jerome. Here we are, all set to go, and there's nothing we can do but wait."

"There's this Miss Burns," Rosamund said eagerly. "Rodney, that should be your job. Find her and make her tell what she knows."

Rodney considered for a moment. "All right," he

agreed. "I'll track down Miss Burns. But she is so honest, so impeccable, that I simply can't believe she was involved in this mess. It's impossible. The woman I'd like to lay my hands on is the office girl who appeared for one day and then managed to vanish off the face of the earth. But I don't even know her name. I don't know what she looked like."

"I have a picture of her," Hal told him. "I got shots of the office, of your brother, and of the girl. They are in my files. I'll show them to you."

"What was she like?" Rodney asked.

Hal shrugged. "Anybody. Nobody. Colorless, unattractive, with dull brown hair, thick glasses, dowdy clothes. Nothing you'd remember at all, aside from that wild hysterical fit." He stood looking intently at the wall. "There was something—something odd about her voice when she spoke. She stuttered."

According to the Long Island telephone directory, Miss G. Burns was still to be found at her old address. There was nothing odd about that. The surprise would have come from discovering that she had moved. In an increasingly restless world Miss G. Burns continued to follow the same pattern, day after day, year after year, decade after decade. That was what made her abrupt resignation from Jerome's office so fantastic.

Rodney had vivid memories of her from the time he was ten and paid his first visit to his father's law office. She had seemed as old to him then as she had nearly twenty years later. He could remember still the trim tailored suits, the white blouses that managed to remain crisp and clean even at the end of a hot, dusty summer day in New York City. Her hair, originally a mouse-colored brown, had become an iron gray but it was always arranged in the same way, drawn back tightly into an uncompromising knot. Rodney could not recall ever seeing a single lock out of place.

She reported at the office at a quarter of nine, though it did not open until nine, dusted her desk and her employer's, dusted the telephone and then wiped it with a damp cloth, prepared an array of sharpened pencils, opened and sorted the mail, and made a list of appointments for the day. She remembered the birthdays of the members of the family and reminded Rodney's father several weeks in advance. She made his dental appointments and told him when it was time to have his checkups with his physician. If he said his health was perfectly good she simply snorted, made the appointment herself, and saw that he kept it.

She had remembered, too, the dental appointments for the two motherless boys. She had noticed when they needed their wardrobes replenished, and looked up suitable summer camps. She had inspected their report cards and been dissatisfied when they did less than their best. Not that she had praised them when they did their best. That, she implied, was only to be expected of them.

In a world that changed almost from day to day, she had remained the fixed, immovable factor. And then she had behaved in an inexplicable, uncharacteristic manner.

For a long time after his talk with Rosamund and Hal Perkins, Rodney lay awake, thinking about Miss G. Burns and about the office girl who had come from nowhere and disappeared into nowhere during that short, twenty-four-hour period when Jerome had been blinded.

And then at last he let himself think of Tony Carew. For weeks he had shied away from the thought of her because it was too painful, but now—if the mystery surrounding Jerome could be cleared up—he could go back to her. At least he would have a chance to try to win her.

All the following day he dialed Miss Burns's telephone number diligently but there was no reply. It was not until six o'clock in the evening that he heard her voice, crisp, impersonal, unchanged.

"This is Miss Burns speaking."

"This is Rodney Meredith."

There was a startled gasp and then no sound at all from the other end of the line.

"Miss Burns! Miss Burns!"

"Yes?" she said. And she was a stranger.

"I was afraid we had been cut off. I want to see you. May I come out now? Perhaps you'll have dinner with me."

"Oh, no, I—That would be impossible."

Rodney's hand tightened on the telephone. She was afraid of him. Afraid!

"It's terribly urgent," he said. "I've got to see you—for Jerome's sake. I won't take up much of your time."

"You can't come here," she said in the decisive tone he remembered. When she spoke in that voice there was no budging her.

Rodney thought quickly. Incredible as it seemed, she was in a panic at the thought of having him in her house.

"Miss Burns," he tried to speak as quietly as possible, "if you won't see me at home, will you let me call on you at your place of business?"

"Why do you want to see me?"

"I can't explain over the telephone. I wouldn't take much of your time. And in your office—wherever it is—at least you needn't be alone with me, you know."

She heard the bitterness, the reproach, in his voice. After a moment's thought she gave him, still reluctantly, the name and address of the welfare organization by which she was employed.

"I can see you at twelve tomorrow, if you like."

The welfare organization was on a side street and Rodney had some difficulty in finding it. Most of the social workers were at lunch but he saw Miss Burns at once, sitting at a desk halfway down a long, rather bleak room.

As he approached she looked up and studied his face for a long moment. Then she indicated the chair beside her. "Sit down, Rodney." She did not offer to shake hands. "If you have anything to say, I hope you will tell me as quickly as possible. My case load is very heavy and I have no time to waste."

"Social work is a new departure for you, isn't it, with your law training and experience?"

It was the wrong thing to say. Her lips compressed. "At fifty years of age," she said tartly, "a woman is lucky to find any employment at all. I'd used up most of my savings by the time I got this job. In the circumstances, a recommendation from Jerome wouldn't have done me much good."

At least she had made her enmity clear. She

would do nothing to help him. Nonetheless, he would not leave without trying.

"I've come to ask your help," he said quietly, and saw her mouth tighten. "You know about the burglary in Jerome's office, five years ago, of course."

"I read the papers."

He leaned forward and saw that, instinctively, she drew back, pulling her chair farther away from him.

"Why did you resign like that, without any warning?" he asked her.

For a moment she stared at him in perplexity, then she said in a tone of contempt that was like a whiplash, "Really, Rodney, I'm ashamed of you. To use tactics like that! I don't know what game you're trying to play."

He wanted to get up and walk out. Instead he said patiently, still quietly, "Why won't you answer my question?"

"You know as well as I do," she snapped, "that I didn't resign. I left for my regular three weeks' vacation. In the following morning's mail there was a note from Jerome saying he hadn't wanted to hurt my feelings but I was getting too old for the job and he no longer needed me. He enclosed a month's salary."

He stared at her unbelieving. "Are you telling me that Jerome fired you?"

"Didn't he tell you that?"

Rodney ran his fingers through his hair. "Look here, Miss Burns, there's some terrible misunderstanding somewhere. He got a note from you the next day, resigning, saying you no longer wished to work for him. No explanation. Nothing."

"But I didn't—are you telling me the truth, Rodney?"

"Have I ever lied to you?"

She shook her head slowly. "I thought you and your brother were like your father, men whose word was as good as their bond. And then—"

"Miss Burns, that money you say he enclosed—was it a check?"

"No, the money was in cash."

"Did you keep the note?"

"I always keep records," she said and he smothered a smile. "It's at home in my filing case. Now what is this all about? Why, after all this time, are you raking up the whole ugly business?"

"Because I didn't know how to tackle it before," he said slowly. "It was only a couple of days ago that I learned enough about the situation to know Jerome had been the victim of a very slick, very ruthless frame-up. Why didn't you even call to ask for an explanation? You must have felt that Jerome owed you that."

"Because," she said tartly, "when I picked up the paper the next morning I read about the burglary in his office."

"Well?"

She looked at him steadily.

"I see. You thought he was guilty."

Something in his tone made her exclaim in self-defense, "What else could I think?"

"You knew him," he said hotly.

She was silenced.

"Did you know that when he was found he had been blinded from a blow struck by the burglar, that he is still blind, that he may always be blind?"

For the first time in his long knowledge of her Miss Burns changed color. For a moment he thought that she was going to faint but she was made of sterner stuff than that. It was a long time before she spoke to him, an interval during which she answered telephone calls with all her old incisiveness, with her inevitable fairness, betraying only occasionally the fundamental, if somewhat rigid, kindness that made her tackle social work with justice and helpfulness but without sentimentality.

"I didn't know," she said at last. "Oh, Jerome! My poor boy. I read only that he was found unconscious."

There had been occasions since Jerome's disaster when Rodney had nearly lost his control but never had he come as close as at this moment when the

stern-faced woman looked at him with tears spilling
down her cheeks.

Being Miss Burns, she had no patience with point-
less emotion, and in a few minutes she recovered,
removed her glasses, and wiped her eyes. "Tell me
what I can do, Rodney. I don't understand any of
this."

"I want to clear him. It's as simple as that. I want
to find out who is responsible for that frame-up and
see that he is punished. And I need all the help that
you can give me."

"But I've told you all I know. When I left him that
afternoon he said he hoped I'd have a good rest. Go
out and make some whoopee." A smile trembled on
her lips. "You know what nonsense he talks. Well,
the next morning I got that letter in the mail. I
thought he had been too cowardly to tell me to my
face. Then I read about the burglary. Naturally I
suspected him of being involved. There could be no
other reason for getting rid of me like that."

"You don't know anything else at all?"

She shook her head.

After a long thoughtful pause he said, "What do
you know about the man Simon Cranshaw who
seems to have been my brother's friend, and about
his niece Eve who was engaged to him, and about
those bearer bonds? And who, except yourself, could
have known about them?"

"I never knew about them," she answered promptly. "If they were in the office I never saw them. That's
one reason—perhaps the chief reason—why I believed
Jerome was guilty. He had never kept a professional
secret from me. I had free access to his personal files; I
handled his banking; I balanced his checkbook. If
those bonds had been there—"

"They must have been there," Rodney said heavily.

"Simon Cranshaw," Miss Burns said, "was a real
estate man in California. Jerome met him when he
took that long vacation after he had pneumonia and
the doctor said he must get away for at least three
months. You remember?"

Rodney nodded. "I was away but he wrote me about it."

"He sent me little notes now and then, usually about his practice, sometimes just gay little messages to tell me how well he was and how fat he was growing. You know the way he is."

"The way he used to be."

Miss Burns winced. "He mentioned Simon Cranshaw several times, a 'big wheel'—that's the way he spoke—whom he'd met out there and who wanted him to stay and go into practice in California and be his legal adviser and business manager. Jerome was a bit flattered but he didn't intend to do it; he preferred being his own boss to making any amount of money without independence. Then he met Cranshaw's niece. Eve. If you could believe him, she was a combination of Helen of Troy, Cleopatra, and whoever the chief lovely of the movies is now. Then he wired me that she was going to marry him.

"When he came back he was—well, he could hardly keep his feet on the ground. All I heard was Eve—Eve—Eve. Then I got my vacation earlier than usual because I had had extra work and responsibility while he was gone and—that's all."

"You never saw this Eve Cranshaw?"

"I think she was still in California though they were planning to be married very shortly. That's all I knew. I assume that she didn't marry him."

"She gave him what is called in less elegant circles, the bum's rush."

After a pause she said brokenly, "It doesn't help, does it? And I want so terribly to help."

"At least, I know now why you left, so one point is cleared up. But I still don't know who the girl was who appeared so opportunely to take your place in the office. I don't know what happened to her. I don't know how anyone could have been informed of the presence of the bonds in the office. I don't know how anyone knew where to reach you and prevent you from returning. I don't know what happened to the man Cranshaw or why he turned over those negotiable bonds to Jerome in the first place, then accused him of theft, and finally withdrew his charge, or at least disappeared so there was no one to testify against Jerome. And I don't know what became of Eve."

Miss Burns leaned forward and put her hand over his. For the first time since he had known her the stern, disciplined face was warm with a mother's tenderness.

"You're going to find out, my dear. There's something about you. You're going to find out. And you are going to clear Jerome."

"Are you as sure as all that?" He smiled at her.

"I'm as sure as all that." She did not smile. "And remember that I'll help all I can. Anything. If there is any possible thing I can tell you I'll do it."

Rodney grinned and his face was like a mischievous boy's. "Tell me—what does that G stand for?"

There was a faint blush on Miss Burns's cheeks. "A most unsuitable name," she said in embarrassment. "I was christened Gloria."

"And so," Mrs. Haven said, "I'm having my brother and sister-in-law and nephew for Thanksgiving dinner."

Tony, who had come to have great affection as well as deep regard for her charming landlady, leaned back in her chair and laughed.

"You sound as though it were a disaster!"

"I'm truly devoted to my brother, Tom," Mrs. Haven said. "I suppose it's just my miserable, shameful pride. I can't bear to have my sister-in-law come here and discover that I have no servants. I know how silly it is. Heaven knows values like that aren't important to me. It's only for the sake of my husband. I can't endure the comments Betty will make about the fact that he left me with so little." She looked up with a wry smile. "I am really ashamed of myself."

While she spoke Tony had been thinking swiftly. She knew that Mrs. Perry, Rosamund, and Hal Perkins were going to Catherine Cathcart's house for Thanksgiving dinner; that, for some reason which made them all a little awkward and self-conscious, she had not been included in the invitation. It was, she supposed, because Rodney was to be there with his brother and Rodney did not want to see her.

Or was there something else? For the first time in a long and devoted friendship, Rosamund seemed to be avoiding any personal conversations, to keep the talk strictly on the problems and little amusing incidents of the bookshop.

Mrs. Haven began to laugh. "You're up to something," she said. "I was warned in the beginning that

77

your face always betrays you. You've got a plot up your sleeve."

Tony joined in the laugh. "Wait and hear! It would be the loveliest joke! Why don't you let me pretend to be your maid and serve the Thanksgiving dinner?"

"Tony!"

"No, I mean it. Your family would never need know that you haven't got a staff. For all they could tell you'd have a cook in the kitchen and I'd be combination waitress and parlor maid to open the door. Please, Mrs. Haven!"

Over Mrs. Haven's half laughing, half shocked protests, the girl prevailed. "It's going to be fun," she assured her.

"Well, if you're sure—"

Tony was sure. She got paper and pencil and said in the businesslike tone that always so amused her friends, "Now, what course have you planned?"

"Three, with coffee in the living room."

"Then it's to be a dinner, not a gorge. Sensible woman. With each course prepared, cooked, and served temptingly, three are all anyone but an anaconda needs, and with the terrific prices, about all the average homemaker can afford."

Mrs. Haven looked at the girl who spoke with such understanding of the problems of the "average homemaker." Where had this extremely wealthy young woman with a far larger income than she could ever spend acquired her understanding of the problems of people in a lower income bracket? Certainly there was no condescension in her manner. She accepted Mrs. Haven's problems as though they were her own.

The day before Thanksgiving was the first that Tony had taken off from the shop. After the holiday there would be the pressures and frantic excitement of Christmas sales. Rosamund assured her that she could manage and that, if too many customers came in, her mother would help.

In the basement kitchen, each of them swathed in big aprons, Tony and Mrs. Haven worked quickly and efficiently. The turkey was stuffed and placed in the roasting pan ready for the oven. The celery was cleaned, washed, rolled in a damp napkin, and placed in the refrigerator. The squash, cut and peeled, was left standing in a saucepan of cold water, as were the potatoes and onions. The creamed macaroni, covered with buttered crumbs, was in a baking dish ready for its final browning. Even the tiny sausages which, all brown and crispy, were to garnish the turkey were ready for the frying pan.

Hard sauce for the plum pudding had been forced through a funnel of stiff white writing paper and laid on a glass dish in the form of roses, garlanded with green leaves cut from angelique and centered with a bit of brilliant red maraschino cherry. Lemon, orange, and pineapple juices were mixed for the mint cup; ginger ale and soda, which were to be added when it was ready to serve, were at hand. The mussiness of preparation was over.

Tony stood with a big can of plum pudding in her hand and soberly regarded a large mince pie reposing on the counter and ready to be popped in the oven. She looked at the turkey and sighed.

"I don't think I've ever seen such a tremendous bird going into such a small oven. We'll have to bake the pie now and then heat it up tomorrow after the turkey comes out. Not at all according to Hoyle, I'm sure."

Mrs. Haven was busy filling little china molds with hot cranberry jelly, which would make a glorious bit of color at each place on the dinner table.

"I added a slice of lemon to the cranberries for this jelly," she said, "to give it an added tang."

Tony slid the pie into the oven and turned to survey the room. "Well," she said in a tone of satisfaction as she took off the big apron, "that seems to be that."

"And what I'd have done without you I can't imagine," Mrs. Haven said fervently. "It does seem ridiculous to go to such a great amount of preparation for a meal that people will dispose of in an hour's time."

"Not Thanksgiving dinner," Tony replied. "I always think of that first Thanksgiving, of tables groaning with food from the first harvest, a harvest resulting from men clearing the first fields in a wild country, planting seed under the menace of Indian arrows, surviving that first bitter winter without proper shelter or clothing or bedding. With nothing at all but their courage and faith in the future and in themselves. I guess Thanksgiving dinner is a kind of symbol to me, a tangible sign that men could wrest a living from the most unlikely soil and under the hardest conditions. It always makes me tremendously proud."

Mrs. Haven with difficulty lifted the heavy roasting pan that held the big turkey. "It's a tangible sign, all right," she laughed. "Now, for heaven's sake, child, go upstairs and rest."

Tony dropped a curtsy. "*Oui, madame. Merci, madame.*" She laughed. "That makes me think of Mrs. Hazleton, who has the beauty parlor. Oh," she wailed, "I forgot. I have an appointment to get my hair done." She ran up the stairs, her heels tapping, and Mrs. Haven laughed, her heart warming with affection for the girl who had brought youth and gaiety into her house.

What a delight the girl was. She wished that she could have had a daughter like this, that she could keep her here always. But Tony was bound to marry soon. It was odd that she seemed to have comparatively few engagements with young men. Now and then she went to a theater or to dinner or, more rarely, danced late at a night club. But she appeared to have no particular interest in any of the young men who telephoned so assiduously. Well, Tony knew her own business best, of course, but it was odd that Rosamund Perry should be the one to marry first.

ii

"*Bonjour, madame,*" Mrs. Hazelton said as Tony came breathlessly into the beauty parlor. "Today I've given you my best operator, Cecily Ann. I hope she'll take care of you to your satisfaction."

"I'm sure she will," Tony said with a smile.

"*Merci, madame,*" Mrs. Hazelton replied, and having exhausted her French returned to her own chair.

As Cecily Ann turned the chair for Tony the latter looked at her. She was older than she had appeared from a distance and there was a curious hardness about her face. She was, or she had been a few years earlier, an extremely pretty girl. What had aged her was not a matter of years but of experience.

While she brushed Tony's hair she met her eyes in the mirror with calculating scrutiny.

"You run the bookshop next door, don't you?" She spoke with an exaggerated Southern drawl.

"Yes." After a moment's silence Tony said, "I own that great Dane, too."

"Oh." There was a flicker of the girl's long artificial lashes.

"Mrs. Hazelton said you complained about him."

"It wasn't on my account," Cecily Ann said in her slow voice. "He scared away the customers."

"What customers?" Tony asked.

"I don't remember their names now," the girl said vaguely.

"You didn't have any trouble with him yourself, then?"

Cecily Ann hesitated. "He jumped me once. After that I hardly dared go outside. He was always— prowling."

Tony stared at the girl's reflection in the mirror, her brows drawn together in a frown. "That's odd. He's never frightened anyone before."

There was an almost imperceptible shrug of the operator's shoulders, a faint touch of impertinence in her manner. "I wouldn't know about that. Anyhow, I reckon there always has to be a first time."

"Yes, of course." *She's lying,* Tony thought in surprise, but what possible reason could she have for inventing that story about Mister Duffy?

Cecily Ann worked on her hair with deft fingers. She was, as Mrs. Hazelton had said, exceptionally competent. A rather stocky man went through the room, wearing a white coat. The blond operator's ridiculous lashes fluttered.

"Hello, Frank," she drawled.

He turned toward her. "Hello there, Cecily Ann."

The big blue eyes gave him a long look that brought color creeping up over his cheeks. "You look right perky," she said. "Any luck?"

"That's right. Saw a man today and got the financing all straightened out. Looks like we're in business. We'll start manufacturing in another three months. This time next year the No-Age cream will be famous."

"That's wonderful." The tone managed to convey the idea, *You're wonderful.*

The man paused awkwardly, straightened his necktie and then went on, obviously flattered by the girl's interest in him, her extravagant admiration of him. In the mirror Tony saw the cold, watchful eyes follow him speculatively. If I were Mrs. Hazelton, she thought, I'd get rid of that girl. She may be a fine operator but she's a troublemaker if I ever saw one.

When Cecily Ann had combed out Tony's hair she studied her in the mirror. "With your looks, I can't imagine why you waste time in a bookstore."

Tony smiled. "What would you do?"

"Go where the money is," the girl said briefly.

I'll bet you would, Tony thought as she paid her bill and added a tip, which Cecily Ann deftly slipped into the pocket of her uniform.

Next morning, smiling to herself, Tony dressed in the black uniform with a tiny crisp white apron and white lace cap which she had bought as a surprise.

"My dear!" Mrs. Haven exclaimed when she saw her. She began to laugh.

In the kitchen, the trim uniform covered by a big apron, Tony busily prepared grapefruit for the first course. Standing at the counter she looked up through the ground-floor window onto the small backyard. A light early snow hung on the branches of a little maple tree, it sparkled on window ledges. Long spikes of ice fringed roofs and gutters.

Children in bright new snowsuits played in the next yard. They shouted and laughed, tumbled and rolled in the fluffy snow; their eyes sparkled like diamonds, their cheeks were like roses, their snub noses looked for all the world like red cherries. Watching them, Tony thought wistfully that it would be wonderful to have children of her own; wonderful if this Thanksgiving were to be celebrated in her own house, with her own family around her, with her own husband at the head of the table, carving the turkey.

Is that, she wondered, such a lot to ask? She thought of Cecily Ann saying, *I'd go where the money is*, thought of the calculating way she had watched Frank Hazelton. She shook her head to drive away unpleasant thoughts. Then she arranged the fruit in tall glasses and garnished it with cherries. She regarded the result with satisfaction.

"Tony," Mrs. Haven protested as she came down the steps to the basement kitchen, "I meant to do this myself."

"All finished," Tony said cheerfully. "I'm glad you are starting with grapefruit. This won't take the edge from appetites. Everyone will be ravenous for the turkey. I always feel as if I'd been cheated when my hostess serves me soup before the national bird. And generally thick, filling soup at that."

Mrs. Haven looked at the electric clock over the stove. "They'll be here any minute."

Tony nodded and removed the heavy apron. "I'll just take one last look at the table," she said, and ran lightly up the stairs to the dining room. There were silver dishes of candies in green and red, amusing place cards, and tall red candles highlighting red roses in the center of the white tablecloth.

The doorbell rang and she went to open it for a small bustling woman, a tall heavy-set man in his late fifties, and an equally tall and extremely handsome man of thirty.

She led the way to the upstairs bedrooms and assisted Mrs. Holbrook with her coat. Betty Holbrook said sharply, "Be sure to hang it carefully. Don't let it brush against anything. That's my new mink."

"Yes, madam."

Mrs. Holbrook looked around the room and nothing escaped her eyes from the furniture to the pictures on the walls and the appointment of the dressing table. She helped herself to powder, looked up at the tall, slim girl in the dainty white apron and cap.

"That will be all," she said curtly.

"Thank you, madam."

Tony reached the head of the stairs just as the Holbrook men came out of the back bedroom, which was now her own and in which she had put away any personal things that might betray the fact that she occupied the premises.

Mrs. Haven's brother gave her a swift look of approval and went rather heavily down the stairs. The son, Carter, who had not seen her face before, took a long look and his lips formed an approving whistle.

"And where," he asked, his voice carefully low, "did Aunt Jane find you?"

With her eyes demurely downcast Tony hastened to the basement. She could hear Carter Holbrook's voice raised—deliberately raised, she thought—in a question.

"Aunt Jane, where did you find that beauty?"

"Now, Carter," his mother said petulantly.

Tom Holbrook laughed. "Trust Carter not to miss a pretty face."

"Pretty! That girl is beautiful. She's a raving beauty. This situation deserves a little research and I'm the boy to do it."

"I won't have you paying attention to a servant girl," Mrs. Holbrook said.

For the first time since Tony had known her, Mrs. Haven was angry. "Carter won't get anywhere with her," she said confidently.

"Oh, Jane, I wish you hadn't said that!" Mrs. Holbrook sounded fretful. "Now he'll be sure to try it just to prove that you're wrong."

Tom Holbrook laughed again.

In a few minutes, after she had loaded the dumb-waiter, Tony appeared in the doorway.

"Dinner is served." She did not look up as they passed her, Mrs. Haven with her brother, Mrs. Holbrook with her son, though the latter was frankly staring at her, with admiration in his eyes.

While she removed dishes and served the courses Tony heard enough of the conversation to understand more fully than she had before why Mrs. Haven, in her loyalty to her dead husband, had tried to conceal from her sister-in-law her comparative poverty.

"I see you still use the Holbrook silver," Betty commented.

"Of course. I've always loved it, I remember it from my grandmother's house."

"It's all right, of course," Betty said, "but I must say I preferred selecting my own pattern."

"I suppose I'm a traditionalist," Mrs. Haven said with a smile.

"I know. Old furniture. Old silver. Sometimes I think your husband didn't add one new thing to this house."

"Betty!" her husband warned her.

Mrs. Haven looked up serenely. "He added happiness," she said.

Betty Holbrook was silenced.

When Tony had served coffee in the formal drawing room she returned to the kitchen to put the dishes in the electric washer. She had given Mrs. Haven her solemn promise not to wash them. In her own room she changed to a dark-red wool sweater and skirt, put on a short car coat, pulled the hood up over her dark hair, and slipped quietly down the stairs.

She closed the front door behind her and bent over to step into her boots. The door opened and Carter Holbrook came out hastily, sliding his arms into his overcoat.

"Where are you going?"

"For a walk," she told him. Belatedly she added, "Sir."

He grinned. "Let me walk with you."

Recalling Mrs. Holbrook's voice with her scornful comment about "that servant girl," Tony shook her head.

"Please," he said. "I'd like to very much."

For a moment she hesitated, then she smiled mischievously. "Of course," she said, and he fell into step beside her.

They walked through the crisp light snow, feeling the wind cold on their cheeks, drawing in the fresh air. At first they did not talk at all. When at last he spoke he said with cheerful impersonality, "It's good to get out, isn't it? I should have been an outdoor man. A hunter or trapper, perhaps."

"Or a lumberjack," she suggested.

"Or a forest ranger."

"Or a whaling captain."

He laughed, caught her arm as she slipped at a crossing, tucked his hand companionably under her arm. They walked on in friendly silence.

While Tony was serving Mrs. Haven's Thanksgiving dinner, Catherine Cathcart, assisted by Rosamund and Mrs. Perry, was serving dinner at the old house in Westchester.

"I never get used to all this space," Rosamund told her sister after they were seated at the big round table. "That kitchen of yours is almost as big as our whole second floor at home. I should think you'd walk yourself to death."

Sam, for all the banter of the Meredith brothers about his hopeless blundering, had turned his hand to everything from peeling potatoes and basting the turkey to cleaning up the kettles.

He snatched Jerome's plate from Hal, who was carving, and cut the turkey, buttered a roll, poured the gravy.

"The kitchen is much too big, I suppose," Kathy admitted, pushing back the hair from her flushed face, "and by modern standards of efficiency I suppose it's awfully old-fashioned and inconvenient, but I love it. I've always thought a kitchen was the real heart of the house, the place where the family gathers and gossips and—oh, I don't know—sort of belongs together. Of course, when we bought it, we wanted a big house because we planned to have a large family, but—things don't work out the way you expect."

"No, they don't," Jerome said.

"Mom, can I have another slice of turkey?" Dennis asked.

"Pass your plate," Hal said. "There's a piece here with your name on it."

"Where?" Dennis demanded. "I don't see it."

After dinner they all gathered in the kitchen to do the dishes. Only Jerome hovered in the background and then drifted aimlessly off. Kathy sent an anxious look after him and gave Rosamund an appealing, if wordless, message.

Rosamund handed her dishtowel to Hal. "Here," she said, "you might as well get in training. A good husband should be an expert dishwasher."

He groaned aloud. "What am I getting myself into? A henpecked husband married to one of those managing women." His voice raised in lamentation. "Oh death, where is thy sting?"

Rosamund found Jerome sitting in a big chair in the living room, with Dennis curled up at his feet.

". . . and," Jerome was saying dramatically, "just then he looked up and saw the panther crouched to spring, its tail lashing. He reached back of him, moving as quietly as a shadow, and—"

Rosamund choked back a giggle. "Even a crouching panther," she said, her voice low, "can't compete with three helpings of turkey and two desserts."

"Is he asleep?"

"He certainly is."

"Just as well," Jerome confessed with a grin. "I didn't know what we were going to do in order to cope with that panther."

There was a jingle and Rosamund laughed. Mister Duffy had brought his leash and dropped it at Jerome's feet.

"Hey, there," he complained. "How can I walk after all that dinner?"

"Be good for you," Rosamund said briskly, welcoming this unlooked-for opportunity to talk to Jerome alone. "Just what we both need."

She ran to get a coat, cap, and mittens. Sam brought Jerome's heavy coat and gloves. With the thick leash in Jerome's hand they started out. For a few minutes Rosamund watched in silence, tears stinging her eyes, as he strode confidently along with Mister Duffy. There was more color in his cheeks than when she had first seen him. He had, as she had observed at dinner, taken more part in the conversation, shown more interest in things and people, in politics and art, in all the gay conversation that had gone on around him.

She had wondered how to approach the subject. Now, without stopping to shape her words, she said, "Jerome."

"Yes?"

"It's about Rodney. I want to talk to you about him."

"What's wrong with Rodney?" he asked sharply.

"Nothing is wrong. That is—something is wrong, in a way. He has fallen in love with Tony Carew, my dearest friend."

"I guess that weeks ago," he said drily, and the flat sound, the bitterness were both back in his voice.

"And Tony is in love with him," Rosamund said. "Rodney doesn't know; at least, if he does know, he isn't doing anything about it."

"I'd say he is acting like a sensible man, but I suppose you wouldn't like that."

"No," Rosamund agreed quietly, "I wouldn't like that."

"Sorry. I've become a bit of a misogynist, I'm afraid."

"I don't mind. Go on and hate women, if it amuses you. But I don't think you should hurt Rodney."

"Hurt him?" Jerome was both startled and angry. "I'd never do anything to hurt Rodney."

"He'll never ask Tony to marry him until he can make things right for you."

"What do you mean by that?" The blind man had turned, gripped Rosamund's arm.

"You're hurting me, Jerome. If you'll try to be calm, I'll tell you."

"Sorry."

Mister Duffy jerked at the leash and they walked on again.

"Hal recognized you when we came up here before, you know." Before Jerome could comment Rosamund told him hurriedly about their long conference and how they had consulted Rodney. "He wants to clear you. So do we. But we need your help."

Following Mister Duffy's brisk lead they walked at a fast pace along the country lane.

"That is very good of you," Jerome said at last, "but perhaps you had better not interfere."

The hair-trigger temper flared off. "Interfere!" Rosamund blazed. "You don't do a thing to help yourself and so someone has to do it for you. Interfere! You make me so furious! I'm not doing this for you, anyhow. I'm doing it for Tony, because she deserves to be happy, if anyone does. She makes happiness possible for other people, and that's a rare quality, though you probably don't know it.

"Hal is doing it because he's stupid enough to think you deserve it. So far as I am concerned, you're just a—just a goose with its head in the sand."

Jerome released his hard grasp on her arm and leaned back, shouting with laughter. "A goose with its head in the sand. A goose!" When he had recovered he said, "All right, Rosamund. God knows whether you are right or wrong about this thing but you can count me in."

Now that her temper had exploded, Rosamund, as usual, was miserable and ashamed. "I'm sorry," she said in a small voice.

He chuckled. "Poor Hal! What that man is letting himself in for." He called, "Mister Duffy!" The great Dane, who had been let off the leash, came back and Jerome groped for the collar, snapped on the leash. "We're going back. We have things to do."

ii

"And that," Hal concluded, "is all I know about it. I dug around in my old files and found prints of the pictures I took in your office."

He handed them around. Everyone had gathered in a circle in the living room. There were several shots showing the chaos caused by that frenzied search; there were several of Jerome lying unconscious, his head in a pool of blood; there was one of the temporary office girl, wearing a shapeless dress, drab hair pulled back in a knot, steel-rimmed glasses covering her eyes.

"I didn't realize it had been that bad," Kathy said in a shocked voice. "Jerome, it's a wonder you weren't killed. That awful wound on your head."

"I'm hard to kill," Jerome said. Unconsciously his fingers touched the scar that had so narrowly missed his temple, a red scar with four tiny white indentations.

Mrs. Perry looked up quickly as she heard her daughter's voice. She took the prints that were handed her without comment. It was Kathy's life, after all, and she wasn't the kind of mother who thought she knew best about how her grown children should behave. But a blind man who hated women! Oh, dear, she thought in distress. She looked at the prints, took one of them to the window to study it more carefully.

"That's queer," she said, startled. "I've seen that girl before."

"Are you sure?" Hal asked.

She nodded. "Yes, I'm sure. You see that odd line from the nose to the corner of the mouth? The tiny ear set flat against the head? I'm positive."

"Where did you see her, Mother?" Rosamund demanded.

Mrs. Perry continued to stare at the picture. She shook her head. "I don't know," she admitted at last. She passed the prints to Rodney, who looked at the picture of the missing office girl.

"Who was she, Jerome?" he asked.

His brother shrugged. "I didn't know a single thing about her except that her name was Martha Kumer."

"How did you get her?"

"She just walked into the office that morning. I had called an employment agency and asked for temporary help while Miss Burns was on vacation, and they said they didn't have anyone who could handle legal work but they'd try to find someone. Then this girl showed up. I took for granted that she was sent by the employment agency, but, of course, I don't know. I was so darned upset. There was a letter in the mail from Miss Burns, who said she wasn't happy on the job any more and she was not going to return. Just like that."

"This is where I come in," Rodney said. "I saw Miss Burns the other day."

When he had finished his story there was a long silence.

"So," Hal said at last, "we have someone getting Miss Burns out of the way, getting your Martha Kumer very much in the way. All right, Jerome, let's hear your version."

"Well," he began slowly, but the flat tone was gone from his voice, it was alive and interested, "I came in that morning knowing Miss Burns had gone on vacation. I'd tried to get a replacement the week before and, as I said, the agency wasn't hopeful. Then this Kumer girl appeared, most opportunely."

"I wonder how she knew there wouldn't be another girl," Hal said, "by the time she got there?"

"She was waiting at the door when I arrived. All she said was that she had come to try out for the job. When I got in I found Miss Burns's note and I was flabbergasted, and I suppose that's why I didn't pay more attention to looking up the girl's credentials."

"What do you remember about her?" Rodney asked.

"She was there only one day," his brother reminded him, "and this was five years ago. She was efficient. I remember that. A homely girl, badly dressed, with such a stutter that I had to take over all the telephone calls myself."

"Go on," Rodney said.

"She was slow, of course, which was natural. After all, she was tackling a new job and legal work is complicated and has to be absolutely accurate. There was a brief that had to be in the mail that night and she had made some mistakes in it, so it had to be typed over again. That's why we happened to be working overtime. She didn't seem to mind at all."

"In other words, if she hadn't had the brief as an excuse she'd have found something else," Hal said.

"That's guesswork," Jerome said. "I was in my office." Suddenly he smiled and his smile was like Rodney's. "Well, actually, it was just a little cubby-hole with beaverboard walls. Miss Kumer was typing. I heard the door open; someone came in and spoke to the girl. I didn't hear what he said, just a murmur—then—I had turned away from the door, reaching for a law book on a shelf on the wall behind my desk. And whammo!"

He clutched his head, remembering that terrible blow. "I must have been knocked out temporarily."

"Temporarily!" Hal's voice was sharp.

"Yes. I came to, lying across my desk, with the grandfather of all headaches. I opened my eyes and the light hurt them. I couldn't remember—then I heard the noise in the outer office, heard the man say, 'Damn, it, they have to be here! Use your head.'

"I tried to get up and found I couldn't make it. I reached for the telephone and called the police, trying to keep my voice low. Then I heard something—raised my head—there was someone in the doorway—"

"Did you see who it was?"

"Just a black shape, so far as I was concerned. I still couldn't focus. I tried to get up." After a pause he said, "That's all I remember."

"But you were found in the outer office, on the floor beside the secretary's desk," Hal pointed out.

"I don't know how I got there," Jerome said slowly. "I'm pretty sure I got that second blow on my head when I was at my own desk."

After a pause, Hal said, "What has me running around in circles is the timing."

"The timing?" Rosamund asked.

"Well, look. Jerome called the police. There was a prowl car there within three minutes, at most. Say another minute to get up to his office. In that time he was struck for a second time, moved to the outer office, the intruder presumably found the bonds, and then got clear away."

"Are you sure there was a man?" Kathy asked.

"I don't believe any woman could have dragged Jerome across the room in that amount of time. What's your weight?"

"About a hundred and ninety, as a rule," Jerome said.

"Now about the girl. How come she was still there when the police arrived?"

Jerome hesitated. "All I have to go on is what they told me. I was unconscious for a couple of days. I can't figure it out unless she had to cover for him some way by making such a scene—they tell me she carried on in a hysterical way—that he had a chance to escape."

"Taking a risk, wasn't she?" Hal commented.

"People take a lot of risks for two hundred thousand dollars in bearer bonds," Jerome reminded him.

"So now," Hal said, "we come to the bearer bonds. What do you know about them, Jerome? Did you really have them in your possession or was that fellow Cranshaw lying?"

"No," Jerome said, "that's one time when Simon Cranshaw didn't lie. I had the bonds." Aware of the tension in the room he said in discouragement, "There's not much point in going on with this, is there?"

"Jerome!" Rodney cried in protest. "Are you completely out of your mind?"

Kathy got up impulsively and went to sit curled up at Jerome's feet. She put out one small hand and covered the fist that was clenched on the arm of the chair. "We believe in you, Jerome. Can't you understand that? We believe in you. But speaking with complete detachment, I think you're the most thick-headed, stubborn goon I ever came across. Could you, for Pete's sake, just once in your life cooperate without putting up an argument?"

Nothing stirred in the room for a long time. Then Jerome's taut fingers opened, his hand moved, tightened over Kathy's.

"All right," he said. "This is the story of Meredith the sucker. I went out to California because I had been run down for a long time and the doctor said it was that or a hospital. I met Simon Cranshaw. He was a real estate man with big holdings, plunging rather heavily in some big housing developments. At least," Jerome added wearily, "that's what he told me. How much of it was true, if anything, I don't know. In the first place I wasn't particularly impressed by him but he seemed to like me. I'm only human. I was flattered. He took me to lunch. He took me to the theater. He took me to dinner. That's when I met his niece, Eve."

He drew his hand away from Kathy's and she got up to return to her place beside Rosamund on the shabby davenport.

"Eve," Jerome said again, his face brooding. "She was the prettiest, sweetest thing. I fell for her. Hard. After I met Eve I thought Cranshaw was wonderful because she did. Never questioned anything he said. Believed in him wholeheartedly. From then on I saw Eve every day. By the end of a couple of weeks we were engaged. I told her I was just getting started and hadn't much to offer her, but she said that didn't make any difference.

"Only thing I held out over was when Cranshaw said he wanted me to give up my New York practice and join him. I was determined to hang on to my own independence. That was the one time Eve and I ever had an argument—until the last one.

"Well, the night before I had to leave for New York, Cranshaw took Eve and me to dinner. Afterward he asked if I would do him a big favor. Naturally," Jerome laughed at himself, "I jumped at the chance. He had this big package, two hundred thousand in bearer bonds, and he wanted me to bring it back to New York with me, to keep it safe at my office until he came for it.

"I told him it was risky to the point of madness. I didn't want any part in it. But he and Eve talked me over, against my better judgment. Cranshaw said he needed it for some big deal he'd be making in New York. Had to have cash and it would be safe with me because no one would know I was carrying it. Anyhow, I'd be saddled with it only for a few days. He and Eve would be in New York within a week.

"There's no excuse for me. Down in my heart I knew no legitimate deal would be handled in that way. Something was wrong with the whole setup. Either Cranshaw had got that money dishonestly and was trying to unload it as fast as he could or he was going to use it in some way that wouldn't stand the light of day.

"No excuse for me at all. But Eve said, 'You can't let Uncle Simon down, Precious,' and, of course, I couldn't.

"Well, I came back to New York, scared out of my wits at carrying so much in negotiable bonds, and put the stuff in a couple of cardboard files on the shelves with my law books. I figured no one would think of looking there; less danger of theft than in my safe. No one would ever guess where the stuff was. I didn't even tell Miss Burns, because I knew she'd think I was crazy. And then—we had the burglary."

He went on more slowly. "Well, you know pretty much what happened. Cranshaw read the papers about the burglary, came to New York on the next plane, and said I'd faked the whole thing to get my hands on his money. I was in the hospital, but under technical arrest, released on bail, and then—before the case came to trial, Cranshaw just—disappeared."

"And Eve?"

"She believed I was the thief. She told me so. She came to the hospital and questioned me like a district attorney about the burglary, wanting to know exactly what I had done, what I had heard, what I had seen. Then she said I'd got what I deserved; that I'd end as a—as a blind beggar."

"I didn't know," Rosamund said, aghast, "that anyone could be so vile."

Kathy, seeing the expression on Jerome's face, realized that he had endured as much as he could. She broke in hastily. "We've had a mystery of our own up here." She told them about the man whom Mister

Duffy had attacked, and went to get the scarf as a proof that there had really been a prowler.

"A forty-dollar scarf," she said as she displayed it. "Worn by a prowler! Only why anyone would try to get in here simply baffles me. This is the quietest neighborhood."

"Why anyone would try to get in!" Hal exclaimed. "But that's exactly what we said about Jerome's office. An unlikely thing unless—"

"Unless the man with the imported scarf had something to do with the burglary," Rodney said in excitement.

Jerome shook his head. "I can't see any connection. I haven't a single scrap of evidence. I don't know who the burglar was. There would be no point in it."

"Hey, wench," Hal protested, "what are you doing? That's evidence."

Rosamund was carefully folding up the scarf. "I'm going to take this back to New York, go to the shop where Kathy saw one like it, and try to find out who purchased it. With anything as expensive as this, there must be comparatively few sales. It's no bargain counter item. Some clerk might possibly remember."

She looked at her watch. "Heavens, we've got to start back." She managed to keep her tone light but she was remembering that Hal had told her someone might not want Jerome to regain his sight. Warm as the room was, she was shaken by a chill of fear. Suppose that prowler had intended to see that Jerome remained blind?

Long after the guests had gone, Kathy and Jerome sat before the fire. She got up at last. "The room is getting chilly. I'd better put on another log."

He stretched out his hand, groped for hers, found it. "It will always be warm where you are, Kathy. Thank you."

"For what?" she asked in surprise.

"For being you, exactly the way you are."

Tony stood in front of her mirror in the bedroom at Mrs. Haven's house adjusting a perky green hat over her dark hair. The matching suit was deceptively cut, exquisitely simple and devastatingly becoming. She became aware of the droop of her lips, the lost look in her eyes.

"You stop it," she told herself impatiently, "I have no use for women who bog down in self-pity. All right, Rodney has dropped out of your life. You'll never see him again. Never. Never. But you have to go on living, just the same; you have to look for new interests, for something else to fill up that empty heart of yours. And don't tell me it can't be done, my girl," she added severely. "Just look at Mrs. Haven. You don't see her wallowing in self-pity. Her life was smashed and she got to work to pick up the pieces and build something new out of the wreckage, something good and solid."

She switched her thoughts angrily away from Rodney Meredith. No one can go through life with an aching heart. But it wasn't just Rodney, of course, though his disappearance was the hardest to bear. There was Rosamund, her dearest friend, from whom she had had no secrets, no reticences, and now there was an intangible wall between them. For some reason she had lost Rosamund's confidence.

She gave the hat a final twist, sprayed perfume behind her ears. Smile, darn you, she snarled to herself, and found that she was laughing.

Mrs. Haven looked up as she came into the small sitting room, pulling on gloves.

"You're going out?"

Tony nodded. "I'm having dinner with Carter."

"I'm so glad you're taking time off for a little fun after the way you've worked since Thanksgiving."

Tony laughed. "I don't mind the work, and the shop is simply booming. This is the busiest season of the year, you know."

"Tony," Mrs. Haven said abruptly, "this is inexcusable impertinence on my part. I have no right—"

"You can say anything you like to me. I hoped that you knew that."

"Thank you, my dear. It was just—how long is this joke to go on?"

"Joke? Oh, you mean about my being your maid? Why, I don't know."

"You're thinking about my pride, aren't you? Well, the thing has become absurd and it must stop," Mrs. Haven said vigorously. "I believe you ought to tell Carter the truth. He's not like his mother, you know. We can't carry on this deception any longer. It's not fair to him."

"All right, I'll tell him it began as a joke on my part," Tony agreed.

"Tony." The older woman hesitated. "What do you think of my nephew?"

"He's one of the most attractive men I've ever known," the girl answered promptly. "Nice-looking, nice manners, nice company." An impish smile touched her mouth for a moment. "In the beginning I think he wanted to impress the poor working girl, but he's not like that now. I really enjoy going out with him."

Mrs. Haven laughed.

"What's funny about that?" Tony demanded.

"Your coolness. Your detachment. You aren't a bit in love with him, are you?"

Color flamed in Tony's cheeks and died out again. "I really like him very much."

"Carter," his aunt said drily, "may not feel quite so detached. In fact, I think he's falling more in love with you every day. It must be quite a new experience for him. I've watched his performances in the past. As a rule it's the girls who fall for him while he remains impeccably polite and not at all impressed."

"Oh, dear," Tony said in such a tone of distress that Mrs. Haven had to laugh again.

"And his mother is simply wild," she said in a tone of mischievous satisfaction. "She called from Boston yesterday and talked for half an hour, blaming me for having a pretty waitress and for throwing her in Carter's way, because young men are so impressionable and don't know how to protect themselves from women's wiles."

Tony gave a soft gurgle of laughter. "Poor Carter! He must be at least thirty. I don't understand mothers like that, do you? The ones who try to impose their values on their grown children. If by the time the child has become an adult he hasn't learned the basic values, he never will. And it isn't as though Carter were dependent on his mother in any way."

"Far from it," Mrs. Haven agreed. "He is making as much money as his father right now. Probably more, though I must say he doesn't flaunt it."

"What is his business?" Tony asked. "He never mentions it."

Mrs. Haven smiled. "He probably doesn't feel that the feminine brain could cope with it. He's a business consultant, whatever that means. Betty has her heart set on his marrying some girl from the Social Register. The fact that I'm in it and she is not has always been simply torment to her." She broke into laughter. "My dear, when I think what she would do if she knew about your social background and the Carew fortune! Anyhow, Carter is sweet to her and patient with her, but he continues to live his own life without making an issue of it."

The doorbell rang and she smiled. "You had better answer, as long as I'm not supposed to know my nephew is taking my maid to dinner."

"I'll tell him tonight," Tony promised, blew her a kiss, and ran down the stairs to open the door for Carter Holbrook.

Each time she saw him, and she had had half a dozen dates with him since Thanksgiving, she experienced a first moment of surprise over his good looks. In the intervals, it is true, she tended to forget all about him, though he had been a pleasant and amusing companion who never referred to her supposedly subordinate position in his aunt's house and, after one abortive attempt, had never tried to make love to her. They were simply good companions.

He stood in the doorway, very tall, his heavy overcoat making him seem bigger than ever, his eyes alight as they looked at her. They smiled at each other and he took her arm to help her into the big Cadillac at the curb.

"I've discovered a wonderful French restaurant," he told her. "I hope you'll like it."

"I'm sure I shall."

"Aunt Jane didn't cause you any embarrassment because you won't be serving dinner tonight?"

This was the perfect opening for her confession. "Carter, I'm really sorry about this. It started as a joke, you know; something I thought would be fun to do. And somehow it got out of hand."

"What did? Going out with me, you mean?" he asked, sounding so disturbed that she realized his aunt had been right. Carter was falling in love with her.

"You see, your aunt was wonderful when I was looking around desperately for some place in the neighborhood where I could stay. She let me have that spare room of hers, and we got to be friends. She's a lovely person, Carter. Well, when Thanksgiving came and she was having her family for dinner I suggested—just for a lark, you know—that I pretend to be her maid. And after that the thing just drifted on, I guess."

"Well, I'll be darned." After a moment Carter began to laugh. "Well, I'll be darned! You know, I simply couldn't figure out how a girl as lovely as you are, and with that quick, cultivated mind, could be content to do housework. Any movie scout getting a glimpse of you would camp on your doorstep until he had you in Hollywood."

"Not me," Tony said emphatically. "I like housework but I'd loathe living in a goldfish bowl."

"What a girl!" Carter parked the long car and followed Tony into the restaurant. It was a misleadingly simple-looking place, with no garish decorations, no orchestra, no entertainment. But the tables had the greatest luxury New York City can offer, space between them, so that strangers did not bump elbows while they ate; the room was quiet; the food was perfect.

Tony looked up from her soup into the good-looking face that was watching her thoughtfully, with a puzzled expression. "What's wrong?"

"I was just wondering," he said slowly, "how much my mother had to do with—that little joke of yours."

When she made no comment he said, "Look here, I'm not going to criticize her. Only there are some things that count a lot to her, money and social position and what other people think. All that jazz." He added a trifle defensively, "Lots of people are like that. Perhaps most people are like that."

She nodded.

"And Aunt Jane was left pretty hard up by her husband. That always rankled with Mother. Not for the wrong reasons, honestly, but because she thought Aunt Jane would have been so much more comfortable, so much happier, if she had married a man who could give her more. One of the wealthiest men in New York proposed to Aunt Jane and she turned him down flat. Naturally it upset Mother."

"But, Carter," Tony protested, "no one could have given her more than her husband did. She was a supremely happy woman. In fact, her life was so rich and fulfilled that even now, when he has been taken away from her, she can never really be alone again. He's there always—to have and to hold."

"And that's what you would like, isn't it?" he asked abruptly. "You who would honestly rather do housework than live in a goldfish bowl."

"Yes, that is what I would like," she said quietly. "How did you know?"

He half smiled, half frowned. "I don't know. I seem to have a lot of perceptions about you, though I've never been particularly clever about people. I wonder why that is."

When she made no reply he said, half seriously, half teasingly, "Why do you think that is, Tony, my beautiful?"

There was a note in his voice which she had never heard there before. Behind the laughter there was a profound seriousness.

"Carter," she said quickly, in an attempt to sidetrack him, "what is it that you want most?" She forestalled the inevitable personal comment by adding, "You say most people want money and social position and public approval, the things that are too often called success. How about you?"

"I don't believe I've ever particularly thought about it," he said slowly. "Sure, money is fine. I like the things you can buy with it. But money in itself, for itself? No, I don't see that."

"But Mrs. Haven says you are doing awfully well for so young a man."

"I suppose I am, but not just for the money." He frowned, crumbled a roll, trying to think it out. "There are two things about money," he said at last, "the power that goes with it and the excitement of getting it."

"And which matters most to you?"

"The excitement," he said in a tone of surprise. "You know, it's queer; I've never realized that clearly before." He grinned at her. "And while we are in this mood of confidence, what do you really do for a living?"

"I run a bookshop," she said, "with a friend of mine. Oh, you know her, of course. Her mother and your aunt are old friends. Rosamund Perry."

"Of course I know the Perrys. Known them for years and years. But why a bookshop?"

She told him why, her voice eager and excited, while he watched her face, the play of expression, nodding his understanding.

I'm in love with this girl, he told himself in astonishment. For the first time in my life I'm really in love. No passing infatuation. I want to marry her, to have her with me always.

For a moment words trembled on his lips and then he checked them firmly. This would take thinking out. A wife wasn't a girl you met and had a couple of dates with and forgot. She'd be there always, a part of his life. *To have and to hold*. He hadn't thought of marriage that way. Was it a promise or a trap? Would it mean a richer life or all sorts of unforeseen and bothersome complications? Could he continue to treat his job as though it were an exciting gamble or would he have to sacrifice all the thrills for a dull, pedestrian existence?

He could foresee his mother's reaction if he were to tell her that he was going to marry Tony Carew. Even when she knew that Tony wasn't her sister-in-law's servant she would still regard her as a penniless girl, a nobody. There would be an unpleasant time for everyone, for Tony most of all.

And there was his work, too. So far he had been extraordinarily lucky for a man of his age; even his proud mother would have been astonished if she had known how much money he could lay his hands on, how thick his investment portfolio was. And the excitement. A girl who preferred housework to Holly-wood might not understand the irresistible lure of that excitement. In fact, there was something about Tony that made him sure she would not understand it.

He looked across the table at her, at the unforget-table face, at those extraordinary clear gray eyes. Tony. He'd never find another girl like her. Never in his life. The miracle was that he had found this one. For Tony's sake it might even be worthwhile to give up the excitement, to settle into some kind of groove that had no risk in it.

He forestalled the waiter in pulling out her chair for her. "There's a good picture at Radio City," he said. "Shall we take a look at it?"

The movie was gay and witty; on the great stage of the Music Hall the girls performed with their usual fabulous precision. The theater lights went on and Carter helped Tony with her coat.

"How about a nightclub?" he suggested. "The evening is still young."

"Not tonight, but thank you. I'm not dressed for it. Anyhow, I have to work tomorrow, you know."

"You're sure?"

She nodded and he drove her reluctantly down to Nineteenth Street, held the hand she offered him, and then bent forward with sudden determination. She turned her head away, avoiding his lips.

"Please don't, Carter." There was an edge of impatience in her voice. "We've had this out before."

"You don't give a guy much of a break," he grumbled.

Not much of a break, he thought to himself after he had left Tony at his aunt's house. There weren't many girls who would have dismissed him so casually. He was perfectly aware of his good looks, his excellently cut clothes, his luxurious car. No girl could say he didn't provide her with a pleasant evening.

With a shrug he put her out of his mind. Tony Carew was beginning to occupy too much of his attention and, like her, he had work to do. When he let himself into the smart bachelor apartment he occupied on Beekman Place the telephone was ringing. The man at the other end said, "I've been trying to get you all evening."

"Had a date," Carter said briefly. "Just got in. Anything new?"

"It's in the bag. The reports are in and look better even than we hoped. There's a fortune in this thing. For my money—"

"For whose money?" Carter asked drily.

The other man laughed. "Anyhow, we've got it made."

"You're overlooking the risks, aren't you?" Carter said.

"Since when have you been scared away by risks?" the other man scoffed.

Carter was silent. A man who married a girl like
Tony Carew would take on a long-range responsibility. He would take pride in providing her with a life
of financial and social security. She would, as he was
well aware, grace any circle. Her unstressed dignity
and pose were rare qualities in a young woman who
had had few advantages. He would always be proud
of her. It mattered, more than he had realized, that
she should be proud of him.

And yet their standards were worlds apart. How
capable would she prove at understanding the im-
pulse that drove him.

"Well?" the other man said impatiently.

Without a word Carter put down the telephone.

ii

Tony led her customer to the desk where Mrs.
Perry was helping out during the Christmas rush.
"Mrs. Perry will wrap it for you," she said, and
turned to the next impatient woman.

The Good Companions Bookshop was thronged
with customers. As usual a small crowd was examining the Christmas cards on display at the back of the
shop. Mrs. Perry had been appalled by the size of
the initial order but Tony's judgment had been more
than justified. The cards, expensive as they were by
usual standards, were being snatched up. More than
one customer had said, "I'm going to keep one for
myself and have it framed."

Harassed mothers were looking along the shelves at
bright-jacketed children's books. The night before,
Rosamund had said with a giggle, "Just once I'd like
to meet a mother whose child is not old for his age or
brighter than the average." Now she was explaining
to a customer, with all the tact and patience she
could summon up that, no matter how beautiful the
illustrations might be, a book for six-year-olds would
not have much appeal for a twelve-year-old.

"May I help you?" Tony asked a woman who was

standing in the way of other customers who were trying to see the bookshelves.

"Oh, yes, I want a book," the woman said brightly.

Tony bit her lips. "What kind of book?"

"Well, anything you have that's on the best-seller list. I don't know what people would do without best-seller lists, do you? They save all the trouble of thinking for ourselves."

Rosamund had led her troubled customer to the desk where her book was to be wrapped, and had turned to see which person had been waiting the longest. There was a babble of voices:

"Well, something light and amusing. I hate gloomy books, don't you? . . . He doesn't really like anything except mysteries but I think he should improve his mind, whether he wants to or not. . . . Honestly, the price of books! It's outrageous. Why for that much money I could get something really nice."

"Less than a theater ticket, less than a restaurant meal," Rosamund pointed out, "but it lasts. It's always there to enjoy over and over. The meal took perhaps an hour to cook, the play three months to produce, and the book a year or more to write."

"Oh. Well, I declare, I never thought of that. Here, it's my turn next. I've waited longer than she has."

Tony had learned, in her few weeks of experience, how much discourtesy is showered on sales clerks. At first she had been indignant, now she merely felt sorry. If only people could realize, she thought, the extent to which good manners smooth the way and make life pleasant and bearable for themselves as well as others.

Slowly the crowd thinned out as women drifted home to prepare dinner. Tony looked around in relief as the last one went out. She drew a long breath. After the battle of voices, the jostling, the pushing, the "I'm first" manner of so many impatient and discourteous shoppers, it was good just to enjoy rest and quiet and peace.

She was about to draw the blind and lock the door when it opened with a gay jingle and Carter Holbrook looked in.

"Hello there," he said. He surveyed the shop in curiosity. "So this is your place of business. I've passed it so many times before. I wish I had known it was yours. I'd have become your most faithful customer."

Tony straightened tired shoulders, smiled at him. "And what may I do for you, sir?"

"Tony," Mrs. Perry called from the middle room, "do come in and have a cup of tea. You need a little rest before dinner. Oh, sorry, I didn't know you had a customer."

Carter looked questioningly at Tony, such an appealing look that she laughed in spite of herself. "I have a customer for tea," she called, and took him in. There was a fire in the grate, and Mrs. Perry had cleared books off a small table, covered it with a white cloth, on which she had set out a tea service and paper-thin sandwiches.

"Hello, Carter," Mrs. Perry said.

Tony sank down in a chair and took gratefully the cup Mrs. Perry handed her. The latter had greeted Carter with her usual warm friendliness, but Rosamund, after a first surprised look, behaved with a restraint that was unusual to her. For some reason she did not seem to like Carter, at least as a caller on Tony.

Tony was too weary to talk but Mrs. Perry carried the conversation easily, telling the young man some of the amusing incidents that had occurred during the day. Rosamund, who had kicked off her shoes and sat with her feet curled up under her, stared at the fire, forgetting to drink her tea.

At last she stirred, sighed, set down the cup, put on her shoes. "Well, it's like washing dishes; you hate the darned things, but if you leave them they'll still be waiting for you in the morning. Leering at you. I might as well get it over." She went out for a big apron that covered her dress and began to put the stock in order.

"Here—" Tony struggled wearily to her feet—"I'll help."

"Neither of you," Carter said firmly, "is going to stir. Go back to your chairs and collapse. Just give orders and Mrs. Holbrook's little boy will carry them out."

He ignored Tony's rather feeble protests and put books back on shelves, straightened a table display that had been disarranged, gathered up odds and ends of paper and twine and cards that had been dropped on the floor.

In some amusement Tony watched Rosamund's hostility fade as he went cheerfully about the work, keeping up a running commentary of funny remarks that made them all laugh.

It was when he reached the back of the room and was beginning to put the Christmas cards in their proper places that he stopped to examine them closely.

"This is beautiful work, Tony," he called. "But, my dear girl, with an artist of this caliber you must have paid so much for them that there won't be any profit. Unless you are handling them merely as a prestige item. They are exquisite. I'd like to get some myself. More than that, I'd like to meet the artist."

"I didn't pay half what they are worth," Tony replied, "and you've already met the artist. Mrs. Perry."

Carter came back to the fireplace. "Well, of all the dark horses! I've never heard a word about this. It's a conspiracy. Your work is enchanting, Mrs. Perry. What I can't understand is why I haven't seen it before. I'm a collector in a small way and I haunt the galleries."

"I haven't exhibited," Mrs. Perry admitted. "As a matter of fact, I haven't done any painting for years, except for occasional sketches, until just recently. It was Tony who got me started again."

"Bless Tony!" he said fervently.

Rosamund's eyes came up to his face in a startled look and then turned to Tony.

"Have you done anything else?" Carter asked.

"A few things."

"I have a friend who owns a gallery," he told her. "He believes the trend is beginning to drift back to the representational. He'd like to see what you have."

"But there's so little, really," she protested, a faint flush on her cheeks.

"He means it, Mother," Rosamund said. "Get them, won't you? Or shall I?"

"Well, I—" Mrs. Perry got up a trifle self-consciously and went back to the room that was used for exhibiting paintings. She returned with some canvases and an easel, which Carter took from her and set up in the best light.

"There's very little," she said again, and set the first canvas on the easel. He made no comment and she removed it, set up another and another. There were six in all.

When she had finished, Carter said, "Will you let me tell my friend about you, Mrs. Perry? Let him come to call on you and see for himself?"

"You think they're—good?"

"Very good. And you have something that is all your own, the way you have used light, for instance." He picked up a small canvas that showed a farmyard, a pool of water with the light touching it. "How did you get that effect? Anyone looking at it will know the rain has just stopped, though there's no suggestion of rain. They will know that the pool will dry up in hot weather, that it will become an obstacle in winter. How did you do it?"

"I saw it and then remembered. That's all. I can't talk about these things. Anyhow, there's no point in talking. Either a painting conveys its meaning without any explanation or, in my opinion, it's a failure. When art doesn't communicate it doesn't do anything except, maybe, relieve the feelings of the painter."

"Do you have anything else?" Carter asked.

"Nothing finished. I do sketches first and then work from them, as a rule."

At his insistence she brought out her portfolio of sketches and Carter looked through it. There were quick, clever drawings of children playing in

Gramercy Park, of two women holding what appeared to be an acrimonious discussion, of Cecily Ann pausing to look into the bow window of the shop, of the charming old-fashioned summerhouse behind Kathy's house, of lower Broadway with the skyscrapers seeming to lean forward as though to crush a tiny hurrying throng below, of Mister Duffy with a small kitten nestling beside him.

When at length he took his leave, Mrs. Perry was glowing.

"Oh, Mother," Rosamund was saying breathlessly. "Oh, Mother! How wonderful for you!" She turned to Tony. "How nice he is. How terribly nice."

Tony rocked with laughter. "What a change! You were bristling like a cat facing a dog when he first came in. Then he came, he saw, he conquered. At first I thought you weren't pleased to have him come to the shop."

"It was only because—" Rosamund broke off awkwardly. "The question, after all, is—conquered whom?"

Tony had no comment to make.

xii

Conquered whom? So far Tony had not found an
answer to the question though she was aware that
she could not postpone doing so indefinitely. Day by
day, Carter showed more clearly his feeling for her.
She'd have to make up her mind. He was, she
thought, one of the best-looking men she knew. He
had liked her when she was, as he believed, a domes-
tic servant; he accepted her now as a penniless girl
struggling to establish a small bookshop. It wasn't, at
any rate, the Carew money, for he knew nothing of
her background, that attracted him, and she had
always been aware that her money was bound to be
an important factor with the men who displayed
interest in her.

His manner, for all its growing warmth and tenderness, had been maintained at a level of easy, happy
companionship. And he had done for Mrs. Perry
what no one else could do. He had been as good as
his word. The night after his impromptu call at the
bookshop a Mr. Revlin had telephoned and asked to
see Mrs. Perry about her work. He had come and had
been, Rosamund related exultantly, most enthusias-
tic. In February he was going to give her a one-man
show at his gallery, and as soon as the Christmas rush
was over, her mother was going to devote all her
time to her painting.

"What's he like?" Tony asked.

"Short and stocky with a Van Dyke beard, and a
very impressive manner. At first I thought he was
rather stuffy and artificial but afterward I thought
he was a prince among men."

112

Tony laughed, then sobered. "We'll have to handle things," she told Mrs. Perry, "so you won't do another scrap of work in the shop."

Rosamund agreed. "Thank heaven, Tony, you decided not to keep open in the evenings or we'd never get any Christmas shopping done. How is yours going?"

"I'll finish it all tonight," Tony said with determination.

"But you're so tired."

"Choosing things for people you like is such fun that I won't be tired after I've started," Tony assured her.

It was getting started that was the problem. She took a long hot bath to bake out the tiredness, gulped a hasty sandwich and a glass of milk over Mrs. Haven's protests.

"My dear, you mustn't go out without more food than that."

"But there's so little time," Tony said, "and the stores will be jammed."

"Well, for this once—but if you're going to neglect yourself while I'm away—"

"I won't. I promise."

Tony bundled up and set out for her evening of Christmas shopping. There had been a great deal of discussion about Mrs. Haven going away. For several weeks, she had had a hacking cough and she had been losing weight. Her doctor insisted that she go South for at least two weeks.

"It's not necessary. Anyhow," she insisted, "I'm not going to leave you alone in this house."

"But there's nothing to be afraid of," Tony had assured her. "I shan't mind a bit."

"I don't like it. I feel responsible for you. Suppose anything should happen."

"Then I'll get Mister Duffy back and keep him here while you're gone. He's as good as any army for protection and it would be such fun having him."

And in the long run Mrs. Haven agreed, though somewhat reluctantly. Her bags were packed and she was to leave in the morning. At the last minute she had asked, "But where are you going to spend Christmas, my dear?"

"With a friend," Tony assured her.

After all, she reminded herself, Mister Duffy was a friend, wasn't he? And the soreness around her heart came back. This would be the first Christmas in five years that she had not spent with Rosamund and her mother. This annual engagement was so taken for granted that her other friends had long since stopped inviting her for the holiday. But now the Perrys studiously avoided any mention of Christmas. She knew why, of course. They were going to Kathy's, and Rodney would be there with his brother. Rodney.

Tony found herself walking faster and faster, as though trying to run away from the memory of Rodney. Rodney saying, *Oh, Tony, I do love you so*. Rodney saying, *I can't ask you to marry me*. Rodney who had not come back. Who was never coming back.

Shopping at night during the Christmas season resembles a five-thirty subway mob combined with the strenuousness of a football scrimmage. Tony forced her way down aisles, held up presents to catch the eyes of harassed and over-worked clerks, went through the turmoil of noise in the toy department at Macy's, where her ears were bombarded and deafened by the sound of mechanical toys, the shouting of barkers, the irritable yelling of tired customers.

Three hours later, she gathered up the last package, gaily wrapped, tied with wide red ribbon, and added it to the pile in her arms.

As she stepped out of the warm, stale atmosphere of the store, the night air struck her face, cold and crisp and tingling, and she breathed it in greedily. She was not heartsore now. She had been too occupied to think about herself and she was weary of turmoil and pushing and frayed tempers. But she was glowing with pleasure as she went over in her mind the presents she had selected, after so much anxious care, and thought of the pleasure they would give. The difficulty had been to restrain her generous impulses and not to buy the extravagant gifts she had wanted. They would only have caused embarrassment and awkwardness and a kind of restraint.

Standing on the street, she remembered the tradition of our ancestors, who at midnight on Christmas Eve flung open the door to let the spirit of Christmas come in. It had, she thought, entered her own heart.

On the corner a Santa Claus in a red suit and a frankly unbelievable beard rang a bell over a Salvation Army kettle. Laughing, Tony juggled her packages precariously, until she could reach her purse and drop money into the kettle. She called a gay, "Merry Christmas!"

For a little while, before returning home, she stood on Fifth Avenue, listening to the carols piped from a department store, looking at the enormous Christmas tree at Rockefeller Center, at the shoppers who, however tired their feet might be, however much their arms might ache with the packages with which they were loaded, were in a gay and laughing mood.

She stood looking down at the skating rink, at the brightly dressed skaters swirling over the ice, and then her gaze sharpened. From where she stood she could look past the rink into a restaurant on the lower level. At a table looking out at the skaters sat Mrs. Hazelton's blond operator, Cecily Ann. Tonight she wore a smart mink hat over her bright hair and a mink coat was draped over the back of a chair.

Then the girl stood up and Tony, in shocked disbelief, saw her companion. It was Frank Hazelton, the chemist husband of the owner of the beauty parlor. Cecily Ann gave him a languishing look and made a laughing comment but Hazelton, to judge by his expression, was not amused. He paid his check and followed her angrily toward the door.

As Tony got out of a taxi at the Nineteenth Street house there was a deep bark.

"Watch it, lady!" the cab driver exclaimed. "Looks like a man-eater."

Tony laughed. "That's all right. He's my dog."

Hal Perkins, who had been holding the leash, took the packages while Tony and Mister Duffy greeted each other. He unlocked the door for her.

At her invitation he came in and she made coffee and cut a lavish slice of the cake Mrs. Haven had baked. He sprawled in a chair in the informal sitting room before the fire, smiling at her, munching his cake, while Tony checked her list against the great pile of wrapped presents. Looking at his kind face with its laughter lines, Tony thought, "How lucky Rosamund is! He'll be good to her all her life."

"I can't tell you how grateful I am, Hal. It was so kind of you to get Mister Duffy for me."

"It was a pleasure," he assured her, "and I enjoy driving that Lincoln of yours. Anyhow, neither Rosamund nor I would feel comfortable at the idea of you staying here alone."

"How are—things?" she asked.

"Fine. Just fine. I must say Jerome looks better every day. If only the poor devil could regain his sight he'd be able to start writing some more children's stories. He keeps Dennis fascinated for hours with the tales he spins."

"I got him a tape recorder for Christmas," Tony said, "but I hardly know him and I don't know how to give it to him so that he would be willing to accept it. I was wondering—do you suppose you could tell him it's an old one from the newspaper office, one that was discarded or replaced or something?"

"A tape recorder! What a magnificent idea, Tony! Just the thing. With that he could go ahead with his books even if he can't see."

"That's what I thought. Can you manage it somehow for me?"

"Of course I can."

"It's that big package on the floor beside the couch. You can take it up when you go to Kathy's for Christmas."

There was an awkward silence while he went over to pick up the tape recorder.

"This is going to give a lot of pleasure, young lady."

"I hope so. I suppose Rodney will be with his brother for Christmas."

"Yes." Hal took an unnecessarily long time lighting his pipe. "You know, don't you, that Rosamund is absolutely sick at not having you with us. Kathy sent the warmest possible invitation to you but—"

"It's because of Rodney, isn't it?"

Hal nodded. "Look here, Tony, the situation must be as clear to you as it is to us. Rodney is head over heels in love with you, but the guy has a real problem. As long as he has Jerome to look after, to support, he can't marry. So it's a lot easier for him to stay away from you. Far away. Those are the facts, gal."

Suddenly Tony leaned forward, looking at him, her face flushed and more lovely than he had ever seen it. If Rodney had been there at the moment he would not have been able to hold by his resolve. Hal stood up, returning her look gravely.

"Hal," she said, her voice choked, "it's a terrible thing to be a girl. There's nothing I can really do but wait, is there?"

"Not unless you want to make it harder for Rodney," he said seriously. "I don't suppose you understand, but a man has a lot of pride."

"So," she told him, "has a woman."

He put his arm around her, gave her a brotherly hug. "Maybe I'd better have a talk with Rodney. According to Rosamund, he's getting some real competition these days from that Carter Holbrook. Good looks, good family, good income, car a mile long."

When she had walked Mister Duffy, Tony went to bed but not to sleep. For the first time she thought of Rodney not with longing but with a stirring of anger. It was not love that kept him from her, it was pride. It was time, she decided, that he remembered that she, too, had pride.

ii

The following night Tony went to a dinner party given by some old friends of her family. It was long since she had spent an evening among the very wealthy. Somewhat to her surprise she found herself thinking of Carter Holbrook and his comment about the things that money could achieve. There was little of ostentation in the big Park Avenue apartment. What generations of money had brought here were a lack of awareness of it, gentle ease of manner, quiet assurance. Only on the walls, lined with fine paintings, were there any indications of great wealth.

Conversation flowed lightly during the perfect but unobtrusively served dinner, with the women's shoulders gleaming, jewels sparkling, the men's dinner clothes immaculate under the great chandelier.

After dinner a celebrated violinist played for them. This was the circle in which Timothy Carew's granddaughter had grown up and she slipped back into it now as though she had never been away. How far from this room were the bustle of the small bookshop, the struggle of the Perrys to keep a roof over their heads, the Salvation Army kettles on the corners watched by shivering elderly men in Santa Claus costumes.

Drifting, as good talk does, lightly from subject to subject, it touched on the new Hartford Art Gallery at Columbus Circle, on the changing tastes in painting. Percy Rolf, who had been her grandfather's partner, showed Tony a new acquisition.

"Seventeenth-century Dutch. My wife was appalled. Not because she doesn't love it but because sixty-five thousand is a steep price."

For a long time Tony stood before the small canvas with its typical Dutch interior, a woman doing embroidery with the light from a window falling on her face, a baby in a cradle on the floor, which she was rocking with her foot.

"I suppose you're sure it's authentic," she said.

Rolf laughed. "I got this from the Trendham Galleries. Their reputation is impeccable. If you trust your dealer you are all right."

"Do you know anything about the Revlin Galery?"

He shook his head. "Must be one of the newer, smaller ones. Why? Are you becoming a collector?"

"No. But a friend of mine is going to hold a one-man show there in February. She's really good. I hope you'll come to see her stuff."

"Be glad to," he assured her.

It was late when the door of Tony's Lincoln was opened for her by the doorman of the apartment and she drove the big car south.

She turned into Nineteenth Street and saw the Cadillac parked outside the house, saw the man waiting patiently at the wheel. She pulled up behind him, shut off the lights, got out to lock the car. For this one night she would leave it on the street. She didn't want to walk home alone.

As she came around the Cadillac the door opened and Carter got out. He stared at the sable coat, at the diamond bracelet that clasped a slim wrist, at the Lincoln. His expression changed.

"Carter?" she exclaimed in surprise. "What on earth are you doing here at—why it's nearly eleven-thirty."

"I know. I got to worrying about you being alone in the house when Aunt Jane was away and I came to make sure you were all right. I didn't get any answer, just a big dog that raised Cain when I rang."

"But of course I'm all right," she assured him. "Have you been waiting long?"

"Since eight o'clock."

"How dreadful! Then you must come in, at least for a minute."

She unlocked the door. Mister Duffy stood at the foot of the stairs, his ruff standing up, growling deep in his throat. Behind her, Carter halted abruptly.

"Mister Duffy!" she said sharply. "Quiet, sir." He growled again. She put out a hand and rested it on his head. "What's got into you?" she asked in surprise. "This is a friend."

"A great Dane, isn't he?" Carter said. "There are a lot of them around these days. Do you think you ought to have a vicious, dangerous dog like that, Tony?"

"He's not vicious or dangerous. I've never known him to be unfriendly before." But she remembered then Cecily Ann's accusation and wondered whether it could possibly be true that Mister Duffy attacked innocent people.

In Mrs. Haven's sitting room, she knelt to light the fire and then got up to take a chair facing Carter, with Mister Duffy at her feet, his eyes fixed unblinkingly and unnervingly on the guest. An emerald green dinner dress fell in long graceful folds to the matching satin slippers.

"Are you allowed to keep a big dog like this in New York?" Carter asked in some surprise. "I should think it would be most difficult."

"I keep him in the country," Tony explained. "He is with me now only because your aunt is away." She looked up to find Carter looking at her steadily.

"You're quite a girl for jokes, aren't you?" he said, and she realized that there was no amusement in his face.

"What do you mean?" she asked in surprise.

His eyes moved from the sable coat to the diamond bracelet to the Paris gown. "And," he said, as though he had spoken his thoughts aloud, "that Lincoln at the door. To me these things spell money. Big money. For a girl who is struggling with a bookshop—"

She told him then. "Rosamund Perry is my dearest friend, as her mother is your aunt's dearest friend. She and Mrs. Perry were going to lose their house. I couldn't offer them money. They not only would have refused it but it would have made a—a breach in our friendship. But in this way—and anyhow, Carter, I love the shop. I think it is worth doing for its own sake. I could never have been satisfied to live the life of a debutante. I realized that tonight when I went back, after such a long time, to have dinner with the Rolfs, my grandfather's old friends."

"Percy Rolf?" he asked, startled.

She nodded.

"Then you must be Timothy Carew's granddaughter."

She nodded again.

"I didn't know."

"Of course you didn't."

"The reason I came tonight—oh, I was really worried about you, that was true enough—but the chief reason—" He fumbled in his pocket, took out a small jeweler's box, opened it to show her a solitaire diamond ring. "This was for you. I wanted to ask you to marry me, Tony. But I suppose, with all this, you wouldn't look at me."

"That's hardly fair, is it?" she answered. "If you have learned anything at all about me, you must know that I wouldn't be influenced by money or the lack of it."

"Then," he said eagerly, "will you marry me, Tony? I love you very much."

She shook her head. "I'm terribly sorry. Believe me, Carter. Terribly sorry."

"You don't like me at all?"

"I like you immensely. You're one of the nicest friends I ever had. And I'm so grateful for what you've done for Mrs. Perry, but—"

"I could teach you to love me, Tony," he said earnestly. "I know I could. I've never thought for a single moment I wanted to be tied down by marriage. I've never taken a girl seriously in my life. But I'd do everything I could to make you happy. I'd rebuild my life the way you wanted it to be."

"I'm sorry," she said again. "I'm sorry."

"I'm desperately in earnest. I didn't know it was possible to care so much for a girl. There's nothing I wouldn't do to win you."

"Oh, Carter!" There were tears in her eyes.

"Is there someone else?"

She got up and Mister Duffy was on his feet instantly, standing between her and the tall young man. She found herself thinking of Rodney and of Mister Duffy's instant capitulation to that elusive young man.

Carter looked down at the jeweler's box, smiled wryly, shut it and dropped it into his pocket.

"There doesn't seem to be anything else to say, does there?" he said bitterly.

"Except thank you with all my heart," she told him. "I am proud, more proud than I can express, that you wanted me for your wife."

At the gentleness in her voice, hope came back to his face. "Won't you take a little more time?" he implored her. "Won't you give me a chance? I don't ask a promise of you; just a little time." There was a wry little smile on his mouth. "I've been learning lately that being single is a lonely way of life. Perhaps you may find it so, too. If you do, I'll be waiting."

He saw her hesitation, took a step toward her, and Mister Duffy growled.

He laughed suddenly. "I'll be back, you know," he said without giving her a chance to protest. "I'll be back when you've got rid of that elephant. No man can talk to his girl properly with something like that in the way." He smiled at her. "Good night, my lovely Tony, and Merry Christmas. I'm going to Boston to spend the holiday with my family but I'll see you as soon as I get back."

He ran down the stairs and she heard the front door close behind him. Slowly she followed to shove home the bolt. The motor of the Cadillac came to life. Mister Duffy growled deep in his throat.

xiii

It was Christmas Eve. The bookshop had closed at four o'clock and Rosamund, Mrs. Perry, and Hal Perkins said good-by to Tony before they set off in her Lincoln for Catherine Cathcart's house, the trunk of the car and half the back seat stacked with packages to which Tony had added her own contributions.

Rosamund had flung her arms around Tony and her cheek was wet with tears. "I can't bear to leave you at Christmas."

Tony managed a light laugh. "Don't be a little goose."

"At least, I hope to heaven it's the last one we'll ever spend apart. You are family."

"Stop worrying and tell Hal to drive slowly. The weather forecast sounds bad."

The weather forecast couldn't have been worse. It was to be a white Christmas. No doubt about that. But the temperature was to drop close to zero and the snow now sifting so lightly might become heavy, with high winds and little visibility. Blizzard ahead, one broadcaster had warned gloomily.

Tony stood laughing and waving at them as they drove off. Then she went back to Mrs. Haven's empty house. She had assured them all that everything would be all right, that she would have a wonderful time. Now she closed the door, pretenses gone, and let loneliness creep around her. Never before had the house been so silent. It seemed almost to listen.

She went slowly up to the sitting room with its warmth from the blaze of logs in the fireplace. The air was scented with the spicy Christmas fragrance of the greens she had arranged on the walls, the gold and orange of kumquats and tangerines in the wreath over the mantel. Alone or not, she had done her best to bring some vestiges of the spirit of Christmas into the house.

In the street night had already come, the darkness lighted by the snow that was falling like a diaphanous veil. Knowing that the highways would be thronged with people leaving Manhattan for the holiday, that there would be more drunken drivers than usual because of the inevitable parties, that the weather forecasters had threatened heavy snows over the whole of the northeastern section of the country, Tony wondered whether the Perrys would make it safely. Then she recalled Hal's reliable, dependable driving and felt reassured. Nothing would happen to them. There were snow treads on the Lincoln, antifreeze in the gas tank, chains in the trunk.

From the church on Fourth Avenue she heard the carillon ring out with "Silent Night." Some restlessness made her get up and go downstairs. Something dark stood outside the door.

For a moment she was aware of fear and then she laughed at herself. She squared her shoulders, went to look more closely. At the sight of the broad shoulders, her heart lurched. She flung open the door.

"Rodney!"

He stood smiling at her a little diffidently, as though unsure of his welcome. "I couldn't leave without bringing you a small Christmas remembrance."

He came into the foyer and rested his present on a long table. Against the dusky glow of the darkened room glistened a Christmas tree. A silver tree. From the gleaming star at the top it rippled, dripped, cascaded, streamed silver. It bore silver fruit, it shed silver light, it showered silver cornucopias, it dangled silver bells.

In the very middle of the tree the branches had been cut away. In the hollow thus fashioned had been set a small painting of the Correggio Virgin adoring the Child.

Tony had seen the picture many times. She could remember clearly encountering the original in the Uffizi in Florence. But never before had she felt it. Now the half-sad, half-sweet rapture of passionate devotion, the dewy melting eyes, the delicate smiling mouth of the Virgin as she knelt before the Child lying on a fold of her intensely blue mantle; the appeal of the tiny arms outstretched to His mother, the tenderness expressed in the lovely hands extended above Him, tugged at the girl's heart. It seemed to her absorbed fancy that the figures shed their own radiance. The picture set in the heart of that silver tree reminded her that the coming of the Christ Child and not the exchange of gifts was the heart of Christmas festivities.

Tears blurred her vision, spilled down her cheeks. "Oh, Rodney." She turned toward him, her hands outstretched, and then, somehow, she found herself in his arms, felt his lips on hers.

When at last he released her he said rather breathlessly, "Tony, my beloved, I didn't mean to do it."

At the sight of his expression, half exultant, half distressed, a smile lurked in her clear gray eyes.

"You didn't mean it, then?"

He returned the smile reluctantly. "Of course I meant it. But I intended to wait." There was incredulity in his shaken voice. "Tony, you love me!"

"From the first minute," she told him, meeting his eyes bravely.

He caught her hands, held them so tightly that he hurt her. "I don't deserve you. No one could deserve you. But some day—when Jerome is all right—may I come back and tell you all the things I want so terribly to say now?"

She remembered in a sort of wonder that not long before she had intended to show him that a woman, too, had pride. Now it did not matter at all.

"There isn't anything really that you need to say, is there, Rodney? Only—don't wait too long."

He bent over her hands, held them to his lips. Raised his head listening.

"They are singing carols in the park. Will you come with me?"

She nodded. In a few moments she joined him, wearing a close red hat, a bit of holly tucked in the collar of her coat, suggesting an animated Christmas decoration. Snow fell softly, windows in apartments around the park held burning candles in rigid squares, in towering pyramids, in rare candelabra. Garlands of green adorned iron balconies. Snow sifted like silver dust on the shoulders of the passers-by, transformed commonplace iron fences into fantastic convolutions.

The Christmas tree in Gramercy Park was lighted and a group of choristers had gathered around it. Tony slipped her big key in the lock. They made their way through the deepening snow to the tree, while the voices chanted:

> *It came upon the midnight clear,*
> *That glorious song of old,*
> *From angels bending near the earth*
> *To touch their harps of gold.*

Tony's voice rang out clear and high; Rodney's deeper voice swelled triumphantly in the familiar carol; the snow fell whitely over tree and carolers, performed magic tricks with hedges and paths; made crystal stars on shoulders.

Tony raised her eyes, looking slowly around the square. Behind open curtains, for on Christmas Eve one must not shut out the night, men and women were arranging decorations, fixing strings of lights, hanging stockings on mantels, piling gay packages beneath the Christmas trees.

Rodney's hand reached for hers, held it firmly. Their eyes met in a long deep look, with delighted awareness that they had discovered each other, with unshaken confidence that their future together would be good.

"It's going to be a white Christmas," he told her in a whisper. "Tony, why don't you drive up to Kathy's tonight with me? Spend Christmas there with us. Everyone wants you."

"Even you?"

"Especially me, as you know very well."

"I'd love it," she said breathlessly, "but they aren't expecting me."

"What difference does that make? They want you. Surely you know that. You'd be as welcome as Santa Claus. In fact, without you—"

"I'd have to go back to the house to pack a bag, collect Mister Duffy, and call Kathy. I simply couldn't barge in at the last minute without notice."

"That's the girl! Then let's go."

As they started down Irving Place the voices from the park rose joyously:

> *Oh little town of Bethlehem,*
> *How still we see thee lie!*
> *Above thy deep and dreamless sleep*
> *The silent stars go by.*

They had nearly reached the darkened shop with its sign, The Good Companions Bookshop, when the sound of the Christmas carol was submerged in the high, terrifying snarl of a police siren. A prowl car drew up at the curb and Tony began to run.

"It's the shop!" she exclaimed.

But it wasn't the bookshop. The police car had stopped at the beauty parlor and a uniformed man was banging on the door.

"Open up, there!" he called.

"What's wrong?" Tony asked.

"Keep moving, lady. Just keep moving."

"But the lady owns the bookshop next door," Rodney explained.

"Oh. Burglar alarm went off," the policeman said. "Someone set if off just now."

Tony looked in alarm at Rodney. "Suppose he got into our shop first?" she demanded. "We don't have a burglar alarm and we didn't have a chance to deposit today's money. It's still there in the cash register."

"You shouldn't do things like that," the patrolman admonished her. "That's why banks have slots for night deposits."

Tony hesitated. "Rodney, it's silly but I'm nervous about going in. Will you get that money from the cash register while I go home, pack a bag, and telephone Kathy that I'm coming with you? You can meet me at the house."

She handed him the key to the shop and went quickly down the street. In the quiet that had followed the police siren she could hear the voices from the park once more and her heart sang with them: "Silent night, holy night." Nothing—nothing in the world—could dim this moment.

ii

As Rodney slipped the key into the lock of the bookshop he heard one of the patrolmen from the radio car say, "The guy's trapped. He won't try to get out this way; that's a cinch. And there's no way out in back except through the basement of one of the Fourth Avenue buildings and they are all locked at this hour."

Rodney closed the door of the shop behind him and stood listening. Some instinct made him pause in the dark with his hand on the light switch. Then he heard a snap that sounded loud in the silence of the night, loud in the darkness. Someone had forced a window at the back of Tony's shop. The burglar, warned by the police siren, had escaped from the beauty parlor and was trying to get out through the bookshop, probably by way of the basement and the areaway.

Rodney opened the door quietly, ran to the police car, and said in a low tone to the man behind the wheel, "He forced the lock of a window at the back of the bookshop."

The man nodded, spoke briefly into the two-way radio, and climbed out of the car, drawing his revolver. "We'll handle this," he said. "Keep out of the way."

But Rodney was already inside, groping his way through the shop, trying to remember from his only visit how it was arranged, a futile effort because all he had noticed on that occasion was Tony herself.

Someone was moving in the back of the shop, groping his way forward just as Rodney was groping his way to the back. Rodney knocked against a table, making a loud scraping sound, and the noises from the intruder stopped abruptly.

Then, throwing all caution aside, Rodney plunged forward. Someone was breathing so near him that he could have touched him. He leaped. There was a grunt. Then something struck his head and he fell into darkness.

When he opened his eyes a uniformed man was looking down in disgust. "I told you to leave it to us," he said.

"Did he get away?"

"Sure he got away. Went through the areaway while I was trying to find out whether he had killed you."

"I'm sorry," Rodney said.

Unexpectedly the prowl car man laughed. "From the look of that head of yours, you'll be a heap sorrier in the morning."

Rodney put his hand to his head, felt the warm stickiness, saw the blood. "Good lord!"

"Yeah. Next time, you mind your own business." The words were stern but the policeman's expression was friendly.

He asked routine questions which Rodney answered quickly. Tony would be worrying, wondering what had delayed him, whether the shop had been broken into.

"Did he get anything?"

"Broke open the safe in the beauty parlor. Don't know yet if anything is gone. We'll call the owner, get her down here. Can you handle yourself?"

"Sure. Sure," Rodney said readily. He stood up, an

operation that required more assistance than he had expected, and held on dizzily to a chair.

"How about that broken window?"

"There will be a man on duty here tonight," the policeman assured him.

Rodney started slowly down the street. For some reason he didn't seem to be able to focus. The street lights had a way of wavering, of making strange patterns. Perhaps it was because the snow was thicker. The sidewalk under his feet moved up and down like a scenic railway. It was all very confusing.

When he reached the house on Nineteenth Street, Tony had the door open before he could ring the bell. She looked at the blood on his forehead, at the blood dropping down his cheek.

"*What happened to you?*"

"I ran headlong into the burglar, got clobbered, and let him escape," he said in disgust.

With infinite care she supported his staggering weight into the house and pushed him gently into a chair. It would be impossible to get him up the stairs. Swiftly she ran up and ransacked the medicine closet, got antiseptics, bandages, adhesive, scissors. She was relieved when she came back to find him still on the chair, his hands gripping the arms, head back, the blood almost covering one cheek. For a heart-stopping moment she thought his eye had been damaged and then realized that the blood seeped from a cut on his forehead.

With deft, gentle hands she wiped away the blood, cleaned out the cut, bandaged and taped it. After a frightened look at the colorless face she went in search of brandy and forced a little between his lips. He swallowed with difficulty and then tried to focus on her.

"Can you help yourself at all?" she asked anxiously.

"Of course."

"If you'll lean on me I'll get you out to the car."

"What are you going to do?" His speech was thick.

"Drive you up to Kathy's," Tony said briefly.

Rodney was dimly aware of Mister Duffy nuzzling his face, of Tony pushing him firmly away, of her dropping her suitcase into the back of the car. He heard her voice coaxing him to move over in the seat, and after what seemed to be an enormous and perplexing struggle he got into the passenger seat while someone with a riveter set to work on his head.

The Chevorlet moved slowly away from the curb. Now and then, Rodney opened his eyes, startled by the snarl of an ambulance siren, the rumble of a snowplow, the stopping of the car for a red light.

He tried to see where they were going but something was wrong with his eyes or else the snow had grown very heavy. All he could make out was a swirling white blanket that drove at the windshield, shutting out the world.

His last thought was that some darned woodpecker had taken his head for a tree. Tap. Tap. Tap. Pound. Pound. Pound. Something warm trickled down his face. He moved a hand sluggishly, felt the substance that stuck to his fingers. Blood.

He didn't rouse at all when Hal, Jerome, and Sam lifted him from the car and carried him into Kathy's house.

Jerome had ignored the protests of the others. "I'm stronger than either of you," he insisted. "With Sam leading the way, I won't fall over anything or let him drop. For God's sake, let me help. He's my brother."

Rodney did not rouse when they placed him gently on Jerome's bed, when Kathy took off the bandage and replaced it.

"I shouldn't have brought him here," Tony said remorsefully.

"Best thing you could have done," Kathy assured her. "That cut's not deep and it is perfectly clean. He'll be all right, though he'll probably have a frightful headache in the morning from the lump on the back of his head."

"What's wrong?" Jerome asked, hearing the curious tone in Kathy's voice.

For a long moment Kathy stood looking at Jerome's forehead. "Yes, I thought so."

"*What is it?*"

"It's just about the strangest coincidence I ever heard of," Kathy said. "The mark on Rodney's head is exactly like the scar on yours."

With Rodney quietly settled for the night and in a deep sleep, the others gathered around the fire in the big living room. Tony had arrived so late that the Christmas tree had already been decorated and the smell of the spruce boughs was sweet and pungent in the warm room. The gay red stockings with their sprigs of holly and little bells were fastened to the mantelpiece. There was no light in the room except that of the blazing fire and the small colored bulbs that had been strung on the tree. At the top, almost touching the high ceiling, gleamed a large star, in which a light had been set. Around the foot of the tree Christmas packages were piled and stacked and heaped.

At first, Mister Duffy had displayed too much interest in the packages, sending some of them tumbling down, but after some difference of opinion he consented to be drawn away and now he was lying at Tony's feet.

Kathy looked around her and gave a little sigh of satisfaction. "This is just the way it ought to look on Christmas Eve." She got up to turn on an outside light. "The snow is so heavy that the balsams must have a foot of snow on every branch. It's too beautiful to bear!"

Then she bit her lip. She had forgotten temporarily Jerome's blindness and that his beauty was denied him. She came back soberly to her chair by the fire.

"Ouch!" she said as she stumbled over a sled for Dennis which had been placed at a little distance from the other packages so that he would not break anything in his first excited leap for it. She sat rubbing her ankle.

Side by side on the couch sat Hal and Rosamund, his arm around her shoulders. The rest were quiet, deep in their thoughts, contented at being together, congenial even in their silence, weary from the strain and the exertion of the past week.

It was Jerome who spoke first, "Kathy," he said, "tell me about that cut on Rodney's head."

"Well, it's like yours; the same size, not bigger than a dime, and with the same four little indentations in it. Exactly the same!"

"It's a fantastic coincidence," Hal said slowly. "I can't for the life of me see why the guy who struck Jerome in his office five years ago should turn up at Mrs. Hazelton's beauty parlor. Granted there was a robbery each time but—darned if I understand it." He turned to Jerome. "What is it about you Meredith men anyhow? There's a common denominator somewhere. Bound to be. Your office gets burglarized, and you get hit. The bookshop gets robbed—or I suppose it was—and Rodney gets hit. Someone tries to break into this house when you are here. What's the connection?"

"There can't possibly be any connection," Jerome said. "That doesn't make sense. In my case, it was Cranshaw's bonds. But why the same man—no, it's not possible."

"Wait," Rosamund said excitedly, "I've been meaning to tell you ever since I got here." She looked around, her green eyes sparkling and demanding their attention. "Sensation, ladies and gentlemen! I've found out who bought the scarf the prowler left here."

"Good girl!" Hal exclaimed, his arm tightening around her. "Keep on like this and I'll begin to think I'm getting a bargain in you after all, though there have been times when I wondered about that."

"How can you be sure it was the same scarf?" her mother asked.

"Fish or cut bait, woman!" Jerome said, pretending

to snarl. "How long are you going to keep us in suspense?"

Rosamund caught her breath as though she had just become aware of an unexpected obstacle. Then she said firmly, "I took the scarf to the shop where Kathy saw them on display. No one else in New York handles them, which simplified the problem. The clerk had sold four, three of them to people who had regular charge accounts; the fourth one was on record because the buyer ordered it sent to her hotel. So they had her name and address—by the way, she was staying at the Pierre, no less, so she's really living high. I called there and found that she had checked out, leaving no address."

Hal's hands encircled her slender throat. "Talk, woman, before I strangle you."

Rosamund took a long breath. "The woman who bought the scarf worn by your prowler was named Eve Cranshaw."

She should have been satisfied with the sensation she caused. The greatest of actors in his greatest scene could not have done more. There was a confused babble of voices. Kathy, after an anxious look at Jerome, whose face was colorless but without expression, sat with her small hands clenched on her lap.

How long was that really evil woman going to cast her spell over him, to hurt him? How lovely she must have been to look at. And no one, Kathy admitted dolefully to herself, has ever thought I was beautiful. When Jerome could see again—and somehow, some day, he *must* be able to see again—he would look at Kathy and realize she wasn't beautiful. Just a good, useful sort of face, she told herself savagely.

Finally Tony asked aloud the question they were all thinking, her quiet voice managing without difficulty to still the confusion.

"But what does it all mean?"

One thing, Hal pointed out, was that there was now a definite connection between the theft of the bonds and the prowler who had tried to enter the Cathcart house.

"In other words," Jerome said flatly, "it was Simon Cranshaw who stole his own bonds and blinded me."

"But why?" Rosamund demanded.

"A lot of possible reasons," Hal told her. "He may hav been afraid, for some reason, to be known to have them in his own possession, afraid someone would steal them from him; or possibly, they may have incriminated him. By turning them over to Jerome, whom he could trust, he knew they would be safe. Then, by staging the burglary, he could get them back and still not be known to possess them."

"It might have been that way," Jerome admitted. "What I can't see is why he would come up here. Oh, it would have been easy enough to keep tabs on me, to find out where I was living, all that. But there's nothing—I don't have a scrap of evidence, I don't know a thing that could be of any conceivable value to him or a threat to him. I just can't see it."

Hal said bluntly. "There's one thing you could do that would be a real threat to him. Regain your eyesight. Then you would be in a position to identify h'm. And Eve."

"But if she's using her own name, the question of identity doesn't arise," Jerome protested.

"What about Cranshaw? By this time, he may have built a new personality. That is, if he's what I think he is, a crook on a really big scale."

"I—see."

Sam, who had been lounging against the wall, clenched his fists. "Just let them try to get at Jerome. Just let them try."

"Hold on," Jerome said quickly, "there's still something wrong with this picture. Cranshaw is an exceptionally small man, not over five feet five. How could he have dragged me out of my office?"

"All of which brings us," Hal said, "to Kathy's queer discovery that the wound on Rodney's head looks just like the scar on Jerome's. To me that means another man in the picture, someone working with Cranshaw. You're sure about the similarity, are you, Kathy?"

She nodded emphatically. "I'm positive. I've noticed that scar so often, with those four tiny white indentations, wondering what could have caused it." She added hastily, almost stumbling over the words, "Not that it is disfiguring. Not in the least."

"O God," Jerome exclaimed in despair, "do you suppose Rodney's eyesight is impaired?"

Tony spoke quickly. "The blow was struck higher up and he can see. Of course he had trouble focusing, but that's because he hit his head when he fell and he is slightly concussed. You'll find out tomorrow."

"But why was the man who blinded Jerome in The Good Companions Bookshop? Unless," Hal added grimly, "he followed Rodney and is trying to wipe out the Merediths."

Kathy turned to Tony. "Just what did happen?"

"The man broke into the beauty parlor next door and set off the burglar alarm on the safe. By the way, Rosamund, we must have one installed. The radio car came just as Rodney and I were passing the shop, and Rodney went in to get today's money out of the cash register. You remember we hadn't deposited it. Evidently the burglar was startled by the police siren, tried to escape through our shop, ran into Rodney, and knocked him out.

They were silent for a while, pondering. Hal shook his head. "It couldn't have been that way. If we're dealing with the same man, he's after big stuff. Those bonds, for instance. What could he get from a small beauty parlor? At most, fifty to a hundred dollars for the day's take."

"But there *was* something," Tony exclaimed eagerly. "Something big." She told them about the new formula for a face cream that, Mrs. Hazelton and her chemist husband believed, might well make them a fortune, put them in a class with Elizabeth Arden and Dorothy Gray and other top names in the field of cosmetics. A cold cream that covered signs of aging and made a woman look much younger.

She caught her breath as she remembered. "And," she went on excitedly, "Mrs. Hazelton told me that people had tried to break into the shop several times, and they were worried for fear the formula might be stolen."

"Several times," Rosamund said. "Look here, Tony, doesn't it strike you darned queer, if Mrs. Hazelton was afraid of burglars, that she was so determined to make you get rid of Mister Duffy? No burglar would ever try to get past him. Never in the world. With that tremendously loud bark and his size he seems like a man-killer."

Mister Duffy, hearing his name, raised his head and wagged his tail lazily.

"But it wasn't Mrs. Hazelton who wanted to get rid of him. It was Cecily Ann, that Southern girl who works for her. She told me herself that Mister Duffy had jumped on her, nearly scaring her to death—" Tony's voice faded out.

Jerome, leaning forward, his hands tight on the arms of his chair, said urgently, "What is it?"

"Cecily Ann," Tony said slowly. "The night I went Christmas shopping I stopped at the skating rink in Rockefeller Center. You know how you can see down into the restaurants? Well, at a window table I saw Cecily Ann with Frank Hazelton. She was wearing a mink coat and a mink hat. She was flirting with him but he was angry. Simply furious, to judge by the way he acted."

"Do you think," Rosamund asked, her voice rising in excitement, "she was trying to persuade him to give her the formula?"

"I don't know. But from his expression I don't think he was willing to do what she wanted."

"I should hope not!" Rosamund snapped. "Cecily Ann and her phony looks, her phony accent. That drawl of hers is so slow it takes her an hour to get out a sentence. And Mrs. Hazelton is a nice, hard-working, honest woman! No man would exchange her for that girl unless he's a plain darned fool."

"Accent?" Jerome asked.

"Southern, but strictly from South Brooklyn, if you ask me," Rosamund replied.

Kathy looked up as the tall clock against the wall stirred wheezily like a weary old man and then bonged twelve times.

"Merry Christmas, everyone!" she exclaimed.

"Merry Christmas!" they replied in chorus.

"I hate to say it but you ought to be warned. Dennis will probably be up and clamoring to come down before it's light in the morning to see what Santa Claus left him. I'll just take a look at Rodney to make sure he's all right before we go to bed."

"Christmas," Hal snarled. "Bah! Humbug."

For a moment Tony stood beside Kathy as she tiptoed across Rodney's dim room, with one light carefully shaded. Once he stirred restlessly and groaned.

When they had gone out, Tony said in a whisper, "Are you sure he's all right?"

"Of course he's all right."

"But he's in pain."

"If I know Sam he'll sit up with him all night. And there's Mister Duffy, of course."

"I know," Tony agreed. "I know. Just the same, I'm frightened."

"Why?" Kathy asked in surprise.

"Because I don't understand any of this. I don't understand those two wounds being exactly alike."

"They're alike because they must have been made with the same weapon," Kathy told her.

"But—"

"And nothing more is going to happen to the Meredith men," Kathy assured her. "Sam and I are going to guard Jerome with our lives, and Hal and Rosamund are working with Rodney to clear his brother. They've been at it for a month."

"Oh, so that's it!" After a pause Tony asked, "But why didn't they tell me?"

Kathy grinned mischievously. "I suspect they thought you'd rather have Rodney tell you himself; that is, when he has something interesting to say."

Sam came down the hall, his face scarlet with cold, his hair and Mister Duffy's coat thick with snow from their excusion out of doors.

"He all right?" he asked, nodding his head toward Rodney's room.

"Sound asleep," Kathy told him. "Good heavens, you look as though you'd been rolling in the snow."

"You may not have noticed it but we're having a real old-fashioned blizzard. Snow must be eighteen inches deep now and it's piling up fast. Like a curtain in front of your eyes. And the wind!" He shivered.

"It's just as well you got here when you did," Kathy told Tony.

"Yeah," Sam agreed. "This is no night for man or beast to be out. At this rate, by morning we'll look like a couple of verses from Whittier's 'Snow-Bound.' All you've got to worry about now is how you're going to be able to leave here."

In the room she was sharing with Rosamund, Tony lay awake for a long time, listening to her friend's quiet breathing, hearing the wind that rose now and then to a scream, now and then sank so that the only sound was that of tiny pellets of ice beating against the window.

How bitterly cold it must be outdoors! She wriggled down farther into her warm bed, pulled a soft comforter higher around her shoulders. Only in the country, she thought, was one aware of weather as more than discomfort; here one knew the rain would make the crops grow, the sun would hold life-giving warmth; the great storms could mean death and disaster to the unprotected, the unsheltered. How brave our ancestors were, she thought with a glow of pride, to choose deliberately that unsheltered life and create out of their heroism and their determination and their hard labor a way of existence new to the world and a beacon light for the future.

It seemed to her that she had slept only a few minutes when she heard Dennis calling urgently, "Mother, isn't it time to get up? Did Santa Claus come last night?"

She blinked at her small travel clock. Seven o'clock. It couldn't be. There wasn't a scrap of light outside.

There was a scamper of feet and Kathy was saying, "Quiet, now. You don't want to wake the others. We'll slip down to the kitchen so you can have your breakfast and be all ready when they come down."

"Oh, Mother, just one single peek?"

"Well," Kathy pretended to consider the matter, "one peek, then."

The living-room door opened, there was a startled gasp and then a squeal. "He brought me a sled! He brought me a sled!"

"Shhh," his mother warned him.

In the bed beside Tony's, Rosamund opened her eyes and laughed. "This," she declared, "is where we arise and shine or Dennis will burst with frustration. Merry Christmas, Tony!"

Warmly dressed in sweaters and wool skirts, Rosamund in green, Tony in red, the two girls ran down the stairs a few minutes later.

Dennis was gobbling up a bowl of cereal so quickly he was nearly choked on it, eager, for once, to end the pleasures of breakfast and get into the living room, which, over night, had been touched with magic.

"Merry Christmas!" they called. "Merry Christmas."

"Santa Claus came," Dennis told them, wide-eyed with wonder. "I listened and listened but I didn't hear him, but he came."

In a few minutes Sam came in. He had already lighted the tree and built a fire in the grate in the living room. He was followed by a sleepy Hal who groped blindly for a cup of coffee and by Jerome, who this morning seemed extremely alert.

"How's Rodney?" he asked at once.

Sam grinned. "He's got a terrific headache but I got up early and made him some coffee and gave him a couple of aspirin. He couldn't remember coming up here at all. Said the last thing that was clear to him was being in the bookshop. I told him Miss Carew drove him up. He's getting dressed but it's a slow process. Every time he moves his head he thinks it's going to fall off."

"His eyes?" Jerome asked tensely.

"Fine," Sam assured him. "Just fine."

Rodney, however, looked anything but fine when he appeared. The blow on his forehead had given him an impressively black eye but the cut itself was clean, closing, and seemed to be healing normally.

"You came after I went to sleep," Dennis said accusingly, looking from Tony to Rodney.

"We certainly did," Rodney said. "At least I suppose so. I might as well have dreamed that trip for all I remember of it."

He looked out of the window, or tried to. Snow covered nearly two-thirds of it. "Good lord, what's been going on?"

"An old-fashioned blizzard," Sam told him. "I came down around four to make myself some coffee. Got one of those all-night stations on the radio. Looks like traffic will be snarled for a couple of days. People already cut off. There's a good two and a half feet of snow right now. And the temperature is four above zero."

"Look," Dennis said, hopping on one foot, tugging at his mother's arm, "it's Christmas! Let's go!"

She laughed down at him. "What are we waiting for?"

She flung open the living-room door and Dennis hurled himself across the room, dragged the sled away from the tree, squatted down beside it, his eyes wide and shining.

"A sled," he said over and over. "A sled. We'll get a harness for Mister Duffy and he can take me for a ride."

"At this point you'd need a couple of huskies to get you through the drifts," Hal told him.

For a while the adults watched as Dennis examined his presents, one by one.

"If life could only be like that always," Mrs. Perry said softly. "All wonder and magic. All like a dream come true."

Within a half hour the living room resembled any American living room on Christmas morning, the floor strewn with tissue paper and bright ribbons, voices raised in exclamations of delight: "How lovely! . . . Oh, I've wanted one of these forever! . . . The package is just too beautiful to open. . . . Look, did you see what Rosamund gave me? . . . Hey, get a load of my loot, will you?"

Mister Duffy, beside himself with the excitement and raised voices and general confusion, knee-deep in Christmas wrappings, was dragged firmly away from the lighted tree, and finally submitted, with a bored and abused attitude, to having a new collar fastened around his neck, on which was inscribed: MISTER DUFFY.

"But look here," Jerome expostulated suddenly, speaking for almost the first time, "are you sure, Hal, that it's all right with your office?"

"Sure, sure," Hal said with a quick look at Tony. "These things change and are improved all the time; they replaced this one a week ago. Nobody wanted it, so—"

Rodney took a quick look at the shining new case that held the tape recorder, another look at Hal. The latter shook his head warningly and winked.

"I'll show Sam how the thing operates," Hal said easily, "and then you'll be on your own."

"Well, I hardly know what to say." Jerome was shaken, a little embarrassed. He had removed the dark glasses absently, and his eyes, as deep a blue as Rodney's, seemed to see them all. "This is really terrific."

"It's no free gift," Hal warned him. "We all expect you to put another best-selling juvenile on that machine in short order."

"I'll do my darndest," Jerome promised.

By midmorning comparative quiet had fallen over the house. Dennis and Sam were absorbed in repairing a mechanical toy that had already lost a part. The rest were sitting around in lazy contentment, now and then exclaiming over their presents, now and then listening to radio reports on the blizzard.

"There's one thing sure," Kathy announced, returning from the window, "there's no possibility of you getting away tonight. This side road is one of the very last to be plowed because there are so few houses on it; actually, there are only two others. It's fine for me," she added hastily. "There's plenty of room and plenty of food and plenty of fuel for the oil burner, thank heaven! Whatever may be going on around us, we can be sure we'll be snug and warm and safe."

Rosamund reached out to touch wood. "You should be careful about saying things like that; the brownies might hear you and jinx you for it."

Rodney had come back to curl up at Tony's feet in front of the fire. Nothing had been said between them and yet everything was changed. This place near her belonged to him and he claimed it naturally. It's curious, she thought; I had expected that great happiness would be shot through with excitement, not that it could be so deep and quiet. She tipped back his head to look at the scar, from which he had removed the bandage.

"It's the same as Jerome's," she said. "Just the same. Those four tiny points. What could they have been? What did it feel like when you were hit?"

"Curtains," he said with a grin.

They speculated about the weapon that could have caused such a scar, but nothing seemed to fit the case. It was Mrs. Perry who, after examining the scar on Jerome's head and the cut on Rodney's, said, "You know, it could have been made by a ring with large prongs to hold a big stone."

"A ring like that would be awfully conspicuous for a man to wear," Hal objected.

"And it would still have to be worn by a strong man. There was a lot of power behind the blow," Rodney said.

"It might not be a ring he wore all the time; just when he was—well, on a job of that sort. With the stone removed, heavy prongs could be an unpleasant weapon."

Rosamund leaned back in her chair, taking a long breath. "I'm so happy at this exact moment," she declared, "that I can hardly bear it. Let's forget all the mystery for today. Everything is working out. Everything. Hal and I will be married in two months—"

"Seven weeks less two days," he corrected her. He

had been looking through his wallet. "Oh, here they are. For a moment I thought I'd lost them."

"Lost what?" Rosamund asked.

"I've made reservations for a certain young couple on a ship for Nassau in seven weeks less two days."

Rosamund sighed rapturously. "I'm almost afraid I'll wake up and find it's all a dream. The Good Companions Bookshop is becoming a real success. We've already had customers there from all over the city, not just the neighborhood. And Mother's one-man show in February will help her terrifically in establishing a reputation. I just know it will."

Kathy sat up abruptly. "What one-man show? Who's been holding out on me?"

"Heavens, didn't you know?" Rosamund squealed. "I guess we've just been so frantic at the shop we forgot to tell you." She explained about the one-man show that was to be held at the Revlin Gallery in February. "And we owe it all to Carter Holbrook."

"Carter?" Kathy said in surprise. "You mean Mrs. Haven's handsome nephew?"

"That's the one. He's fallen for Tony and he dropped in at the shop, saw Mother's Christmas cards, and then insisted on looking at the rest of her stuff. He really went overboard about it. He arranged everything, and Mr. Revlin came down to look at it, because Carter asked him to, and now everything is all set."

Only one person failed to join in the general chorus of congratulation and jubilee. Rodney, after a quick look at Tony, remained gloomily silent. Seeing his expression, Rosamund grinned to herself. It wouldn't do that young man any harm to think he had some stiff competition.

Kathy excused herself to go to the kitchen to serve the Christmas dinner. Mrs. Perry joined her to set the table, using a lace cloth that had been one of Kathy's wedding presents. She put sprigs of holly at each place. They had been working in companionable silence for a few minutes when they heard a sound of hammering.

"What's going on?" Kathy asked, and went to see.

Sam was just getting off a ladder, a sheepish look on his face.

"What?" she demanded suspiciously, "have you been up to?"

He grinned at her. "Very important thing. Almost forgot it."

"What's that?"

He looked up at the arch over the doorway, where he had hung a sprig of mistletoe.

In the living room Rosamund and Hal sat on the couch and Tony faced them, curled up on the floor. In a moment Rodney dropped down beside her. The two couples talked idly, the conversation drifting lightly from subject to subject, revealing how many interests they shared, how many opinions they had in common, where they disagreed.

Only Jerome sat a little apart. At length, with a murmured excuse, he drifted off to his own room, where Sam had set up the tape recorder. He told himself that he was eager to try it out. He didn't, he assured himself, feel left out of things. Not in the least. The last thing he ever wanted was to fall in love with another woman. The very last thing. No, thank you.

Dennis, overtired and overexcited, was experiencing the inevitable letdown. Jerome was shut up in his room, so there were to be no stories. Sam was helping in the kitchen, so there was no one to play with.

"I want to go out on my sled," he declared, loudly and defiantly. "Me and Mister Duffy want to go out with my sled."

"Not today," Rosamund told him. "The snow is as high as you are. Not today."

"But it's a Christmas sled and I want to go out on Christmas."

"Not today. That's final," Rosamund said firmly.

"I will too," Dennis said, but he whispered it to himself.

It seemed that no matter how far the conversation ranged, it always came back to the unsolved puzzle, to the fact that the two Meredith men had the same kind of scars, to the fact that Eve Cranshaw had bought the scarf worn by Kathy's prowler.

"I've been wondering," Rodney said at last, "whether we aren't on the wrong line altogether. The similarity in the scars may be coincidental, it may mean nothing at all. We know now, or at least we have a shrewd guess, that the safe-breaking at the Hazelton beauty parlor was for the purpose of getting hold of that formula. Could it possibly have been Hazelton himself who took it?"

"But he wouldn't have had to set off the burglar alarm," Hal reminded him.

"Unless he wanted an out, a proof that someone else had done the job."

"I can't see that," Rosamund admitted.

"You mean because of Cecily Ann?" Tony asked. "Well—" She considered. "Of course, no beauty parlor operator could conceivably have afforded the mink she was wearing. Neither could Frank Hazelton. And, after all, he didn't need to steal the formula. He was the one who worked it out in the first place. He could duplicate it at any time."

"Oh, I hadn't thought of that." Rodney sat back disgruntled.

Sam appeared in the doorway with Jerome, whom he had brought from his room. "Ladies and gentlemen, dinner is served!" He raised his eyes expressively so that they rested on the mistletoe.

Hal laughed, swept Rosamund up into his arms and kissed her, turned to Mrs. Perry, to Kathy, to Tony.

"My turn," Rodney said. He kissed Mrs. Perry and her two daughters lightly and turned to Tony, a question in his eyes. At her smile, he held her for a moment tightly and kissed her lips.

"Wow!" Sam exclaimed when he released her, and the others laughed.

"What's going on?" Jerome asked.

Rodney led him under the mistletoe. "Over your head," he explained, "there hangs a little twig on which there are some small white berries."

"Oh," Jerome said blankly.

There was a half-awkward pause and then Kathy reached him, stood on tiptoe, kissed his cheek. "Merry Christmas, Jerome." She slipped away almost before he realized what had happened.

"Hey," he protested, stretching out his hand.

She laughed, tucked her hand under his arm, and led him toward the table, pausing to say firmly, "No, Dennis, you know perfectly well that Mister Duffy cannot come into the dining room."

The Christmas dinner was a great success. There was laughter and joking and banter. Only Hal grumbled.

"Serving you cannibals," he muttered, "is the hardest work I ever did. I ought to picket this joint as unfair. I haven't had a chance to get a single mouthful. By the time I've finished one round the first person is ready for a refill."

"That," Rosamund told him severely, "is your third helping. I've been watching you. When we are married, you are going on a strict diet."

Hal let out a cry of bitter protest.

It was Sam who insisted on taking over the ungrateful job of clearing up and washing the dishes. "Have to earn my keep some way," he said, "as Jerome doesn't really need me any longer."

There was a knock at the door. "Who could possibly be coming on a day like this?" Kathy exclaimed. "Why the road hasn't even been plowed yet!"

She opened the door to a man who looked more like a walking snowman than a human being.

"C-c-can I use your telephone?"

"Of course. Come in."

"I'll have to get some of this snow off first, or I'll have it all over your house."

"Snow won't hurt anything," Kathy assured him. "And it's freezing out here."

"Freezing!" The man shivered. "It's dropped to zero and that wind is like a knife. I could hardly see my way through the snow. Haven't known a blizzard like this since I was a boy."

Kathy indicated the telephone in the hallway. "I'm going to get you some hot coffee," she said.

"Bless you," he said fervently. "My name is Chalmers. Dr. Chalmers. I was on my way back from an emergency call when my car stalled in a drift. I've been trying to get it out for the past hour, and then I gave up and just began walking in search of help."

While Dr. Chalmers dialed garages, Kathy brought coffee and insisted on his coming into the living room after he had removed his wraps. When he had emerged from a wool cap, muffler, and topcoat he appeared to be a man somewhat over middle age, corpulent, with a kindly face that looked perpetually tired. He dropped into a chair and sighed with pleasure after the first sip of coffee.

"This is a lifesaver," he said.

Kathy introduced herself and her guests. "Any luck?"

He shrugged. "Only one garage open and they say their wrecker is out and, anyhow, there are four emergency calls ahead of mine. May be hours before they can get here."

Mrs. Perry leaned forward. "You were working for an hour on that car before you started fighting your way through that blizzard? Then you haven't even had anything to eat!"

Chalmers smiled at her. "A doctor's lot," he said cheerfully. "We miss a lot of meals, one way and another."

With an exclamation of distress Kathy hastened out into the kitchen.

"Look here," Rodney suggested, "there are plenty of able-bodied men in this place. Why can't we help you dig yourself out?"

"Not now," Kathy said firmly. She had appeared in the living room, where she set up a small table before the doctor on which Sam placed a laden tray. "This man is going to eat a good hot meal before he takes one more step out of doors."

The doctor shook his head in disbelief. "Of all the places in the world, I landed in this one! And they say there's no such thing as luck."

While he began to eat, Rodney, Sam, and Hal got into high boots and heavy windbreakers and pulled wool caps down over their heads.

"There's only one shovel," Sam said. "I'll bring that from the garage. We'll just have to do our best with what we can find among the gardening tools."

The three men opened the door, felt snow sting against their cheeks and eyes as though it were hot metal, and closed the door behind them. Rosamund watched them through the window as they floundered down the steps and began to push their way by main force against the wind. In a few minutes they were blotted out by the swirling snow. She darted back to her chair with her usual quicksilver grace.

"It's a wonder to me," she said idly, "that Mister Duffy didn't raise a fuss about going with them."

"I know," Kathy said. "He always barks in that frightening way when a stranger comes. That's odd. He didn't bark when you came, Doctor."

"Where is Mister Duffy?" Mrs. Perry asked. "I haven't seen him around since we finished dinner."

"Neither have I," Kathy said. "Where is Mister Duffy? And where is Dennis? *Where is Dennis?*"

xvi

Dennis was nowhere in the house; a few minutes of frantic search revealed that. Neither was Mister Duffy. Neither was the sled. After a brief chaotic search, with shouts of "Dennis! Come back!" Rosamund, Kathy, and Tony put on heavy wraps, boots, and thick mittens.

"Surely the boy will be all right," Dr. Chalmers said.

"He's only four," Kathy told him, white-faced. "He's only four."

"My God!"

At the insistence of the girls Mrs. Perry promised to stay in the house with Jerome while the others began their search.

"There's no need for you to go out," they told Dr. Chalmers as he reached wearily for his coat. "You've had all the cold you can stand for one day."

"And anyhow," Kathy said through dry lips, "we may need you here when—if—" She broke off to cry in protest, "No, Jerome! You simply can't go. It would be suicide. When the men come back—"

For the first time Dr. Chalmers realized that the tall man with the clear blue eyes was blind. He looked at him, thinking he had never seen such torture on a man's face.

The front door closed and they heard the girls calling, "Dennis! Dennis! Mister Duffy! Mister Duffy!"

"Only four years old," Mrs. Perry choked. "The snow is higher than he is."

"Surely," Jerome said, "Mister Duffy will look out

152

for him." He turned toward the doctor. "A great Dane, a powerful animal, and devoted to the boy."

"That's the best hope, I expect," the doctor said quietly. He remembered his own battle through the blinding snow; the drifts, some of them up to his thighs, into which he had stumbled, out of which he had fought his way by main strength. He was aware that it was sheer, unbelievable luck that he had found this warm and welcoming house and shelter when he might as easily have gone around in circles for hours until sleep had overtaken him and he had frozen to death.

He looked at Mrs. Perry, who was pacing from window to window, trying in vain to see through the thick blanket of snow; at the blind man who was suffering agonies from the fact that he was unable to join in the search. *When the men come back.* How that had hurt! Later, perhaps, they would need all their self-discipline, all their control. Something had to be done now to distract their attention.

"I think," he suggested to Mrs. Perry, "that it would be a good thing to make sure there is plenty of hot water for baths, some coffee or hot soup, and a supply of sandwiches."

She got up, grateful to have something to do, to have any task set to occupy her mind.

When she had gone out of the room Jerome's fist crashed down on a table. "God! To be helpless here while everyone else is searching. To be useless!"

"What happened to your eyes?" the doctor asked casually. "They appear perfectly normal." In his easy, relaxed voice he continued to ask probing questions, forcing Jerome's attention, dragging out reluctant answers. "Well," he said at last, "that's interesting. I've seen cases before. Apparently there is no organic trouble at all; no disease. Simply a traumatic shock."

"Simply!" Jerome laughed shortly.

"Simply." The doctor's voice was tranquil. "In other words, you are blind because, primarily, you want to be."

In his outrage and fury Jerome leaped to his feet.
"I want to be!" he shouted. "Do you know what hell
this is? Don't you know I'd give anything on earth to
be out there right now looking for Dennis?"

"You didn't understand me," the doctor said, unmoved by his excitement and his anger. "This is not
a condition that you have brought about deliberately. The answer lies much deeper than that, somewhere in your subconscious. In other words, you had
a profound emotional shock, something happened so
painful that you couldn't look at it. And nature took
over, helped you not to 'see' the thing that you
hadn't the courage to face."

"That's a pretty contemptible sort of man you are
making me out to be," Jerome said.

"Not at all. Just human. We all run away from
something, whether we are aware of it or not; in you
it took a more drastic form. When you can face the
thing you found unbearable, when you're willing to
see it clearly, it is my firm belief that your sight will
return."

"My God! Do you really mean that?"

"Don't misunderstand me. I'm not making a promise, simply holding out a hope. I'm telling you that
the cure lies somewhere inside your own mind and
heart. Things have a way of changing their values
for us. When—or if—the thing that so shocked you
loses its power to hurt, you'll be on the way to cure."

So far the doctor had been successful in holding
Jerome's attention, but now the blind man got restlessly to his feet, began to pace the floor.

"I wonder if they thought of looking in the barn,"
he said. "Dennis might have tried to use the sled on
that slope down to the summerhouse. He loves playing in the brook. Of course, it's frozen over now but
he may have broken through the ice. I wonder if
they know of those places."

The front door opened with a bang and there
were cheerful voices. Jerome swung around, his
blind eyes on the doorway.

"Well, Doctor," Rodney called cheerfully, "we
found your car and we dug it out. Had some trouble

getting it started but it's waiting at the door. And if it hadn't been for the lights in the windows we'd never have found the house. I doubt it you'll be able to get out until the plow comes through." He broke off. "What's wrong?"

Mrs. Perry came running from the kitchen, her eyes red from crying, "It's Dennis! He's lost. Out in the storm somewhere. The rest are all looking for him."

"Let's go," Sam said briefly.

"Wait, you can't go like that. I have coffee and sandwiches ready. You'd better have something before you go out again."

The men drank the coffee, standing about restlessly, eager to begin the search, each of them thinking of a four-year-old lost in the storm, of the snow piling up, of the complete lack of visibility.

"Keep all the lights on," Hal said as they prepared to set out again. "Especially the outside lights. And we will need flashlights. Lanterns would be a lot better, of course."

While Sam unearthed an old-fashioned kerosene lantern and a couple of flashlights, Jerome told them of all the places he had thought of where a small boy might go. The men who had just come in from the darkness, the driving snow, and the bitter zero temperature exchanged glances but did not speak. What possible chance was there that Dennis could survive this storm?

ii

The hours passed in a kind of nightmare. Tony plowed through snow, clawed frantically at snowdrifts, called, "Dennis! Dennis! Mister Duffy! Mister Duffy!" until she was out of breath.

Now and then she returned to the house to get warm, each time with a renewed hope that Dennis had been brought back, each time to look from Mrs. Perry's face to the doctor's to Jerome's, each time to have Jerome suggest another place where Dennis might be. Now and then she encountered the other searchers or saw their lights or heard their voices, calling, calling.

It was Kathy's voice that tore her heart. Kathy was moving more slowly than any of them, overlooking no snowdrift, her hoarse voice calling tirelessly, "Dennis! Come to Mother, darling. Come to Mother."

Tony, forcing her way through heavy snow, almost unaware of the bitter cold, found herself remembering the picture Rodney had given her, the Madonna and Child, the eternal mother in whose face were the rapture of love and the foreknowledge of loss.

"Dennis!" Kathy called, summoning a small boy who did not hear, who did not answer.

Tony rubbed hr face briskly because it was beginning to grow numb. She ought to go back once more to the house. She could see lights, a lot of them. Her heart leaped. They had found Dennis!

She stumbled against someone and a strange voice said, "Hey there, lady. Be careful. Don't slip." A flashlight turned on her, then turned on the face of a trooper.

"You'd better get back inside," he said. "You're going to be frostbitten. There are three of us on the job, and the neighbors for miles around are turning out. The Boy Scouts are searching. A bunch of college boys on their way to a skiing resort have joined the party. There must be thirty people on the job, You go back, lady."

Tony protested. She couldn't leave Dennis in the night and the darkness and the killing cold.

"Go back, lady," the trooper said again gently. "There's nothing you can do. Not on a night like this. When we find him—you'd better be there. Someone ought to be there with his mother."

"There's Dr. Chalmers," Tony said.

"Well," the trooper considered, "perhaps he could help put her to sleep. What she's going to need more than anything else is an understanding friend."

He didn't need to explain. Tony turned and forced

her way back toward the lighted house, tears freezing on her cheeks.

If it weren't for this horror, she realized, this would be a miraculous sight. Lights crossing and recrossing, like some elaborate duel, through the snow. Voices shouting. Such a lot of voices.

A light touched her. "Oh, it's you," Kathy said, her voice colorless and flat and dull.

Tony's arm went around her. "We're going back," she said firmly.

"No, no! I can't leave him out there. Dennis!" her voice roused in a despairing cry.

"Come, dear, we're going back." Tony slipped an arm through Kathy's and led her, stumbling, up the steps and into the house.

At first the bright lights made her blink. Then she saw the young men herded into the kitchen, drinking the coffee Mrs. Perry was busy pouring for them, eating sandwiches. From their talk she realized that these were some of the college boys who had set off on a skiing trip. In the beginning, the search had been an adventure and the sight of Tony made it a rewarding one. But their high spirits fell and they were silenced when they saw Kathy's gray, stricken face.

"No word?" Kathy asked uselessly.

Seeing the tragedy in her face they were silenced; then they wrapped up and went out again into the night. Dr. Chalmers started toward Kathy but somehow Jerome found her first. He took her in his arms, rocking her gently.

"Kathy, Kathy," he whispered, his cheek against her hair. For a moment she tensed and then she collapsed against him, all the tears she had withheld pouring out with great sobs that shook her slight body.

"Best thing for her," the doctor said.

Tony helped Mrs. Perry in the kitchen and finally drove her out to rest. She made sandwiches, served coffee, washed dishes, moving like an automaton. Faces came and went. Each time anyone entered the kitchen Tony looked up with a flare of hope, turned silently back to pour coffee, cut sandwiches, her heart growing cold within her.

The night wore on. The Boy Scouts had been sent home. Some of the neighbors had given up. Rosamund came in and dropped exhausted on the kitchen floor, her face pinched with cold.

"Hal made me come back—he was afraid I'd get pneumonia. But I can't stand it in the living room, looking at Kathy; she's—dying right in front of my eyes."

"He can't have gone far, he's so tiny," Tony said. "He can't. Where's Mister Duffy?"

iii

For hours Rodney had been moving slowly, using a flashlight, calling constantly, even though he no longer hoped for a reply. It had been Jerome's suggestion that the searchers fan out, each trying to cover a small amount of space, search the snowdrifts, not duplicate one another but not miss an inch of ground. Whether it was the concussion or not, Rodney's head was pounding. The lights were like some phantasmagoria. Was he having delusions?

He stumbled and fell headlong in a drift, his face buried. Slowly he pulled himself up, wiped snow from his mouth and nose and eyes. He bent to rub his ankle. He'd fallen over something sharp.

Something sharp. In a moment he was scrabbling frantically, wiping off snow, hauling out a small sled. The Christmas sled.

"Dennis!" he shouted, a new note in his voice. "Dennis!"

There was no answer. Nothing but lights from the other searchers, distant voices.

"Mister Duffy!"

There was a bark, one sharp bark, but the sound was unmistakable.

"Mister Duffy!" he shouted again.

Again there was a bark but Mister Duffy did not come near him.

"Mister Duffy!"

This time he was answered by frantic barking, but still there was no sign of the dog.

Somewhere a voice shouted, "Hey, that must be the dog."

People were coming closer now, the lights gradually converging on Rodney. He stumbled through the snow. Something moved against him.

"Mister Duffy!" He patted the dog and then yelled, "I've found him!" as he bent over.

The lights were on Mister Duffy now, lights on the snow where he lay, lights on a small boy sleeping with Mister Duffy's big warm body almost covering him, shielding him from the snow, sheltering him from the night, guarding him from the hovering angel of death.

iv

Dr. Chalmers turned away from the small bed on which Dennis slept, looked into Kathy's face on which a kind of white radiance had dawned.

"He's going to be all right. Keep him in bed for a day or so. He has a slight fever but he's a healthy young man and I don't think we need to fear pneumonia."

In the living room below, Mrs. Perry was trying to find words to thank the troopers, the neighbors, the college boys who had helped in the search through the long terrible night.

"That's our job, ma'am," a trooper told her.

"That's what neighbors are for," a tired-looking man assured her.

"Glad to help," one of the college boys said. "But, man, what will you take for that dog?"

When they had gone, Kathy came downstairs. The doctor shook hands all around and prepared to leave. "You go to bed, young woman," he told her severely. "It will be a miracle if none of you get pneumonia. Hot baths all around. I doubt if you'll need sleeping pills." He grinned as he looked at his watch. "Four o'clock."

Rosamund got up, "Scrambled eggs," she suggested. "Come on and help me, Hal."

"Just the thin edge of the wedge, if you ask me," he grumbled. "First I dry dishes, now I'm a busboy. A domesticated slave, that's what I'm going to be."

He moved cheerfully if wearily toward the kitchen, pausing to tighten his hand on Kathy's shoulder as he went past.

Tony sat on the floor in front of the fire, her arms around Mister Duffy. "You wonder," she whispered to him. "You noble old boy."

"Is Kathy all right?" Jerome demanded anxiously.

"Quite all right." Kathy spoke for herself. "No one could be all righter."

"Thank God! I was afraid for a while you were going to break under the strain."

Mrs. Perry laughed. "My girls look fragile but they are like flexible young trees that bend under the storm; they don't crack under it. When it's over they stand as erect as ever."

Jerome gave a half-stifled cry.

"What's wrong?" Rodney asked quickly.

"I don't know." Jerome flung his hand over his eyes. "I don't know. Delusions, I guess." He pulled off the dark glasses.

"What's wrong?" Rodney demanded again.

"The queerest thing. I keep thinking I can see a star, only it would have to be the biggest star in the world. Unless I've gone nuts."

Rodney followed the straining eyes to the top of the Christmas tree where the great star shone serenely.

It was two days before the roads were sufficiently cleared for Kathy's guests to return to New York, two days of exhausted quiet and deep peace. Dennis, aside from a mild cold, appeared to have suffered no damage at all. Mister Duffy had been so praised and petted that he had become insufferably proud of himself.

That first morning, or rather at noon the day after Christmas when they drifted slowly down to breakfast, each of them waited breathlessly for Jerome's appearance. Suppose that flash of light had been only a passing miracle. When he came into the dining room with Sam they looked quickly at him, their hearts sinking, for Sam was guiding him as usual. Then they saw his expression. The lines of strain had gone and so had the cold aloofness. He was eager, almost gay. For the first time since his accident Rodney recognized the old Jerome.

"Well?" he asked eagerly.

"I can distinguish light from darkness," Jerome said. "I can't make out furniture or people but—it's something." He put aside his own preoccupation with the tremendous thing that had happened to him. "How's Dennis? How's Kathy?"

Something in his tone as he spoke of her brought color flooding into Kathy's tired face. "Dennis is in bed," she told him, "and outraged about it, but he's got to stay there for at least a day until he shakes off his cold. And I'm fine. I'm on top of the world. As they say in Scotland, 'I wouldn't call the King my cousin.' "

During those two days, while they were shut in the house, they went back to the mystery of the stolen bonds, to the burglary at Mrs. Hazelton's shop, the intruder at Kathy's, the similarity between the scars on the heads of the two Meredith men.

"If Eve bought the scarf the intruder left here," Jerome said, and for once there was no trace of feeling when he mentioned her, "then it seems to me the whole thing must center around her uncle. Simon Cranshaw is the core of this business."

"I have an idea," Hal put in. "Our newspaper has all sort of correspondents out on the coast. Why don't I get hold of our San Francisco man, who is an old friend, and ask him to find out what he can about Cranshaw? So far we just don't know enough about him to take any steps. Any objections?"

There were no objections. "All right, then. Motion carried. I'll call him as soon as we get back to New York."

"Call him now," Kathy said eagerly.

Hal fumbled in a notebook and found the number he wanted. In an incredibly short time he heard the voice of his friend, speaking as clearly as though he were in the same room and not three thousand miles away. After a brief bantering exchange, Hal told him what he wanted.

"Simon Cranshaw," the man at the end of the line repeated, as he wrote busily. "His niece, Eve Cranshaw. You think he may be a big real estate dealer? You say he left San Francisco five years ago.... Negotiable bonds.... What's that?" he broke off, startled. "Two hundred thousand dollars? What's the matter? Need 'em for your honeymoon? And, by the way, congratulations."

"Of course I don't need them for my honeymoon," Hal said haughtily. "I expect my wife to support me."

The other man laughed. "Okay. I'll get on this at once. There must have been some kind of stir with nearly a quarter of a million dollars doing a disappearing act."

"There's one thing you could do, Tony," Rodney told her when Hal had finished his conversation. "Go to see Mrs. Hazelton; you've got a good excuse because the burglar broke into your shop, too. Tell her about seeing Cecily Ann with her husband."

"That's a cruel thing to do," she protested.

"Not as cruel as it will be if he takes the formula and runs off with the girl," Hal pointed out.

Nonetheless, Tony was in a reluctant mood when she opened the door of Mrs. Hazelton's shop the morning after her return to New York.

"I haven't an appointment," she began.

"That's all right, Miss Carew," Mrs. Hazelton said. "I have plenty of free time today. The rest of the week will be hectic with people getting fixed up for New Year's, and how I'm going to manage I don't know. I've been on the phone for an hour trying to get some good operators."

"What's happened to Cecily Ann?" Tony asked quickly.

"She left without notice on Christmas Eve. Said her fiancé wanted to get married right away. No advance notice. Nothing. Walked out on me. And such a good operator, too. A lot of my customers came here just because she was so good. A real flair for styling, you know. Well—"

She put Tony in the chair, draped a towel around her shoulders, began to brush her hair. In the mirror Tony saw the older woman's face, drawn and white.

"You look awfully tired," she said sympathetically.

"Tired? I'm just about ready to drop." This morning Mrs. Hazelton didn't bother with her scanty French. She was too worried for that. "I guess you didn't know we had a burglary here on Christmas Eve."

"Yes, I did. I was just walking past when the police cars came. The man escaped through my shop. Did you lose anything?"

Mrs. Hazelton shook her head. "He opened the safe, but there was nothing to take except my record books."

"He didn't get the formula, then?"

"The formula?" Mrs. Hazelton said sharply. "How did you know?"

Tony smiled at her. "You told me yourself. Don't you remember? Said it was going to put you up among the big names."

"That's right. I'd forgotten. Frank always tells me I talk too much." There was a curious expression around her mouth when she mentioned her husband.

"But how did you manage to protect it?" Tony asked.

"Well—" Mrs. Hazelton looked a little embarrassed. "Frank would about have blown his top if he'd known at the time but, you see, what with two other attempts to get into this place, I was afraid of losing that formula. So I took it out of the safe without saying a word to Frank and I hid it in an old teapot."

She looked up in surprise as Tony burst into a gale of laughter. Then she smiled reluctantly. "I guess it was funny at that. But anyhow I saved the formula."

"So, after all, Mr. Hazelton can't be angry with you."

"Well, he—Frank's odd. He's—I don't know—he used to be the cheerfulest man I ever knew. Just couldn't make him mad if you tried. Now he's irritable. On edge."

She met Tony's look of understanding in the mirror and a dull flush crept over her face. "I guess you noticed something," she said heavily. "It just never entered my head. Frank's always been so reliable. But, of course, Cecily Ann is a mighty pretty girl. Maybe he couldn't of helped falling for her. I don't believe he thought she was really engaged. I guess maybe he believed she liked him quite a bit."

There was an awkward silence while she shampooed Tony's hair. When her eyes met again in the mirror she said, "Marriage takes a lot of adjustments, Miss Carew. I suppose right now I ought to tell Frank I'll never forgive him, but—" Unexpectedly the words burst out in a flood. "But the truth is I'm that grateful he didn't go away with her. I don't care so much about anything else. At first, when the

burglary happened, I thought he might of been looking for the formula to take away, him and Cecily
Ann. Then I knew it wasn't true. He might be taken
in by a pretty face and pretty ways but get down to
brass tacks and he wouldn't do a really bad thing.
Just silly, maybe, and he'd be sorry afterward."

"You know, I believe that's true," Tony said impulsively. "I've been wondering how to tell you, but I
believe you'll understand and see it the way I do."

She described Cecily Ann's attempts to flirt with
Frank Hazelton in the beauty parlor, his embarrassment and pleased vanity. Then, more slowly, groping
her way, she described the scene she had observed
from the skating rink: Cecily Ann and Frank Hazelton quarreling at the table, the girl wearing a mink
coat.

"Well, there's one thing sure," Mrs. Hazelton said,
"Frank didn't give her that mink coat. He couldn't.
We don't have that kind of money. So maybe she
was putting the idea up to him, that he turn over the
formula and maybe she'd go away with him or something, and maybe—"

"And he turned her down," Tony said with an
assurance that brightened the eyes of the older woman. "I'm sure of that."

"So it must of been the other man, the fiancé,"
Mrs. Hazelton worked it out slowly, "who gave her
the coat, who tried to take the formula. A real crook
he must be."

"Did you ever see him?"

"Just once, driving Cecily Ann along Fifth Avenue. Car a mile long it seemed to be."

"And she never told you anything about him?"

Mrs. Hazelton shook her head. "Just that he made a
lot of money. She never really talked much, you
know. That slow Southern drawl of hers. She never
said a lot."

On her return to the bookshop Tony reported the
conversation to Rosamund.

"It just gets more confusing, doesn't it?" Rosamund
said at last. "We still don't know who the man was

who struck Rodney; all we know is that he must be the same man who blinded Jerome."

That night the two young couples went to dine with Mrs. Haven, who had just returned from the South, and Rodney was to take Mister Duffy back to Kathy's later.

Mrs. Haven listened in amazement as they poured out the story of Dennis's disappearance, and how Mister Duffy had saved his life; of the attempts to rob the beauty parlor, and of the mystery of the man who had struck Rodney.

"Well," she exclaimed at last, "a lot seems to have been going on since I went away. What happens now?"

"I've left your telephone number with my office," Hal told her, "in case my San Francisco friend calls me. I hope you don't mind."

"All I'd mind would be missing part of this thrilling story," she declared.

They had finished dinner and were in Mrs. Haven's little sitting room when the telephone rang. She answered it and said, "Hello, Betty. . . . Yes, a fine trip. . . . Perfectly recovered. . . . What joke? . . . Oh, Tony Carew . . . Yes, it's true that she is Timothy Carew's granddaughter and his heiress. No, of course not; it was simply a lark. . . . Yes, she really is beautiful."

Mrs. Haven's eyes flickered over Tony's face, smiling. "Yes. . . . No, I don't know how often she has seen Carter. I don't feel that it concerns me. She is my guest and that is all. . . . Nonsense, she spent Christmas with the Perrys. . . . I'm sorry, Betty, I can't ask you to visit me just now. I have a great deal to do for the next week or so." She put down the telephone, tried to smile. "Well, the murder is out," she said lightly.

"It doesn't matter in the least," Tony assured her.

"You don't know Betty." A moment later the telephone rang again. Mrs. Haven answered and then handed it to Hal.

"Hello, Jack." Hal's fingers signaled for pencil and paper, which Rodney pulled out of his pocket.

"Okay, go ahead. Simon Cranshaw—what's that? . . .
Known as a slick operator, was he? . . . Some very
dubious deals but nothing that could be pinned on
him until. . . . Uh huh. Uh huh. . . . Any suggestions
as to how he got away with those bonds? . . . I see.
Now have I got this straight? Cranshaw got a lot of
people interested in what was to be a thriving housing development and demanded cash down because
he had a big deal on in South America and he
needed cash for it. Collected the money and
vamoosed. Then the people found the land was to
become part of a new speedway. No land. No money. No Cranshaw. Yeah. . . . He left San Francisco
when? . . . I'll be darned. That was the day before
Meredith's office was raided. So he could have been
in on the stealing of his own bonds. Then he did the
vanishing act because he didn't want his San Francisco victims on his trail. . . . My, my, what nice
people you get out there."

The voice at the other end of the telephone went
on. Now and then Hal scribbled a note. Then he said,
"Can you describe Cranshaw? . . . Uh huh. . . . Now
about any partner, any other man tied up with him
on these deals. . . . Well, can't expect everything.
How about his niece, Eve Cranshaw?"

After another pause Hal said, frowning, "That's
queer. This niece Eve seems to have been seen with
him a lot. Lunches, dinners, theaters. That's how
they got my friend Meredith all tied up in knots. . . .
You're sure there was no lovely blond niece? . . .
Office girl? Describe, please, . . . Scandinavian. Very
blond. Very beautiful. Name, Ingrid Larsen. Big blue
eyes. . . . Oh, heavy Scandinavian accent. Well, that
lets out an idea I had. . . . What's that? Hold on a
minute."

Hal handed the telephone to Tony, who said eagerly, "I am Antoinette Carew and Hal's trying to help
us. It's terribly important. Are you positive about
that Scandinavian accent? . . . You danced with her
once at a night club. . . ."

Tony looked around the room, her gray eyes

widening as she listened. "Thank you," she said at last. "Thank you very much."

When Hal had terminated his telephone call, Tony said, "Cranshaw's office girl, Ingrid Larsen, spoke very, very slowly, with a heavy Scandinavian accent, but he's not sure whether the accent was genuine."

They looked at her in bewilderment.

"Cecily Ann is a blonde, blue eyes, very pretty, very unscrupulous, who has a phony accent and speaks very, very slowly."

"Well?"

"She's the one who got rid of Mister Duffy," Tony went on impressively. Hearing his name, Mister Duffy raised his head, his tail wagged lazily. "She's the one who claimed he was always prowling. She's the one who, on an operator's salary, has a mink coat. She's the one who told me, 'I'd go where the money is.' "

Rodney stared at her incredulously. "Tony," he exclaimed, "are you trying to say you think Cecily Ann is really Eve Cranshaw?"

Hal intervened. "That's the idea that's been growing in my mind. According to my newspaper pal there is no niece of Simon Cranshaw. The one who called herself Eve may have been—well, any-one."

Mister Duffy growled, the ruff rising on his neck.

"Quiet, Mister Duffy," Tony said.

He was on his feet, barking.

"Quiet, sir!"

There was a ring at the doorbell. Mrs. Haven got up. "I'll answer it." They heard her go downstairs, heard her exclaim in surprise, "Carter! How nice."

"Just got back from Boston," he said in his pleasant voice. "I wanted to see how you were after your Southern jaunt. You look very perky."

"I'm fine. How thoughtful of you." There was a touch of amusement in her voice, indicating that she was not deceived by her nephew's sudden interest in her welfare. "Do come up. I have some guests whom you will like. Oh, of course, you know Rosamund Perry."

"Since she was a baby," he said, laughing as they reached the sitting room.

"Hello, Carter," Rosamund said.

"Hello there, Redhead." He shook hands with Hal. "Still hanging around this gal?" he joked.

"Can't break an old habit," Hal grumbled.

"Tony, you know Carter, of course."

She held out her hand, smiling. For a moment he stood looking down at her, his heart in his eyes.

Mister Duffy tugged at his leash. "Lie down, sir," Tony told him sternly. He dropped down on the floor but he kept his eyes fixed unwaveringly on Carter Holbrook.

"Mr. Meredith," Mrs. Haven said, "I want you and my nephew, Carter Holbrook, to know each other."

The two men shook hands. "Meredith?"

"Rodney Meredith."

"I've seen you somewhere before, haven't I?"

"I don't think so."

Carter sat down, taking a chair as far as possible from Mister Duffy. "That animal of yours doesn't like me," he complained, half laughing. "I seem to have bad luck with great Danes."

"I won't hear a word against this one," Tony warned him. "The other night he saved Dennis's life." She described how Mister Duffy had protected the small boy from the blizzard. "At this point I think he's pretty swell."

"I guess Kathy does, too," Carter said. "What a thing to happen! Kathy must have been almost out of her mind, but she has always been a little stoic."

"She still is," Rosamund assured him. "After her husband died she tried to put the pieces together again as gallantly as possible.

"How is she managing with that big house of hers?"

"Oh, she decided to rent some of the rooms. And that worked out wonderfully. Rodney's brother and his man are living there. I'm so glad, because not long ago there was a prowler who might have broken in if they hadn't been there."

"They—and Mister Duffy," Tony said, reaching down to touch the dog's big head.

"A prowler. At Kathy's?" Carter was surprised. "I remember the place as way off the beaten path."

"There was a prowler all right," Rosamund told him. "He left a scarf behind, caught it on that big barberry bush at the edge of the terrace when he made his getaway. But you can imagine how grateful Kathy was to have two men in the house that night, even if Jerome couldn't really help much."

"Jerome? Your brother?" Carter said sharply.

"Yes."

"An invalid, I take it."

"Blind," Rodney said briefly.

Carter turned to Rosamund. "How is your mother getting along in preparation for her one-man show?"

"So far she hasn't done a thing because of the Christmas rush and inventory. But from now on she'll devote herself to it entirely."

"I hope so," Carter said. "She has genuine talent, you know, a vision that is all her own. Revlin believes she is going to go places."

"Speaking of going places—" Hal got up, pulling Rosamund by the hand. "Tomorrow I have to be a working man."

Rodney got up reluctantly. "And I've got to deliver Mister Duffy to Kathy."

When they had gone, Carter remained standing. Mrs. Haven looked from him to Tony and then, smiling, said good night and went up to her room.

Carter turned to Tony. He was very white, with a look of strain she had never seen in his face before. "Have you a new answer for me?"

"I'm sorry, Carter."

"Don't decide yet," he implored her. "Give yourself—and me—a little more time. Just a little more time. A week. A month." As she started to protest he stopped her, a gentle finger on her lips. "A month," he repeated. "Just let me hope that long."

"It isn't fair to you, Carter."

"Let me be the judge of that." He crushed her hand in his, started toward the door, turned back.

"That fellow Meredith—the way he looked at you—you aren't interested in him, are you?"

"Carter, I haven't given you the right to ask that."

"What do you know about him? If his brother is the Jerome Meredith I think he is, he was mixed up in an off-color operation a few years ago. Do you know how many ways there are for an unscrupulous man to scrape acquaintance with a great heiress? Do you realize how plausible such men usually are? For heaven's sake, be careful, my darling. Be very sure! I have an uneasy feeling that something is going to happen."

"Do stay for dinner tonight, Tony," Mrs. Perry said. "That is," and she looked around her helplessly, "if you can find any place to sit down."

Tony looked in the clutter and confusion in the Perry living room and laughed. Over chairs and couches and tables were strewn materials for Rosamund's trousseau. Against the wall and propped against the furniture were the canvases for Mrs. Perry's one-man show.

"It's a madhouse," Mrs. Perry declared. "Why I ever let myself in for this thing I can't imagine. I must have been demented."

Tony laughed at her. "You love it," she contradicted. "You wouldn't miss this chance for anything. How are you coming?"

Mrs. Perry looked around. "I have nine canvases. When I've finished that portrait of you, Tony, there will be ten. I wish I knew how much space I'll have and what the lighting will be like."

"If Rosamund can manage here, I'll go up to the gallery tomorrow afternoon and find out," Tony promised her.

"Wonderful. Those are all I'll have except for that rather offbeat thing I want to do."

"What is that?"

"An idea I had one day when Cecily Ann stopped to look in the window of the shop. Before Thanksgiving. She paused abruptly and her body was posed at an odd slant. There was just something about the lines—I saw it as design rather than portraiture—but I've gone through all my sketches and somehow or
172

other I've lost it and I can't remember exactly the quality I wanted to catch."

"But how could it disappear?" Rosamund asked, looking up from the tissue paper in which she was carefully packing a filmy negligee. "You've never removed it from the sketchbook, have you?"

Mrs. Perry shook her head. "Actually, I've never even shown my sketchbook to anyone but you and Tony, Jane Haven and her nephew Carter. Oh, and Mr. Revlin from the gallery, of course."

"Then it simply has to be there," Rosamund said firmly. She stood up, holding some shimmering material in front of her. "What do you think of this, Tony? I saw it today and I couldn't resist it. Won't it make a stunning dinner dress?"

"Lovely. That pale green is wonderful with your hair. What style did you have in mind?"

While the two girls discussed cut and line and pattern, Mrs. Perry went through her sketchbook again. Then she gave an exclamation.

"Oh, here's another sketch I did of Cecily Ann one day. It got stuck in that pocket at the back of the sketchbook. It's not the one I was looking for, but—" She broke off, staring transfixed at the sketch. Then she said in a voice so choked the girls barely recognized it, "Rosamund, call Hal. Call him now."

"Mother, what's the matter?"

"I want to see that picture he took of Jerome's missing office girl, Martha Kumer. I want to see it right away."

"He's coming to dinner, you know."

"Tell him to bring the picture without fail."

Mrs. Perry refused to say anything else. While the two girls attempted to bring order out of chaos and clear out the living room she busied herself with dinner.

When Hal arrived he kissed Rosamund, grinned cheerfully at Tony, and said to Mrs. Perry, "Don't tell me you want to do a portrait of Martha Kumer. If there ever was a homely wretch—"

Mrs. Perry took the picture from him and went to hold it under a lamp. Beside it lay her sketch of

Cecily Ann. After a long scrutiny she said queerly, "I knew it! I told you I'd seen Martha Kumer before. Do you see that line from the nose to the chin? Do you notice the tiny ear set flat against her head? It's the same woman: Martha Kumer, Cecily Ann, Eve Cranshaw."

ii

While they were at dinner, still discussing Mrs. Perry's fantastic discovery, the telephone rang. Rosamund called, "Tony, it's Rodney for you."

"A fine thing," Rodney said when Tony had answered. "Here I've been waiting and waiting at Mrs. Haven's and you vanish completely."

"Come over here, won't you, Rodney? We've got something terrific to tell you."

He arrived within a few minutes, in time to join the others for Mrs. Perry's special dessert, pineapple upside-down cake, and coffee.

While he ate they poured out the story, showed him the pictures. Mrs. Perry pointed out the similarities.

"These are highly individual," she told him; "they aren't points that can be altered. Two women might have one of them in common but not both. The possibility of that much similarity except in identical twins is astronomical."

Rodney looked from the sketch of the pretty blonde to the shot of the drab, brown-haired girl; from the high heels to the flat walking shoes; from the smart dress to the shapeless one. He shook his head.

"I realize you have trained eyes but I can't see any similarity between those two women. And if either or both of them turned out to be Eve, why on earth didn't Jerome recognize her? He worked for a whole day with her. I don't see how a man could fail to—well, sense the presence of the woman he loved."

"Remember," Tony said, "he was upset about Miss Burns's unexpected resignation and he had a lot of work to get done with untrained help. Disguised as she was, and not suspicious of her, anyhow—"

"Also," Rosamund said in excitement, "you remember the one thing he recalled most distinctly about her? She stuttered."

"So she did," Hal agreed. "I was there at the time the burglary was discovered. I heard her myself."

"Eve Cranshaw spoke very slowly; Simon Cranshaw's office girl, with her Scandinavian accent, spoke very slowly; Cecily Ann, with her Southern accent, spoke very slowly. Perhaps it was the only way she could conceal a stutter," Tony pointed out.

"I wish," Rodney said, "that Jerome could see these two pictures for himself."

"How are his eyes?"

"Better every day. He can make out the shape of furniture and people though he says it's truly seeing through a glass darkly. Of course, he can't distinguish faces." He grinned. "But I've noticed how hard he tries to see what Kathy looks like."

"See here, Rodney," Hal said, "sometimes shock treatment is the best thing there is. Why don't you call Jerome and put it to him?"

iii

"It's stew tonight," Kathy said apologetically. "After turkey and ham and the roast of beef, I thought we'd just have a simple country supper. Do you mind?"

"It tastes fine to me," Jerome said, "but that goes for anything you cook."

"Mister Duffy likes stew, too," Dennis piped up.

"Mister Duffy has had his supper and—Dennis, I've told you before not to let him in the dining room."

"Aw, Mom!"

"Out he goes."

"Mister Duffy saved my life," Dennis said craftily.

"Out," Jerome said.

Dennis shot one look at him from under thick-lashed eyelids and then meekly led Mister Duffy out to the kitchen.

"You're good for Dennis," Kathy said. "He always obeys you without question and, thank goodness, without resentment."

Sam came in. "Rodney's on the phone for you, Jerome." As the latter pushed back his chair with an apology, Sam added, "Something is up or I miss my guess. He's always so darned quiet, but right now he's practically quivering with excitement."

"Jerome," Rodney's voice came over the wire, "we've come up with rather a poser here."

"We? Where?"

"Well, Mrs. Perry, really." Rodney hesitated for a moment and then went on with a rush. "It's like this. She has just been comparing pictures of Cecily Ann with those of your one-day office assistant, Martha Kumer." He paused again. "The thing is—she thinks they are the same person."

The silence seemed to be endless. At length Rodney called anxiously, "Jerome! Jerome! Are you still there?"

To his immense relief he heard his brother laugh, his old laugh, gay and lighthearted. "I've just hit earth! That explains a lot, doesn't it?"

"Well—you're all right?"

"Don't worry, Windy," Jerome said quietly. "I couldn't, as Kathy says, be all righter. The queer thing is that, somehow, I think I knew it all the time. I don't mean that I realized it clearly, that I told myself, 'This woman is Eve.' But something made me suspicious and I couldn't take it, I guess. I just blotted it out of my consciousness because it hurt too much. Well, what do you know! At least it simplifies things; we have only one woman to look for instead of three." He laughed again. "Wait until Kathy hears this."

"Oh," Rodney said softly, "so that's the way it is."

"Well, after all, I'm not in a position to declare myself now. Not until I find out how much sight I'm going to regain. Not until I'm self-supporting again. But—that's how it is."

"Good luck to you, boy!"

Jerome came back to the table, picked up his fork, and began to eat. Kathy looked at him, saw that he was trying to hold back a laugh.

"If," she said ominously, "you go on acting like a—a mystery man for one minute longer, I'll throw something at you."

He chuckled. "Kathy! I'm surprised. Self-control. Self-discipline. Never pry into other people's affairs. Never reveal vulgar curiosity."

"I could shake you!"

He leaned back in his chair, laughing. "Well, I couldn't have held out much longer, anyhow. What do you think Mrs. Perry has turned up? She believes my missing office girl, the Kumer woman, is really Cecily Ann, and therefore—"

"Therefore?"

"Eve Cranshaw, or whatever that Swedish name she had." He chuckled. "Like Cleopatra, she certainly has her infinite variety."

Kathy toyed with the stew, crumbled a biscuit, said nothing.

"Aren't you interested?" Jerome said at last, with gentle mockery in his voice.

"Yes. Yes, of course." She made a tremendous effort to steady her voice. "Cleopatra! She must be a fascinating woman. Once a man loves her—"

"He feels the impact," Jerome said with no particular emotion. "It depends on the man, of course. Now you take Caesar and Antony. Antony never got over her, but Caesar—well, he seems to have lost interest and suffered no particular damage."

"Mom," Dennis said, "you spilled your glass of water."

"It's all right," she said.

"It is all right, isn't it, Kathy?" Jerome asked. "I

mean—Eve, or whoever she really is, carries trouble with her like Typhoid Mary. But at least I'm immune now. Do you know why I'm immune, Kathy?"

She said nothing at all.

Dennis, looking from one to the other, said, "Can I be excused? Me and Sam want to work on that electric train."

When he had gone Jerome said again, "Kathy?" When she did not answer he got up, made his way around the table, put his hand on her shoulder. "Kathy! I told Rodney tonight how it was with me, but I said I'd wait until I was sure about my eyes, sure about being self-supporting. Right now none of that seems to be so important. Kathy!"

He drew her into his arms. Unexpectedly her hands stiffened held him away.

"What is it?" he asked, still in that gentle voice.

"You mustn't say anything more," she said. "Not until you can see."

His arms fell to his sides. "You are right, of course. Forgive me."

She saw the joy drain out of his face, saw the old aloof mask return, and realized what she had done. "Jerome!" Her voice stopped him on the way to the door. "You don't understand. You don't understand at all. It's because—it's only—I don't want you to say things now that you might not feel after—when you can really see me. I'm not a beauty. I'm not even especially pretty. I could never compete with a siren like Eve."

He was back at her side, reaching for her. "You little goose," he said. "I love you, Kathy. The day I can support a wife I'm going to ask you to marry me. You'd better be making up your mind what your answer will be. I'm a very impatient man."

"I began making it up at Thanksgiving," she said, "and by Christmas I knew what it would be."

"Well?" he said urgently.

She drew away from him. "That, Mr. Meredith," she said primly, "you will find out only after you have proposed to me properly. Now get back to your tape recorder. You've got to finish a story. Remember? And it's time for me to give Dennis his bath. Good night, Jerome."

iv

The Revlin Gallery was a small one on the second floor of a building on Madison Avenue. When Tony went in the following afternoon there was only one customer, who was sitting before a magnificently lighted canvas, studying it carefully, using a pocket lens.

The manager, a small and somewhat stout man with a Van Dyke beard and glasses on a black ribbon, looked up as she came in. Today Tony wore a leaf-brown wool dress with a gold belt and on her shining black hair a tiny scrap of brown hat with a gold feather.

Revlin's eyes widened when he saw her, a reaction to which Tony was accustomed. He left his customer to his study of the canvas and came to meet her.

"Would you rather just look around," he asked, "or is there something I can show you?"

"I'm really here as an emissary from Mrs. Perry, who asked me to discuss with you the amount of space she can count on for her one-man show. My name is Carew, Antoinette Carew."

"I've heard of you from my good friend Holbrook." Revlin shook hands with her. "He told me how beautiful you were but he didn't do you justice." Tony's eyes chilled somewhat. Mr. Revlin was too unctuous. "If you would care to look around for a few minutes, I will be free to discuss any problems that may occur to you." He made a gesture. "This is my only display room. You see, I am starting in a small way. Perhaps you can judge for yourself what we'll be able to do in exhibiting Mrs. Perry's work."

He excused himself and returned to the customer, who was still engrossed in studying the painting. Left to herself, Tony made a rapid survey of the room, decided that in matters both of space and lighting it would serve Mrs. Perry's purpose admirably. Then, as Revlin's voice dropped to a confidential murmur while he talked with the customer, she began to walk around the room, looking at the paintings, trying to shut out the conversation that was not meant for her ears.

There was, she decided, a mixed lot of paintings, a scattering of impressionists and postimpressionists, a few contemporary American painters, some of them good, some of them downright bad.

Her slow walk around the room had brought her behind the customer and for the first time she caught a glimpse of the canvas that he was studying so closely.

"Twenty thousand dollars," he was saying. "That's more than I've ever paid for a painting. For the most part I've stuck to contemporary painters, who—"

Revlin had a fat laugh. "Who needed the money. Yes, I know. Well, of course, my dear fellow, that is the way most of the dealers got hold of the French Impressionists. Bought them from starving painters for a song and then—" He made an expressive gesture. "But here, of course, you haven't the problem of comparatively unknown artists, people whose future remains uncertain, to say the least. Here you have one of the great works of one of the great Dutch masters. Twenty thousand dollars! If you ever want to sell it, which I doubt, you can double your money easily. If it hadn't been for my inveterate habit of prowling around in people's attics, this might have lain forgotten for another hundred years."

The customer took a long breath, stood up. "All right," he said. "I'll take it."

As he stepped away from the canvas Tony looked at it. Looked at the woman sitting in sunlight, looked at the cradle at her feet. There could be no question that it was the same painting. But why on earth had Percy Rolf sold it when he had so loved it? Was it because his wife still felt that he had spent too much money for it? But the difference in price—there was something here she did not understand.

Revlin turned in high good humor. "Miss Carew," he said beaming, "let me introduce Mr. John Dauphin, who is rapidly becoming one of the distinguished collectors in this country."

Tony smiled at him. "You've bought a magnificent painting."

"It's going to be the very heart of my collection." He made out a check and handed it to Revlin. "Will you have it sent to my house?" He gave an address on Central Park West.

A door at the back of the gallery opened and a young woman came out, the type of businesswoman whom Tony disliked, exaggeratedly tailored, wearing a man's shirt and necktie, her black hair cut very short and uncurled, with curious eyes that were almost as black as her hair.

"Miss Jones, Mr. Dauphin has bought the painting. Will you see that it is properly boxed and delivered to him this afternoon?"

The woman nodded, and glanced inquiringly at Tony.

"Miss Carew has come from Mrs. Perry, whose one-man show we are holding in three weeks. She simply wants to look us over." Revlin laughed genially.

The woman looked unsmilingly at Tony, nodded again, and carefully picked up the small canvas, while Revlin attended his customer to the door. There were voices outside and then Revlin returned with Carter Holbrook.

The latter's eyes brightened when he saw Tony.

"Tony! This is my lucky day. Have you come about Mrs. Perry's exhibit?"

"I really just stopped by to see how much space there was, so we could plan the best way to arrange the paintings."

She asked a few questions which Revlin answered, and then she turned to go.

"Hey, where are you off to?" Carter protested.

"I'd better get back to the shop."

He looked at his watch. "Nonesense. It's nearly five.

The place will be closed before you can get there. Come and have a drink with me."

"Well, a cup of tea, if you don't mind."

"Fine!" Carter waved to Revlin and took Tony's arm. As they went toward the door something made her glance back. Miss Jones was standing very still, her eyes fixed on Carter's face with an expression there was no mistaking.

Oh, the poor thing, Tony thought, she's in love with him. She knew the black-haired woman's eyes were following her with no kindly look as she and Carter went out.

Over the teacups Tony tried to carry on a gay conversation but she found it uphill work. Carter's mother's attempts of late to invite Tony to Boston had caused them both embarrassment, though it was not a subject they could discuss.

"Sometimes," Carter said abruptly, "it seems to me that everything has gone wrong since I met you. You're the most wonderful thing I ever saw but you bring me bad luck, Tony."

"I do?" she said, honestly surprised.

He pulled the little ring box out of his pocket and dropped it in again. "I still keep it," he told her, "waiting for a change of heart. But," he went on hastily, as she was about to protest, "you'll have to admit that the obstacles are piling up."

She poured more tea, added sugar and lemon. She did not inquire what the obstacles were.

"Look here," he said urgently, "I know we can't discuss my mother, but you won't let her—well, her interest in my welfare—have any effect, will you?"

She shook her head. "This is between us, Carter, and that's all."

"I wish I could believe that. But there is something else, isn't there?" As she made no reply he went on doggedly, "Rodney Meredith. He's very much in the picture, isn't he?"

"Speaking of pictures," and Tony's voice was cool, unrevealing. "I want to see Percy Rolf before dinner, if it's possible. Would you mind driving me there, Carter?"

"Of course not. Only be kind, Tony, won't you, and have dinner with me later. I'll wait as long as you like."

Reluctantly she agreed, went into the Park Avenue apartment building, and sent up her name. The Rolfs welcomed her warmly. "How nice of you to drop in to see us," Rolf said. "You're like sunlight in this place."

"I'll come back for a really long visit," Tony promised, "but right now I stopped just for a minute to ask—" She broke off, lips parted, eyes widening. On the wall facing her was the Dutch painting, a woman in sunlight, her foot touching a cradle.

xix

The picture at the Revlin Gallery was a copy and Revlin himself was a dishonest dealer. That was the result of Tony's visit to Percy Rolf. Her chief feeling was one of sick despair at the disappointment she was going to have to cause Mrs. Perry after all her hopes, her hard work, her excitement over having a one-man show. Now she had to be told that the dealer was disreputable.

"Tell you what I'll do," Percy Rolf promised before she left. "First I'll see this man Dauphin and look at his painting so there's no possibility of mistake. Then we're going to clamp down on the man Revlin and close that gallery of his up as tight as a drum."

"Oh, poor Mrs. Perry!" Tony wailed. "I'm so terribly sorry for her."

"Suppose I drop in to see her one of these day," Rolf suggested. "If her stuff is as good as you think it is, we'll probably be able to find a sound gallery where she can exhibit."

"Do you really think so?" she asked, brightening.

He smiled at her. "I can't promise. After all, I haven't seen her work, but I do have considerable standing as a collector, and if she's good I believe something can be arranged."

"You're a darling," Tony said, hugging him. "You've made me feel so much better."

"You mustn't try to take on everyone's problems, you know," he warned her.

"You let her alone, Percy," his wife said. "Tony lives the only way she can and be true to herself."

Carter was waiting patiently when Tony left the

apartment building. "Let's drive a while before we have dinner," he suggested.

At her nod he turned toward Fifth Avenue and entered Central Park, white under its blanket of snow. All around the park gleamed the lights of the tall apartment buildings, of the magnificent Fifth Avenue houses, lights from penthouses and the great glaring electric signs from Central Park South.

They drove in deep silence, each of them absorbed in private thoughts. It was Carter who broke it. "You're worried about something. Is there any way I can help?"

"It's just that I have a big disappointment for Mrs. Perry," Tony exclaimed. "I really hate to tell you this, Carter, but your friend Revlin isn't an honest dealer."

"What!" The word was as explosive as though it had been shot out of his mouth. "Revlin! That's impossible, Tony. I know the man. He's a square shooter."

"I'm afraid not." She described watching the sale Revlin had made to the customer named Dauphin, and how she had recognized the painting as one that belonged to Rolf. That was why she had gone to the Rolf apartment. The painting was still there. So the one Revlin had sold as an original was a fake. "Naturally Mrs. Perry can't afford to deal with a man like that," she concluded.

Carter was grimly silent. "Revlin! A man I've trusted. Look, Tony, are you positive your friend is right and Revlin, the expert, is wrong?"

"Percy Rolf is one of the biggest art collectors in the country and no one has ever challenged the authenticity of one single item he has bought."

"I guess that answers me," Carter said gloomily. "I wanted to help Mrs. Perry—well, really, I wanted to do something to please you. But sometimes a guy's luck runs out."

"Out, good heavens, Carter, it never occurred to me to blame you. This must be as much of a shock to you as it is to me."

"It is," he assured her.

"And even more, perhaps, because he was your friend. I guess all we can do is to write it off. Mr. Rolf won't waste any time in exposing the man so he can't do any more harm, and at least he didn't have a chance to cash Mr. Dauphin's check. It was nearly five when he got it."

Carter managed a grin. "Let's forget the failures for a while, shall we? Let's dine at the Carlyle and think of pleasant things. All right?"

When they had ordered, Tony saw Carter look up and frown. "Oh lord," he groaned, "there comes Mrs. Brigson, one of Mother's friends."

A tall, heavy woman stopped at their table and Carter stood up. "Well, Carter," she boomed in a big masculine voice, "it's about time. Haven't seen you in months. Have you forgotten you've a standing invitation to my Fridays?"

"Sorry, Mrs. Brigson. I've been going up to Boston for the weekends."

"That's not what Betty tells me. Says she hardly lays eyes on you. Even for Christmas. Says you've got a girl." She stared appraisingly at Tony. "Hm. You're Timothy Carew's granddaughter. Look just like your mother. Well, Carter, I'll tell your mother I left you in good hands. She'll be delighted."

She moved off like a ship under full sail and Tony, seeing Carter's furious expression, giggled. After a moment he grinned back.

"Was it Shakespeare who said something about all events conspiring against one?" Over crabmeat cocktails he asked, "What's this I hear about a burglary at your shop? Aunt Jane was telling me about it and not a word out of you."

"We weren't really robbed," she explained. "Someone broke into the beauty parlor next door, set off the burglar alarm, and when the police came he escaped through our shop, knocking out Rodney Meredith, who had gone in to get the money out of the cash register."

"Meredith? The big quiet guy who hangs around you?"

"That's the one."

"With the brother, the crooked lawyer, who got messed up in some scandal a few years ago?"

"Don't talk that way!" Tony flared. "It's not like you. Condemning a man without even knowing the circumstances. Jerome Meredith was the victim of a filthy trick."

"You're quite a partisan, aren't you?"

"Yes, I am. I believe in Jerome. He's lived through five long horrible years of blindness, and the worst of it is that the girl he was engaged to is partly responsible, at least, for what happened to him."

"Good lord, Tony! You can't mean that." Carter was horrified.

"At least," Tony said, "there's nothing more she can do to hurt him now. He's gone back to the kind of work he really loves, writing books for children."

"How can he write if he can't see?"

"He uses a tape recorder, then Kathy types the material and reads it back to him for corrections."

Over roast beef so tender it could be cut with a fork, baked potatoes, and asparagus hollandaise Carter said in a worried voice, "I don't like the idea of your shop being broken into, Tony."

"There's nothing to worry about," she assured him. "We weren't meant to be the victims; we were just the escape hatch. The burglar was really after the safe in the beauty parlor."

"A lot of risk for small profits, I should think."

"More than you might imagine." Tony told him about the formula on which the Hazeltons expected to make a fortune and how it had been hidden in a teapot.

"Well, I'll be—!"

Tony laughed. "Isn't that absurd? Of course, she's put it in a safety deposit box now so no one can get at it."

"But how would anyone know about the thing?"

Tony told him about Cecily Ann, her attempts to get the secret from Hazelton, her abrupt resignation on Christmas Eve. She was on the verge of telling him that she believed Cecily Ann to be the mysterious Eve Cranshaw who had involved Jerome Meredith in tragedy, but she refrained because of Carter's obvious antagonism for the Meredith brothers.

Over desert Carter resolutely avoided unpleasant subjects and they discussed Rosamund's approaching wedding, the preparations for the trousseau, and the general happy excitement.

"What do you think she'd like for a wedding present?" Carter asked.

"An electric coffee maker or a toaster or a waffle iron," she answered promptly.

"Sounds rather prosaic," Carter protested.

"But that's what she would like best."

"Okay, if you say so." Carter made a note. "What are you giving her?"

Tony shook her head. "That," she declared, "is a dead secret. I don't dare whisper a word to anyone. Not a soul."

"Where's the wedding going to take place?"

"At Kathy's house. More room there."

"The marriage," he warned, "won't be legal without me. I'll forbid the banns."

Tony laughed. "You'll be invited. There won't be a lot of people, of course. Just family and close friends and a small reception afterward."

"That would suit me," Carter said. "That's the way I'd like it, too." He held her eyes for a moment in an ardent question. Slowly, regretfully, she shook her head.

ii

Next day the sky was clear and blue, the wind was gentle, the temperature rose above freezing, rose into the fifties. One of those February days that make one believe that spring is just around the corner. Usually it is followed by cold blasts and snow, but while it lasts people walk with brightening faces, welcoming this sudden bounty of nature.

Tony, absorbed in thought, became gradually aware of the woman who plodded ahead of her on Third Avenue, her arms weighted down with big brown paper bags filled to bursting with groceries. Then she recognized her, ran to catch up.

"Mrs. Hazelton! Here, let me take one of those. They are too heavy for you."

"Oh, thank you," Mrs. Hazelton said fervently, "I was afraid I'd drop it, my arms were so tired." She shifted the weight of the one she still held and they walked side by side toward Gramercy Park, and strolled down Irving Place toward the beauty parlor.

"How did you manage to get away from the shop during the day?" Tony asked, with her usual friendly interest in people.

"I have two good operators, nice and reliable, so I can have more leisure."

Tony smiled. "You must be getting in training for the time when that formula makes you rich and you won't have to work."

Mrs. Hazelton's face clouded. "Well, I'm not counting any more chickens before they are hatched. Frank thought he had a backer all sewed up but I'm not so sure now. Something seems to have scared the man. He got the idea that someone else is in on the deal. Well, if we don't get his backing, I guess we'll find someone else."

"That's the spirit."

"You get something—you lose something. That's the way life goes." Mrs. Hazelton unlocked the area-way door and Tony followed her into her basement kitchen. She put down the heavy bag on a table and took Tony's. "Won't you stay a few minutes? Have a cup of coffee or something? I baked some real nice gingerbread this morning, if I do say so."

"That sounds fine." Tony settled herself at the kitchen table, as comfortable and at ease as she was in the Rolfs' drawing room. "What did you mean by saying: 'You get something—you lose something'?"

"Well, it's like this. Maybe we've lost the backer we were pinning our hopes on. But—I've got Frank back and that's something."

She poured coffee, cut gingerbread, pulled out a chair facing Tony. "Yes, we had it out, Frank and me. He told me the whole thing. Cecily Ann just about wrapped him around her finger until he didn't know where he was. And then she went too far. She wanted that formula for the cold cream, said she knew someone who could finance it, said—well, she and Frank could maybe go off somewhere and be rich on their share of the profits. *Their* share. The nerve! And that's when Frank balked. Must have been the night you saw them together at the restaurant. She tried every way she knew how to get him to turn it over. Said she had a partnership with two men and they'd never failed to put across really big deals. That's how she got that mink coat, out of her share on a deal."

"Two men?" Tony repeated.

"Yeah. Anyhow, Frank suddenly came to his senses and said he wasn't going to have anything to do with it. Then, four days later, she quit, like I said."

"Did she tell him anything about the men?"

"She pointed out one of them to him once when they were in a cocktail bar. My Frank in a cocktail bar while I was here working my fingers to the bone!"

"Would he recognize the man again?"

"I don't know why not."

Tony finished her coffee, sat back in her chair. "Mrs. Hazelton, if your husband can find and identify that man, I will have your formula examined by expert chemists. If it lives up to what you say, I'll finance the manufacture and promotion myself."

"Then you really are the Carew heiress, like Cecily Ann said?"

"Yes."

"You know how much it would cost?"

"I'll find out."

"Why do you want to do this?"

"To help clear up an ugly mystery that is spoiling the lives of several people."

As Mrs. Hazelton still hesitated, Tony added with a smile, "Including my own."

In an apartment on West End Avenue three people were having a consulation, or rather one person was talking gloomily while the other two listened in silence.

"Of all the rotten luck," the speaker exclaimed. "If the girl hadn't walked in at that particular moment and recognized the picture, we'd have another twenty thousand dollars in our hands."

"How bad is it?" the woman asked, a sternly tailored woman with black hair and strange eyes.

"Bad enough to close up the gallery. Rolf is a fighter and he won't give up. He saw Dauphin, showed him the original, and they sailed in here before I could get to the bank. Said payment would be stopped on Dauphin's check and that the gallery would be fully investigated."

"Well," the other man said, "it was good while it lasted. How much have we cleared in all?"

"About seventy-eight thousand, but when the news breaks, there is going to be a howl and the buyers will all come down on my head."

"So we move fast," the woman commented.

"I don't understand," the man called Revlin complained, "why we've had such a run of bad luck."

"We haven't done so badly," the other man protested. "We've lived high on the hog for a long time."

"The luck's running out," Revlin said. "I can sense these things. You've always thought you were immune, that nothing could catch up with you, but we've just had a sweet little racket swept right out from under our feet. And you muffed that Hazelton formula deal. But good." He looked from one of his companions to the other. "And that goes for both of you."

"There's no point in recriminations," the other man said. "That's the way the cards fall sometimes."

"Especially if you don't know how to deal them."

"Water under the bridge. Forget it. Get the gallery closed up as fast as you can. Sooner you are out of there the better."

"And then what?" the woman asked.

"Then we get a new idea."

"I," the woman said, "am tired of new ideas. I want just one scheme more and then—out. Forever. Something really good. Big money. Big, big money."

"So do we all," Revlin said. "Come up with your idea."

The woman peered at him through those oddly dark eyes of hers. "Antoinette Carew," she said challengingly. "Like I said—big, big money."

Revlin stared at her incredulously. "Kidnaping? You're mad."

She was unmoved. "Am I?"

"There's no money in the world that's worth the risk of going to the electric chair."

"I didn't suggest," she said slowly, "that you kill her."

There was a long silence in the room, broken only by traffic sounds outside, the horns of impatient motorists, the scream of brakes, a television set turned on too loud.

"Can you guess what would happen after we released her?"

"She wouldn't let Rolf take steps—if we had some hostages."

"Sometimes you frighten me."

"So," she said mockingly, "do the Meredith men." She goaded him. "They kind of get in your way, don't they?"

The first man was silent.

The older one looked at his watch. "I've got a queer hunch," he said, "that there's no time to waste. Percy Rolf is famous for the way he handles things at top speed. I suggest we clear out of the gallery tonight; hire a pickup truck to hold the pictures; leave the furniture behind." He reached for his overcoat. "I've got a feeling that time is running out. Let's get going."

"You're scared, aren't you?" There was an undercurrent of contempt in the woman's voice. "By tomorrow there won't be any Revlin. No trace at all." She asked, "Where did you get that scarf? What's the matter with the one I bought you?"

"I lost it."

"How?"

"At the Cathcart house when I was trying to check up on how blind Jerome Meredith really is. That damned great Dane nearly took me apart."

Unexpectedly she put her hand on his arm, looked up into his face. "Still like me?" she asked huskily.

"Even with those eyes," he assured her blandly.

"These darned contact lenses. But at least that colored glass does change the color of my eyes. I suppose now I can take them out."

"Sure," he said impatiently, "but let's clear out the gallery before we do any more fooling around."

ii

Tony, Rosamund, and Mrs. Perry were busy hemming napkins, while Hal was mending a fitted traveling case of Rosamund's, and Rodney was selecting a record for the player.

"The Schubert Trout Quintet," he suggested. "Any objections?" The sound of music filled the room. Then the downstairs bell rang.

At Mrs. Perry's nod Hal ran downstairs, and returned looking rather surprised and accompanied by the Hazeltons. Rodney shut off the player.

For a moment Mrs. Hazelton looked around the room and then, in relief, she recognized Tony. "Miss Carew, this is my husband, Frank."

The chemist, whose face was a dull red from embarrassment, gave her an awkward nod. Tony introduced the others and Hal found seats for the unexpected guests.

"Frank and I have been talking," Mrs. Hazelton began, "and I told him about Miss Carew's offer to finance the formula if he could identify the man who was one of Cecily Ann's partners. And Frank says you must already know him because he saw the man come here."

Hazelton nodded. "One evening, quite a while ago. I figured he wouldn't be a customer."

"What did he look like?" Mrs. Perry asked in surprise.

"Short guy, rather heavy, kind of pompous, held himself like those pictures of Mussolini, sort of tilted back to make himself took taller, glasses on a black ribbon, a Van Dyke beard."

"Mr. Revlin!" Mrs. Perry said in a kind of gasp. "That's Mr. Revlin."

"Hey," Hal yelled, beside himself with excitement. "That's the way my friend in San Francisco described Simon Cranshaw."

iii

Hal, Rodney, and Frank Hazelton had piled into Tony's car the moment it was delivered by the garage.

"But what are you going to do?" Rosamund asked frantically.

"If this guy is smart at all, he's going to be clearing out fast," Hal told her.

"You'll be careful?"

He kissed her lightly. "You're a little donkey. No danger at all. We're simply going to find this guy Revlin and see if Hazelton can identify him as Cecily Ann's partner. That's absolutely all."

"Call me the minute you're through," she demanded.

"The very first minute." Hal turned to Tony. "I'll drop you at Mrs. Haven's so you won't have to walk."

When he had left her at the Nineteenth Street

house he turned north. "Where first?" he asked. "I looked up the guy in the telephone book. No apartment listed."

"The gallery," Rodney suggested.

"It will be closed at this hour."

"With Percy Rolf breathing down his neck he'll be clearing out, or else I miss my guess."

Hal chuckled. "You sound downright belligerent. What's got into you?"

"If he's the man who knocked me out at the bookshop, he must also be the one who blinded Jerome. We have a long score to settle."

"No violence," Hal warned him. "Leave him to the law. That's what it is for. Man's defense against violence and savagery and his own uncivilized impulses."

"You're right, of course," Rodney agreed.

"Sure," Hal assented cheerfully. "Revenge butters no parsnips."

"You know," Rodney commented after a pause, "it strikes me that we are running up against some really big operators."

On Madison Avenue Hal slowed almost to a crawl while Rodney tried to read street numbers. "That's it," he said suddenly. "Middle of the block. There's a place to park near the corner." The men piled out of the car and started back down the block.

Hazelton halted abruptly. "You said it was on the second floor?"

"That's what Miss Carew told me," Rodney said.

"Look," Hazelton said hoarsely, "there's a light up there."

While they stood staring upward, the light went out. They moved back against the wall of the building, waiting. In a few minutes a black-haired woman, her arms filled with canvases, came out and got into a small pickup truck that was parked at the door. She started the motor. A moment later a man, similarly laden, came out of the building.

"That's him," Hazelton whispered, eagerly if ungrammatically.

As Rodney started forward, Hal gripped his arm. "Don't be a fool," he said. "That's not the way to handle it."

"Have you a better idea?"

"I'm going to follow that truck. Hazelton, we won't need you any more tonight; but we'll want you to identify the man later. Okay?"

"Okay." In obvious relief, Hazelton turned east toward the Lexington Avenue subway.

Hal unlocked the car, started it, and slid away from the curb, following at a discreet distance the pickup truck.

iv

Somewhere a voice kept repeating, "Tony! Tony! Wake up."

She opened her eyes and blinked sleepily at Mrs. Haven, who was standing beside her bed, wearing a long housecoat.

"Tony! It's the telephone for you. I hated to wake you but she said it's important."

Tony slid her small feet into slippers wrapped a white wool robe around her, and stumbled down the stairs to the small sitting room, still only half awake.

"Miss Carew?" The woman spoke very slowly and distinctly. An official voice. "This is New York Hospital. A man has just been brought into the emergency ward. I'm afraid his condition is serious. He asked for you."

"Who?" The fog of sleep rolled away, she was wide-awake now.

"The name is Rodney Meredith."

Tony gave a half-stifled cry. "I'll come at once." She ran up the stairs, threw off the robe and dressed rapidly in a blue wool dress with a red belt, gave her hair a quick brush, reached for her handbag.

"What is it?" Mrs. Haven asked from the door of her room.

"Rodney. He's at New York Hospital. An accident. I don't know when I'll be back." Tony ran down the stairs. She started, still running, toward her garage, and stopped abruptly. She had given her car to Hal, who was going to see whether Hazelton could identify Revlin as Cecily Ann's partner. And Rodney had gone with them.

For a moment she waited on Irving Place but it was never a good spot to pick up a cab and she headed toward Fourth Avenue. There must be a cab. There had to be. Rodney! Rodney!

She pulled her coat tighter around her as protection from the wind, drew the collar higher around her chin. A cab approached and she waved frantically, saw that it was occupied, began to walk quickly up the street, pausing every few feet to look back in search of an empty cab.

The street was almost deserted except for an occasional private car. One was heading south. Then, with a sudden blare of its horn, it turned in the middle of the street, drew up beside her.

"Tony!" Carter called. "Tony, for heaven's sake, I thought that was you. What on earth—"

"Oh, Carter," she said as she climbed in beside him. "I was never so glad to see anyone in my life. Will you drive me to New York Hospital at once?"

"Anywhere. You know that. But what is it?"

"An accident. That's all I know. An accident."

"Relax," he told her quietly. "All's well. You are shivering. Half frozen, I suppose. Shock? Well, the car's warm enough."

The car was warm and Tony's shivering subsided. Beside her Carter sat relaxed, driving with easy competence, his eyes on the road ahead. "Oops!" he said as the car skidded. "Getting any warmer?"

"Thanks, much better now." As he pulled up at the curb she protested, "No, Carter. Don't stop. I'm in a desperate hurry."

"I'll get you there, but not half frozen and half shocked. I'll bring you some hot coffee. Won't take a minute."

Before she could protest he was inside the all-night drugstore. In a surprisingly short time he returned, holding the paper cup. "Can you manage that? Careful, it's hot and strong."

"Just what I need."

The car headed east while she sipped cautiously at the hot coffee. It was really hot and strong, bitterly strong. The East Side Drive would be quickest, he told her. Avoid traffic that way. Slowly the hot coffee began to take effect, to bring back a little courage. The tension had relaxed, too.

"Just settle back," he advised her. "The more rested you are, the better you can cope when you get there. Close your eyes."

She smiled at him gratefully. "You're wonderful, Carter." Closed her eyes. Opened them as she heard a heavy rumbling sound. There was a sand truck blocking the way and Carter was swearing softly to himself. She looked around, wondering how close they were to the hospital, caught sight of a street sign.

"Carter!" Her voice was muffled, not as loud as she had expected. "Beekman Place. What are we doing here?"

"You're done up. I'm taking you to my apartment to rest."

"No!"

He parked the car, turned to her, both hands on hers. "Don't be afraid of me, Tony darling. Never be afraid of me. I love you. Right now you've fallen for the Meredith man; you go rushing up the minute you hear anything is wrong with him."

"How do you know," Tony's voice was curiously slow, it was hard to articulate, "how do you know I got a call about Rodney Meredith? I didn't tell you that." She gave a little cry, tried to jerk away her hand. "Don't! That hurts."

"What does?" Carter asked in surprise. He looked at the scratch on her finger, at the drop of blood. "Poor sweet! That was only my good-luck ring." He turned his hand over. He wore a plain ring, and turned inward toward the palm were four steel prongs, but there was no stone for them to protect.

"You! It was you all the time." Tony reached out uncertainly toward the handle of the door; then her fingers opened, her head settled against the back of the seat. She slept.

The pickup truck had parked outside an apartment building on West End Avenue. Hal pulled in to the curb farther down the street and switched off the lights. He saw the man and woman, laden with canvases, go inside. When they were out of sight he strolled up to look in the truck. It would take at least one more load to empty it.

"You stay here," he told Rodney. "I'll look for a phone and call the police."

Rodney settled down to his vigil behind the wheel of Tony's car. In a few minutes he saw Revlin and the girl come out to the truck and load up again, moving quietly, not attempting to talk. He grinned to himself. In a surprisingly short time an unmarked car parked ahead of his and a man walked back to him. A man in plain clothes but with a military bearing.

Rodney rolled down his window. "Police?"

The other nodded. "Lieutenant Murphy. You the one who called?"

"No, here he comes, running."

"He suggested no marked cars, no sirens. What's the scoop?"

Hal came up, grinning. "That's service."

He and Rodney went up to the big car where a second plainclothes man, Sergeant Miller, sat at the wheel, and Rodney made a quick summary of Revlin's fraudulent dealings at the gallery, of his possible identity as Simon Cranshaw who was concerned in the theft of the bonds, and his attempt to steal the cold-cream formula from the beauty parlor.

"Cold cream." Hal shook his head. "Doesn't seem like a reason for a racket."

"You ought to have been around in the days of the artichoke racket," the detective told him. "That was really rough."

Rodney said quietly, "Here they come again."

Revlin and the woman came out to the truck and filled their arms.

"I guess that's it," Revlin said, his voice low but carrying easily in the quiet.

"What about the truck?"

"I'll just move it around the corner and leave it there. Someone will find it. I hired it under another name, anyhow."

As the truck started up, the unmarked car moved smoothly after it. Lieutenant Murphy walked quietly into the building.

"Smooth as silk," Hal said. "Come on. Let's go."

He and Rodney followed Lieutenant Murphy into the building, an old-fashioned walk-up. They could hear the woman's high heels as she climbed, rather slowly, to the top floor; the feet of the detective who followed her were almost silent. A key turned in a lock, and then, as the door opened, the woman gave a startled gasp. "What do you want?"

"Police. We want to talk to you."

"What business—" Her voice rose, was cautiously hushed.

The door closed firmly behind her. Hal and Rodney stood leaning against the wall in the shabby lobby. A few minutes later the door opened and the sergeant came in, leading Revlin, who looked outraged and pompous.

"This," he was saying in a tone of great dignity, "is some preposterous mistake. I'll speak to my friend the Police Commissioner about it in the morning, my man."

"Meanwhile," the detective informed him, unmoved by the threat, "we're going upstairs." He nodded to the two waiting men and allowed them to fall in behind them.

Revlin, aware of their presence, gave them a nervous look; then, with a helpless shrug, he went up the stairs, his arm firmly grasped by the detective.

The latter tapped at the door and Murphy opened it. For a few moments the men stood looking around the room. There were canvases stacked on couches and tables and floor. On the desk were several large account books. Sitting on a chair by the door was the black-haired woman from the gallery, a woman who now had blue eyes.

"Perhaps," Revlin said, still dignified, still outraged, "you'll explain what this is all about."

"You planning to take a little trip somewhere?" Murphy asked.

Revlin made no reply.

"Decided to close the gallery without notice?"

"That's my business."

"Well, not entirely, Mr. Cranshaw. Not entirely."

Before the fascinated eyes of the spectators the dealer was deflated. The color ebbed from his face. The glasses on their black ribbon fell, dangling on his chest. He took his time, lighting a cigarette, a procedure which he regretted because it betrayed that his hands were shaking.

"My name is Revlin."

Rodney saw the black-haired woman give her partner a warning look, as though trying to convey a message. Slowly a look of confidence came over the man's face. He's got another trick up his sleeve somewhere, Rodney thought, instantly alert. He's got a trump card. He's going to get away with this.

He was aware of a sinking of the heart. He had counted too much on finding Cranshaw, on exposing him, on clearing Jerome. But he simply could not believe that this man could have overpowered Jerome, could have struck him that savage blow. He was too small. Something had gone wrong. Terribly wrong.

Revlin—or Cranshaw—readjusted his glasses, and his manner regained its customary pomposity. The telephone rang and he started for it. Before he could reach it Murphy had answered.

"Simon?" said a voice at the other end of the line. "Gallery all cleared out?"

"Yes."

The man and woman listened tensely.

"No trouble?"

"No."

"What's wrong? You don't sound like yourself."

"The police are here."

"Oh." There was a pause; then the other man said, "Then we'll handle it the other way. With hostages. I've got her, and if they arrest you, you'll be sprung in the morning. And Percy Rolf is the man who'll see to it and be glad to."

"Where are you?" Murphy asked.

"Where? Hey, who is this?" The telephone shut off.

"And who," the lieutenant asked, turning to look from Cranshaw to the woman, "is Percy Rolf?" He repeated the conversation.

It was Rodney who cried, "Tony Carew's old friend. *They've got her!*"

The black-haired woman smiled for the first time. Rodney caught at her shoulder, tilted her head back. "Where is she? What have you done to Tony? If you've hurt her—"

She jerked away from him. "D-d-don't t-t-touch me! Why don't you c-c-coppers make him stop?"

Rodney's hand fell away. "Well," he said slowly. He turned to the detectives, who waited stolidly, eyes alert. "Permit me to introduce Ingrid Larsen *alias* Eve Cranshaw *alias* Martha Kumer *alias* Cecily Ann."

"Sure about that?" Murphy asked.

Rodney nodded. "Make them talk! They are holding Tony Carew."

"Simon Cranshaw," the lieutenant said, "I arrest you on a charge of conspiracy to defraud. Unless Miss Carew is safely in our hands within two hours—and I mean safely—you will be charged under the Lindbergh law with the crime of kidnaping, which carries a first degree penalty. Is that clear?"

Cranshaw stared at the carpet as though studying it's pattern, thinking hard. The woman—this, Rodney reminded himself incredulously, was the Eve who had so attracted Jerome—returned Rodney's look, her brows drawn together.

"Who are you?" she asked, her words carefully enunciated, carefully spoken.

"Nemesis," he told her briefly.

Her astonishingly blue eyes opened wide. With a sudden gesture she pulled off the black wig and he saw blond hair. "You're Jerome's brother, the one he called Windy. You look like him." To his stunned surprise her manner was affectionate, gentle. She put her hand on his arm. "My poor darling Jerome. I've missed him so terribly. But I," she looked at Cranshaw, "had to do what Uncle Simon said. I couldn't help myself. I've always loved Jerome. And he loves me."

"Uncle Simon!" Cranshaw snapped. "I'm not your uncle. You're not selling me out. Unless Jerome is more of a fool than I think he is, he won't ever give you the time of day again.

"How right you are!" Rodney said between set teeth.

The police had allowed this unorthodox conversation to go on without interruption. Now at a gesture from Murphy his companion pulled out handcuffs, snapped one on Cranshaw's wrist, one on his own.

"Take them away," the detective said briefly.

"No!" Eve cried.

"Kidnaping."

"No! Not that."

"Well? You have exactly one minute to make up your mind."

The girl looked slowly from face to face, found no help, no sympathy anywhere. She stared at Rodney, eyes as hard as marbles. "You Meredith men!" she said bitterly.

"Twenty seconds more," the detective said.

"She's at C-C-Carter Holbrook's place. He hasn't hurt her." Anger stirred in her voice. "He's c-c-crazy about her."

Murphy held back Rodney, who had moved toward her menacingly.

"It wasn't kidnaping," Cranshaw broke in, knowing the game was lost. "At least, not really. Carter was going to marry her if he could, and if that didn't work he'd get in touch with Percy Rolf, make him pay up to get her back."

"And then what? Did he intend to turn her loose—alive?"

"She wouldn't have let anything happen," Cranshaw said promptly. "He'll have hostages she would like to protect."

"Take them away," the detective said again, and the two prisoners were led out of the room.

ii

At Carter Holbrook's Beekman Place address, the unmarked car turned in at the curb. Rodney and Hal had been permitted to go along. The police car had stopped only once, after a two-way radio conversation, to pick up a doctor who sat beside Rodney in the back of the car, his small black bag at his feet.

"Hold it," Rodney shouted suddenly, "there he goes!"

A long Cadillac had pulled away from the curb, made a light, turned north.

"Sure?" the detective asked.

"Positive. I know the car, the license number, and I recognized Holbrook at the wheel."

"Didn't seem to be anyone with him." The detective hesitated.

"She must be on the floor in the back. He wouldn't dare leave her."

The detective spoke again into the radio. "They'll have a man outside the apartment." The car made a U-turn, went right at the corner. There were few cars on the road at this hour, an advantage in one way, a disadvantage in another. If it was easy to keep Holbrook's car in sight it was equally easy for him to observe that he was being followed.

The Cadillac turned left and Murphy discreetly dropped behind.

"That's a powerful car," Rodney said uneasily. "He could get away from you."

Murphy permitted himself a grin. "You'd be surprised at what's under this hood. Fear nothing, fellow."

The cars, pursued and pursuer, went north. Sometimes the detective almost closed the gap, sometimes he let another car in between, sometimes he dropped a long way back.

They were moving through the Bronx now; they were out of the Bronx, driving through suburbs.

"Any idea where he could be going?" the detective asked.

"Not the faintest. Oh, good God!" Rodney exploded.

"Well?"

Rodney described Catherine Cathcart's house. It was fairly isolated. His blind brother was there. And a four-year-old boy. And a helpless woman. He described the situation laconically, but his anguish came through every word.

"Quite a score these babies are building up," the detective said. "Holbrook is the kind it's a real pleasure to put away for a long, long time. Hostages yet. A little kid. A blind man."

Ahead of them red lights disappeared as the car made a right turn. Again the detective fell cautiously behind. Then Rodney gave a stifled exclamation. "He's going to Kathy's all right. This is the lane her house is on, and it's a dead end."

"Then we've got him!" the detective exclaimed. He spoke into the radio telephone.

xxii

The typewriter clattered steadily, paper was removed, more paper inserted, the industrious typist continued to clatter.

"Kathy," Jerome protested from the doorway, "do you know what time it is? Nearly midnight. You've simply got to stop. When you offered to type my book I never expected that you planned to work yourself to death."

The typewriter stuttered. "Now," Kathy exclaimed, "you see what you made me do? I'll have to erase."

"Not now. Not tonight," he insisted.

"Tonight," she said firmly. She observed his determined face. "Oh, well, I might as well tell you. I've been keeping a secret, Jerome. Two weeks ago I took your rough draft down to your old publisher. That's what I was doing in New York. Because it was so short, and especially because the first one sold so well and had such fine critical acclaim, he broke the rules and read it on the spot."

"Well?"

"He's crazy about it. If we can get finished copy to him within the next few days he'll put an illustrator on the job and he plans a late summer or early fall publication, which is really fabulous."

"He's—taking it, then!" He came toward her quickly, his hands out.

She took them in hers. "I'm so glad for you. So glad!"

"Kathy!" His hands drew her toward him.

She pushed away from him. "No, Jerome. Not now. Not yet."

"Why, dear?" he said gently. "I love you and I think—though heaven knows why!—that you love me. And Dennis is fond of me. Why, Kathy?" Unexpectedly the puzzled look faded, was replaced by a broad grin. "Now let me see," he said deliberately. "Before me there is a very small girl, looks about nineteen, hair so light it's practically platinum, a heart-shaped face, a small nose, an ominously firm little chin, though I can deal with that. Blue eyes with—with tears in them."

"Jerome! How long have you been able to see?"

"My eyes have been clearing up day by day. For the past three days I've been able to see you. I can't read print yet, perhaps I'll never be able to." Gently he wiped away the tears that had rolled down her cheeks. "Kathy!" he said at last.

She walked straight into his arms. Somewhere Mister Duffy growled and then barked. A car door slammed.

"Nearly midnight!" she exclaimed. "What on earth—"

She went to turn on the outside lights, peered out. "It's Carter Holbrook and he's carrying someone—an accident. It's Tony! It's Tony!"

She flung open the door and ran outside. "Carter, what happened? Is she hurt?"

"Just doped, I think. Where can I put her?"

"Right here on the couch."

Sam came in. "What's wrong with Mister Duffy? He's raising Cain." He broke off as he saw the tall man with the unconscious girl in his arms. "It's Miss Carew!"

"Call a doctor, Sam," Kathy told him.

"She won't need a doctor," Carter said.

"It's safer to call one," Kathy insisted.

Carter put the unconscious girl on the couch. "Don't call anyone. She'll be all right when she wakes up."

"She had better be."

Carter whirled around, staring in shocked disbelief at the man who stood in the doorway, blocking any retreat, at the revolver held steadily in the hand of the man in front, at Rodney Meredith, Hal Perkins, and the small man with the black bag in his hand.

The latter brushed Carter aside, bent over Tony, felt her pulse, lifted her eyelids. "She's been doped but she'll be all right. Someone had better make coffee, strong and black and hot. Get her off that couch and start her walking. We want her awake."

"Well," Carter said in relief, "I'm glad I thought of bringing her here. She's in good hands. I'd better get back to the city. I have an early appointment in the morning."

"You won't be keeping it," Lieutenant Murphy told him. "You're going to be busy somewhere else."

Carter mopped his face with his handkerchief, looked from face to face, a very puzzled man.

"Your friends, Cranshaw and Eve, are talking their hearts out at headquarters right now. Don't make any mistake about it, Holbrook; they'll tell everything they know to clear themselves of a kidnaping charge and let you face that one alone. They are willing to settle for conspiracy to defraud. That way they may be able to walk the streets as free citizens again—some day."

"Get out of my way," the doctor ordered them. "Where's that coffee?"

"Just a minute," Kathy called from the kitchen.

Between them Rodney and Hal got Tony off the couch and began to drag her up and down the room, while she sagged against them.

"Keep her moving," the doctor ordered. "Get her awake and keep her that way."

Tony's eyes opened. Closed again. "Let me go, Carter," she mumbled. "Don't hurt me. Please let me go." She stumbled on.

The two detectives moved toward Carter. Then as Mister Duffy barked in a frenzy Sam opened the door for two policeman from a radio car.

"There's some awful mistake," Carter told them earnestly. "You can't imagine I'd hurt Tony Carew. Why, I'm planning to marry her."

"Yeah?" Murphy said.

Jerome lunged for Carter's right arm, forced open his hand, exposed the ugly steel prongs on the ring. "So that's what you struck me with—and Rodney."

"That?" Carter looked at the ring. "Oh, that was an old good-luck piece my grandfather gave me."

"No, Meredith," the detective said sharply, as Jerome lunged at Carter. "Let him alone. He's all ours. Believe me, anything you can do we can do better." He began to laugh. "All right, Holbrook. Let's go." The man went out into the night.

ii

"No," Tony protested. "It's too hot."

"Drink it," Kathy insisted. "Just a little more."

"I must have drunk gallons of coffee and I'm tired. I can't walk any more."

Rodney eased her into a chair but as she leaned back, closing her eyes, he shook her by the shoulders. "Rest if you like, but you must keep awake."

"I'm awake now." She summoned up a smile. "You must have walked me miles and miles."

"Not at the rate you were going," Sam told her. "I've seen an inchworm move faster than that." Now that Tony was alert once more, that her eyes had lost their glazed expression, he, like the others, was relaxed and happy.

The doctor had been driven back to New York by Hal after he had assured them that Tony would be none the worse for her experience. Over the telephone Hal had talked to Rosamund.

"Carter Holbrook! I'm simply stunned. I don't understand a thing about it."

"Neither do I," Tony admitted, when Hal had reported to her. "But tell her I'm all right."

When Hal had gone she turned to Rodney. "Why did he do it?" she asked.

"Later," he promised.

But it was days later before the Perrys, Hal and Tony and Rodney gathered at Kathy Cathcart's house and Rodney pieced the story together for them.

Cranshaw hadn't talked much but Eve—or whoever she was—had given the police most of what she knew. Cranshaw had met her at a cocktail party in San Francisco. They had recognized each other as the kind of people who like to gamble for high stakes, and they had gone into partnership. Their first big scheme together was the sale of lots for a "housing project" and getting paid in negotiable bonds.

Cranshaw, knowing that his victims would go after him as soon as they learned they had been swindled, looked around for a fall guy. He found that in Jerome Meredith, who, once he had met Cranshaw's "niece" Eve, agreed to bring the bonds to New York, though both Cranshaw and Eve had discovered that he wasn't the man to assist them knowingly in any crooked scheme.

Eve had learned from Jerome how his office was run, so she got rid of Miss Burns and appeared as Martha Kumer to set the stage for the recovery of the bonds. It was a calculated risk, but by wearing a wig, a brown sort of make-up steel-rimmed glasses, and not trying to hide her stutter, she believed she could escape recognition for one day.

"How did she meet Carter Holbrook?" Jerome asked.

Rodney shrugged his shoulders. "Carter isn't talking. Denies everything. Not that it will help him."

According to Eve—or whatever her name was—she had heard about one of his operations, a stock swindle, and thought he was just what they needed. A whole lot of Eve's vindictive bitterness now was the result of having fallen in love with Carter and having discovered that he was in love with Tony. When she lost her main hold on him she knew that he could no longer be fully trusted.

Well, the operation had worked out smoothly; Carter came in, knocked out Jerome, and took the bonds. Actually it had been Eve who had suggested

it the first place that Jerome put them in an inno-
cent-looking file rather than in his safe.

They hadn't counted on Jerome's calling the police. Carter got away but the police arrived before
Eve could escape. At any rate, the three conspirators
had divided the bonds and had made a pleasant
profit on a comparatively small degree of risk.

Then Cranshaw made some idle remark one day
about the pictures owned by Carter, who was a
genuine enthusiast. Carter told him that he was careful in buying and explained the methods of some
unreliable dealers. This, Cranshaw realized, could
prove to be a most profitable racket and the two
men set it up. For several years it had pulled in large
profits. Eve, who had no interest in the gallery but
was always on the lookout for a promising racket,
had been in a beauty parlor one afternoon having a
manicure when she overheard the manager talking
with a customer. The manager mentioned Mrs.
Hazelton as having worked for her, said she had left to
open her own shop, and that her chemist husband
had worked out a formula that might make them a
fortune.

"But there was so much sheer chance about the
whole thing," Tony said.

Rodney shook his head. "Rackets grow out of people watching for an opening to fleece someone. If
that's what you're looking for, it's not hard to find."

Eve, now in her guise as Cecily Ann, took a job at
the Hazelton beauty parlor to find out how much
truth there was in the rumor. Mrs. Hazelton not only
told her about it but gave her some of the cream for
her "elderly aunt." This was passed on to a chemist
who investigated and found that the formula was
really effective.

As she had none of the cream left, Cecily Ann
tried to get hold of more and finally turned her
charms on Frank Hazelton. Twice Carter tried to get
the formula by breaking in at night, and twice he
had been foiled by Mister Duffy. So Cecily Ann had
made her complaint and Mister Duffy was removed.
But her charms failed with Frank, and when Carter

made his third attempt, at the time when he was supposed to be spending Christmas with his family in Boston, he had been trapped and had knocked out Rodney.

So the attempt to steal the formula was blocked. On top of that Tony recognized the fake canvas Revlin was trying to sell and the gallery scheme blew up.

"But why me?" Tony asked. "Why me?"

"Eve had wanted one big deal and then to quit the rackets. You had the money. If Carter couldn't get it by marriage he could get it by kidnaping. Rolf would raise anything in the world to save you. And Kathy's isolated house, where there was a blind man and a small child and the sister of your best friend, afforded protection and hostages. If you promised not to give him away, they would not be harmed. He knew you were a girl who would keep your word. Well, Eve faked the hospital call, Carter trailed you, picked you up, and when he brought you that cup of coffee it was doped with sleeping pills."

"What happens next?" Tony said at last.

"The case goes before the grand jury next month. Trial sometime in the late spring probably. You realize, of course, that we will all have to testify."

"That," Jerome said grimly, "is going to be a pleasure."

Tony adjusted the filmy white folds of the dress, straightened the shimmering veil that was like a cloud, and got up from her knees.

"Now look!"

Rosamund turned to look at herself in the mirror, at the bride who watched her with luminous eyes, a smile trembling on her lips. "I look idiotically happy. Do you think he'll like me?"

Tony choked back a laugh. "He'll probably say sternly, 'What is that woman doing here? Take her away.' Oh, Rosamund darling, I do want so for you to be happy."

"*Be* happy? I *am* happy."

From below came the throbbing strings of the quartet that Tony had engaged to play the wedding march and the music for the reception.

There was a tap at the door and Jerome called, "Where's the girl I'm supposed to give away?"

"Just a minute." Tony turned back to Rosamund. "In your suitcase you'll find my wedding present. I'm afraid it looks rather official."

"Official!" Rosamund started out of her dreams to look at Tony in surprise. Tony in an orchid velvet dress, her black hair swept up from her face, her long, clear gray eyes, looked anything but official.

"I've turned the shop over to you," Tony said. "Of course, I'll stay on until you can replace me, but from now on it's yours. And all happiness, Rosamund!"

"Tony!" Rosamund stared at her incredulously, then tears came to her eyes. "Tony, it's too much."

"A bride mustn't cry on her wedding day. In spite of that snow outside, it's all sunshine, Rosamund."

For a moment the two girls clung together. Their friendship and affection and understanding would endure all their lives, but this moment marked the end of a part of it that had been important to both of them.

Again Jerome knocked. "I don't like to disturb you, but there's supposed to be a wedding downstairs."

Tony flung open the door and Jerome offered the bride his arm. Rosamund laid her hand on it and floated down the stairs in her wedding dress. Behind her Tony fell into step beside Rodney, who looked remote and impressive in his formal clothes.

As they passed the landing, Tony could see, beyond the bride's fluttering veil, the minister who waited at the altar of flowers; could see Hal, his face sober but his eyes alight, watching his bride approach him; could see the pleasant man who stood beside Hal, his friend from San Francisco who had flown East to be his best man.

They were crossing the hallway now, passing under the arch into the living room. Tony saw Kathy and Mrs. Perry, half tearful, half smiling; saw Dennis, very spick-and-span in a new suit, wide-eyed over the proceedings; could see Sam leaning against the wall at the back, beaming with pleasure; could see Mrs. Haven, her face sad but her head gallantly erect.

Telling Mrs. Haven about Carter, Tony thought, had been the hardest part of all. She had been deeply shocked, profoundly grieved and shamed, but she had accepted with gratitude and unchanged affection the loyalty of the Perrys. Once, at least, she had seen Carter in jail, where he was awaiting trial. She had mentioned the fact, had not enlarged on it. She had told Tony that she would quite understand if she preferred to leave the Nineteenth Street house, but Tony had stayed on. They had rarely mentioned Carter. Now and then Mrs. Haven had spoken of his mother, who was under a doctor's care; of his father, who had refused to believe the charges against his son until he had seen all the evidence. He had grown old, she said. Very old.

They were in the living room now, pacing slowly up the aisle made by two rows of chairs, to the improvised altar, toward the bridegroom who waited, his glowing eyes on the small redheaded girl. It had not proved possible to have as few guests as had originally been planned. Hal was enormously popular with his newspaper and a dozen or more of his friends had been invited.

Among the unknown faces there was one that Tony was sure she could put a name to: Miss G. Burns. The older woman sat quietly as the four people moved past her, and her eyes lighted as Jerome went by with the bride and Rodney with the beautiful bridesmaid. It was Tony who had suggested that Miss Burns be invited to the wedding.

"But she doesn't know either Rosamund or Hal," Kathy had protested.

"She'll know them before long," Tony predicted.

"What are you up to?" Kathy had demanded suspiciously. "I know you. You're up to something."

"Well," Tony admitted, "I did have a sort of idea. You see, the ophthalmologist says Jerome's eyes have improved greatly but it may be a long, long time before he can read type, and I thought he might need a secretary."

"Tony, that's a stroke of genius!" Rodney exclaimed.

"Ye-es," Kathy agreed hesitantly. "I suppose we really ought to. After all, she lost her job unfairly. But—I sort of expected to do Jerome's typing and secretarial work and reading myself." As Tony laughed she said, "Now what's funny?"

"When are you and Jerome going to be married?"

"Middle of March. After Rosamund and Hal get back. We'll leave Dennis with Mother while we go on our honeymoon."

"And then?"

"We'll be back in time to read the proofs for

Jerome's book. Oh, and did you know he's been asked to do a series of articles? So, you see, we'll be busy. Why are you laughing, Tony?"

"I was thinking of this big house," Tony said demurely, "and how it was planned for a large family, and I thought—maybe—you'd have more pressing duties."

"Oh," Kathy said.

"Oh," Jerome added. In a moment he agreed. "I think we had better get in touch with Miss Burns."

So Miss Burns sat watching the two boys whom she had helped to bring up with severity but deep affection, and closed her eyes in a brief, private prayer of thanksgiving. She had more to be grateful for than Tony had explained to either of the Meredith men, for Tony had insisted on seeing that the savings she had spent during her months of job-hunting were replaced. Her future was secure, her boys were doing well. She was to have a real home. Miss Burns whispered, "Thank you, God, for all these blessings," and opened her eyes as the music came to an end and the minister began to speak the words of the marriage service.

ii

When Rosamund, in a trim gray suit, a blue velvet hat perched on her red hair, had run laughing out to the waiting car, hand in hand with Hal, it roared off. Within a short time the newspapermen had left, taking Mrs. Haven and Miss Burns with them. It was understood that the latter, early in April, was to move, bag and baggage, to the big house in Westchester, where the two rooms now occupied by Jerome and Sam were to be converted into a living room and bedroom for her own use.

Kathy, kicking off her slippers, dropped into a chair with a deep sigh. "Well, everything went beautifully. I never saw a happier bride in my life."

"The groom wasn't suffering any deep depression," Sam commented.

Mrs. Perry groaned. "Talk about the father of the bride! His bank account may be a shambles, but this house—when I look at the buffet in the dining room I shudder."

"Who wants some dinner?" Kathy said.

"No one."

"I do," Dennis said firmly.

"After creamed chicken and hot rolls and—"

"I need some dinner."

"I'll take care of it," Sam said. "And I'll get a head start on the dishes." He gave Jerome a significant look. "Am I the only man in this house?"

Jerome stood up, laughing. "Okay, slave driver. I might as well get in training. I'll wield a dish towel."

"You're too good to be true," Kathy declared fervently.

"You're getting a bargain, lady," Jerome assured her.

Rodney looked at Tony. "If I know the signs, we had better get out of here in a hurry or we'll be roped in and find ourselves helping with the housework."

"Go ahead," Mrs. Perry said. "After all, you'll be running the shop single-handed for the next two weeks, Tony. Get some rest. It's been a happy time, but hectic."

Tony moved over in the front seat of the Lincoln so that Rodney could take the wheel.

"A year ago," he said abruptly, "I was just plodding along, trying to make enough money to look after Jerome and Sam, never seeing Jerome without being sick at heart. Now he's on top of the world."

"A year ago," Tony replied, "Rosamund and I were cramming for spring examinations, thinking of the future, not knowing what lay ahead."

"What did you want most, Tony? Happiness, I suppose."

"Well, not exactly. I was old enough by then to know that happiness is a by-product, not a goal. You don't get it by hunting for it, only excitement; you get it when you are too involved in life to worry about whether you are happy or unhappy. I guess what I wanted most was to make my life count in some way."

"Count how?"

"I didn't know then. I have no special talents. Certainly I couldn't endure being a debutante. But I wanted—I want—to be involved with people." She made a helpless gesture. "It's pretty vague, isn't it?"

"It's not vague. Actually that's the pattern you have already created. Didn't you know?"

When she had been silent for a long time he said, "How do you see marriage, Tony?"

"To have and to hold, for better for worse, in sickness and in health, for richer for poorer, forsaking all others."

They had reached the Nineteenth Street house. In a window on the third floor a light burned, indicating that Mrs. Haven was already home.

"Let's walk a little," he suggested. "Do you mind?"

Silently Tony accompanied him down the street, past the bookshop and the beauty parlor, past the old Washington Irving house, past the newer apartment buildings, to the iron gate of Gramercy Park.

Still silently they strolled along the paths. The park was deserted and, except for the hotels, most of the windows had their curtains drawn against the night.

Several times Rodney cleared his throat as a preliminary to speech and then was silent. "Oh, darn it, Tony," he burst out in despair. "I don't know how to begin. I don't know how to tell you. Except I love you with all my heart. What's a guy to do when he doesn't know how to ask his girl to marry him?"

"Repeat after me," Tony said softly, "*I, Rodney, take you, Tony—*"

If the statue of Edwin Booth had been inclined to bend its head, it would have seen a girl clasped in the arms of a big young man, his head bent so that his lips covered hers. It would have seen the girl's arms reach up around his shoulders. The lights of a car moving up Irving Place caught them in a noose of light but they did not notice it. His arms tightened.

"To have and to hold," he whispered.